# House of the
## *Blue Sea*

Teresa van Bryce

Handwritten Press

First edition, 2016
ISBN 978-1523492312

**Handwritten Press**
**Alberta, Canada**

Publisher's Note: This is a work of fiction. Names, characters, and incidents are the products of the author's imagination and any resemblance to actual persons, living or dead is entirely coincidental. Some of the businesses, locations and organizations in the story are real but used in a way that is purely fictional. Locales and public names are sometimes used for atmospheric purposes.

**Cover art "Beach Walk II" by Mary Ann Hews (Tarini)**
Mary Ann was born in Northern Ontario to Italian parents and paints under her maiden name, Tarini. After a family move to Calgary, Mary Ann began to pursue her love of painting. The Rocky Mountains, Italian landscapes, and people provide ideal creative inspiration for many of her pieces. Mary Ann paints in her studio, but particularly loves the challenge of light, colours and structure en plein aire. She is a member of the Calgary Sketch Club, Calgary Artist Society, and the Leighton Art Centre. www.maryannhews.com

Library and Archives Canada Cataloguing in Publication
Van Bryce, Teresa, author
        House of the blue sea / Teresa van Bryce.
ISBN 978-1-5234-9231-2 (paperback)
        I. Title.
PS8643.A525H68 2016        C813'.6        C2016-900584-4

*For my mother,*
*who showed me it's never too late*
*to embark on a grand new adventure.*

# Acknowledgments

**I am deeply grateful to the following for their contributions to this book:**

The late Nigel Watts, who wrote a little book called Writing a Novel. It was the first of many books I would read on the art of writing fiction, and he had me at *"There are only three rules to writing a successful novel. Unfortunately, nobody knows what the three rules are."*

Rona Altrows, for her writing class that taught me to bring the story from within, and her expertise as an editor that helped me write a better novel without sacrificing my voice.

My beta readers, who took time out of their busy lives to read an earlier draft of the story and offer their valuable feedback: Nora Bitner, Susan Bitner, Julie Brewster, Gord Cochrane, Linda Crossley, Laurana Rayne, Alex White, and Stephanie Phillips and her book club (Colleen Cranebear, Kristine Dow, Margaret Ferrier, Sandra Folkins, Lisa Moore, Barbara Pickering, and Ronda Suitor).

My Women's Fiction Writers Association (WFWA) Critique Group: Krista Riccioni, Chelsea Resnick, and Daniel Aleman for their comments and ideas.

Mary Ann Hews (Tarini) for the beautiful painting that graces the cover.

My writing assistants, Chico and Logan, who were with me every step of the way (under or beside my desk).

And last, but not at all least, my husband, Nollind, for being my best friend and greatest supporter. The adventure continues...

# Prologue

The road, like two dark ribbons on a sheet of bright, white paper, merged into blackness beyond the reach of her headlights. Sandra blinked, then blinked again, squeezing her eyes tight before opening them. Even though she was travelling at just sixty kilometres an hour, the falling snow seemed to drive directly into her eyes, hypnotic and disorienting. She rolled down the car window, the rush of cold air scentless and sharp—but the blast of winter air wasn't working. She was going to have to stop. Probably best not to cross the Canada/US border this late at night anyway. There wasn't much for miles on the other side but wide open Montana cattle country.

It felt like a week since she'd woken up at home this morning and looked out at the coming dawn, the grey light crawling in through the slats of the bedroom blind. It was snowing, and she'd burrowed further down under the covers, pulling them up over her head to block out the light. Rufus whined from his bed on the floor beside hers and she lifted the blanket, patting the mattress to invite him under the covers with her. When the little dog had settled into the curve of her body, they'd both fallen asleep, feeling each other's heartbeats, his wiry coat pressed against her flannel pajamas.

It was nearly noon by the time Sandra dragged herself from the warmth of her bed and headed downstairs to make coffee. Rufus trotted beside, undoubtedly hoping for breakfast, looking up at her with each step. When her bare feet touched the cool of the main floor hardwood she stopped. The cordless phone lay on its back, alone in the middle of the dining room table, noiselessly shouting the many messages it held. She turned and took the first two stairs before stopping again, her hand resting on the railing. Frozen. She stood. And then, just like that, she knew … she needed to get away. She couldn't take one more phone call, one more card, one more well-meaning friend unable to carry on a normal conversation.

Despite the sense of urgency that grew in her as the afternoon wore on, Sandra cleaned the house as she always did before going on a trip—a habit left over from growing up with her mother. If there'd been a fire in the middle of the night her mother would have had to make the bed before escaping the blaze. Sandra filled a duffel bag with a few random items of clothing and toiletries, put Rufus in the car, and set off south on the Queen Elizabeth II Highway.

That was hours ago. The weather was making it slow going, particularly after dark. She still didn't know where she was going, only that she had to go. South. In four hours that was all she'd come up with. South. Out of the cold, out of winter and away from this interminable heaviness.

# *One*

It was like following a house. *On the road … still — Marion and Tom Braithwaite* was written in scrolling purple font across the back of the motorhome. Below the lettering, a multi-coloured graphic of a map of the US had all but a few of the states filled in to show the places they had travelled. Barney. They called their RV Barney. It was grey but with a slight lilac hue, which is why, Sandra assumed, it had been given the name.

How different she felt from four years ago when she'd travelled this same road. When she thought back to that trip it seemed she'd driven the entire way in darkness, but of course that wasn't the case. She'd left home at night in a blinding snow but travelled the rest of the distance in daylight. Darkness had been a state of mind.

She had met the Braithwaites her second trip south. They were on a blog of Baja-bound travellers looking to caravan up for the journey. It was safer that way—of course it was. With a more sane mind, it was clearly a good idea. When she'd first met Marion and Tom they'd chastised her for the reckless behaviour the year before. Sandra was younger than their sixty years by just a decade, but they took her under their wing like a daughter and spoke to her as such.

Almost at the border, a few more miles and they'd be in Mexico, and in those few feet across an invisible line on the earth, everything changed. From Canada to the US was barely noticeable but going into Mexico you instantly knew you had crossed a border. The flat storefronts with bold lettering painted on their faces for signs, small late model cars and trucks replacing the herds of SUVs further north, old school buses used for urban transit, and a general increase in activity and noise that couldn't be attributed to any one thing. Food and music were everywhere. Just try to walk one block in a Mexican town without finding something to eat or hearing music piped out onto the street from a restaurant or store. It was like an assault on the senses, but in a good way. Sandra loved it.

From the Mexican border to the south end of the Baja Peninsula required about twenty hours of driving. They'd done it in two days that first year, she and Rufus, pulling off the road before it got dark; at least she'd had that much sense. She had been looking forward to this year's journey since the first snowflake hit the ground back home, and this time she would stay longer. Life at home wasn't exactly hectic, now that she was more of an arm's length owner in the company without a daily role, but friends, family, animals, and a house offered their own kind of pressure, one that Sandra enjoyed being free of during her Mexico stays. She hadn't brought Rufus along since that first unplanned journey south and, although she missed his constant presence in her day, she revelled in the freedom of daily life in Baja, like she was an observer, dipping in and out of the world as and when she chose, not beholden to anyone or anything.

Four years ago, she wouldn't have thought it possible to feel happy being alone, now it was the key to her contentedness. Each winter she felt more at home, more at peace, the beauty and tranquility of the Sea of Cortez filling the void that had threatened to swallow her each day that first year. She'd drifted through those days in a fog that was finally burned away by the Mexican sunshine in the final week of the visit.

And now Baja drew her like Mecca, its desert landscape and turquoise blue waters pulling at her each winter and inspiring the work she'd begun on canvas her second trip down. It was such an easy place to be inspired, and oh-so-easy to get caught up in the pace of life in Mexico—*mañana*.

Sandra took a deep breath as she climbed out of her SUV; the moist air carried the mingled scents of salt, seaweed and something floral. She stretched her arms above her head and turned slowly in place, taking in the 360-degree view. A small boutique hotel, Casa del Mar Azul rested seaside, its white-washed face looking onto the Sea of Cortez; its backdrop the foothills of the Sierra de la Laguna mountain range. Casa del Mar Azul—House of the Blue Sea.

Mar Azul reminded Sandra of photos she'd seen of Spanish seaside villas. In fact, it was what had drawn her here in the first place. Four years before, on her second night in Mexico, she'd stopped at a small hotel and a brochure in their lobby caught her attention. It had an image of a white and blue villa, sitting right at the edge of the sea. Ever since she'd written a report on the Mediterranean in junior high, Sandra had wanted to visit Spain, but when she swore off flying in her early twenties, she gave up the idea of travel to Europe, unless she wanted to drive across North America and take a boat over the Atlantic. *Visit Casa del Mar Azul and drink in serenity* was written below the photo. It had called to her four years ago, and every year since.

Sandra leaned into the car and adjusted the rear view mirror so she could see herself. The humidity was playing havoc with her straw-coloured hair so she tucked it behind her ears in an attempt to tame the curls and waves. The hours on the road had painted faint shadows under her green eyes, but the heat had given her high cheekbones a natural blush so, all-in-all, she looked presentable.

She pulled her purse and a leather shoulder bag from the passenger seat and took the pebbled pathway to the hotel entrance, the tiny white stones crunching under her canvas deck shoes. The bougainvillea hung thick and fragrant from the roof's overhang, and its bright pink blossoms brushed Sandra's shoulder as she passed. She stopped and leaned her face toward a cluster of flowers and inhaled their honeysuckle-like scent. She closed her eyes, the feel of the air surrounding her like loving arms.

"Ms. Lyall, so good to see you again. Welcome back." Paul was standing in the doorway to the lobby, watching her.

Sandra took the final steps to the hotel, reaching for his outstretched hand. "And it is very good to be back. I've been looking forward to visiting Mar Azul since … well, since I left last year. I was just enjoying the captivating aromas of Cortez."

"Ah yes." He tilted his head back and inhaled. "It's easy to become complacent. Thanks for the reminder. Come in, come in." Paul led her inside and took up his station behind the front desk.

There was something about Paul's face that said *welcome* even before he spoke the word; and the lobby of Casa del Mar Azul reflected his warm nature. Two overstuffed chairs sat along one wall with a rattan table between them covered in magazines, while the walls were decorated with art and keepsakes from Paul's life and travels.

Sandra gestured to the open windows along the side of the lobby. "The weather is perfect, as always."

"I order it up special for your visits. No rain, no storms off the Pacific, and enough wind to keep you cool."

"Well, thank you. This northerner appreciates the refreshing breeze."

Paul Hutchings was an ex-pat from England and his face showed the telltale signs of fifty-plus years of smiling. Sandra's first exposure to British culture had been through her older brother William's passion for everything Monty Python, and Paul reminded her of one of the Python actors, the fair-haired one with the incredibly happy face. (Although Paul's fair hair appeared to be exiting stage left.) When she'd first met him four years earlier, she'd half expected him to break into a chorus of "Always Look on the Bright Side of Life" from behind the hotel desk. Staying at Mar Azul felt like visiting the home of an old friend who was ever so happy to see her; exactly what she needed four years ago and a pleasure that hadn't worn off.

"I've given you the room on the west corner at the front. I recall you being rather a sunset junkie." Paul pushed a key card across the desk.

"Yes, and sunrise. I guess I like the sun, period. And those moments when it's coming up or going down are the most magical. Don't you think?"

"Indeed." Paul nodded and smiled as he typed something into the computer.

"Especially here in Baja where sun means warm. At home the sun can shine beautifully on a day that's minus thirty."

Paul shook his head. "I have no idea how you Canadians do it."

"There's no such thing as bad weather, only inappropriate clothing. At least that's what we tell ourselves."

"But do you believe it?" He raised his eyebrows.

"Not really. If we did you wouldn't find so many of us here in the south for the winter. It would be simpler and less expensive to buy another sweater."

Paul chuckled. "Well, you know your way around so make yourself at home." He glanced up at the clock on the wall. "Sunset is in about half an hour if you want to catch the show before coming downstairs for dinner. I'll send Arturo to get the rest of your bags. Your car is unlocked?"

"It is. Thank you, Paul. But tonight it will be the sunset, a bath and then bed. I'm exhausted, and I had dinner up the road with my Baja caravan companions."

"Still travelling down with the RVers, are you? I guess we'll see you in the morning then. Rest well."

7

An arched doorway led to a hallway that doubled as Paul's gallery, its white stuccoed walls displaying pieces in watercolour, oil, acrylic, and pastel. Each fall the hotel was taken over by a group of artists led by their British instructor, a friend of Paul's, and many of the pieces had been gifted by the visiting artists. At the end of the hallway was a large open porthole that looked out to the Sea of Cortez. Sandra stopped for a moment to take in the magnificent view: shimmering water, azure sky, the pale beige sand of the beach. She turned left and walked past doors with ceramic signs reading *"Picudos"*, *"Dorado"* and *"Cabrilla"* for some of the fish in the area, and smiled as she arrived at the final door, its indigo sign reading *"Pez Vela"*, Spanish for sailfish. She pushed her card into the slot, turned the handle and entered what would be her home for the next two months. Dropping her bags to the floor, she again closed her eyes to inhale the fragrance of the sea as it blew in through the open French doors. *Heaven.*

# *Two*

*What in bloody hell were they squabbling about this morning?* He rolled over and buried his face in the pillow, its balloons of goose down pushing up around his ears. The jackhammer in his head was relentless and his mouth felt like the Mojave—much like most mornings these past few weeks. A few weeks? Was that all? It seemed his life had been over longer than that.

Mark turned his head and opened one eye toward the bedside table. He blinked a few times until the red bars of the LED display formed the numbers 10:10. He'd been in bed for—he scrunched his eyelids, trying to sort the numbers in his head—seven hours. At least, he thought he'd called it a night around half-three, but the wee hours of the morning were a bit foggy. Coffee … that's what the situation called for. The coffee machine should have performed its merciful magic by now.

He spread his fingers and pushed his hands into the mattress, raising his torso … and dropped back to the pillow with a groan. If he were at home he'd simply call for Marcia (or was it Marissa?), to fetch him a cup; in this tropical hellhole he was on his own. He rolled onto his side and swung his legs over the edge of the bed, sitting upright. It was then he realized he was still wearing his chinos from the night before. "Sleeping in our clothes now are we? A new high." He rubbed his face with both hands and pushed his fingers through a nest of graying brown hair.

Outside, the squawking of the gulls hit a new crescendo.

"Shut up you blasted birds! Get off my verandah!" Mark picked up a shoe and hurled it at the open window, tearing a corner of the screen from its plastic frame. "Messy, noisy, winged demons!" The seagulls continued, seemingly unperturbed by the sudden appearance of flying footwear. He threw the second shoe, striking the wall next to the window. "Flying vermin!"

Mark leaned forward and pulled a shirt from the stack of clothing on a chair next to the bed. Holding it in front of him, he appraised its level of wrinkled-ness and sniffed each of the armpits. "Good enough for this day." With the buttons still fastened, he pulled the shirt over his head as he stood and shuffled toward the living area. His left arm shot through the sleeve opening just as he walked through the bedroom doorway, slamming his hand into the frame. "Damn!" He yanked the garment the rest of the way on and surveyed his throbbing hand, exploring it with the fingers of the other. No blood, nothing broken. He could still hold a cup of coffee.

There was no familiar aroma of Jamaican Blue drifting from the kitchen and no orange rescue light on the coffee machine. He walked to the counter and smacked the side of the machine, hoping for one small miracle in an otherwise dismal morning. Nothing. His eyes drifted left to the scene in the kitchen. Empty wine bottles stood upright on the counter like the last surviving soldiers of the battle surrounded by casualties: oyster shells, a half-eaten plate of fish and rice, a wine glass stained red, a cell phone, and paper, lots of paper. Reams of type-covered paper were strewn everywhere—on the counter, the floor, the stove top, even in the sink.

He stood amidst the rubble and turned a slow circle. *Right. Best get this ruddy mess cleaned up. But first, must have coffee.* He opened the cupboard and observed the space on the shelf that normally housed a bag of coffee beans. "Damn it!" He slammed the door and stood staring at it, daring it to open and again reveal its dearth of coffee. He squeezed his eyes tight and pressed his thumb and forefinger to the bridge of his nose. The gesture seeming to trigger the first pleasant thought in his day: *Paul would have coffee on.*

# Three

Sandra had risen early to get started on her first painting of the trip, setting up her easel and paint box on the upper deck of the hotel. The rooftop offered a better view and more privacy, but the breeze was up this morning and she didn't want it pushing canvas and easel face-first onto the floor. A group of visitors from Denmark had just checked out and the hotel was temporarily quiet, reducing the chance of an audience. She didn't really mind people watching her work, but she was aware of how it changed her focus, especially in the early stages of a painting. She would inevitably worry that the person looking over her shoulder was critiquing her unfinished work and her tendency was then to paint faster, or fill in areas that were undeveloped.

Just after she'd arrived the day before, Sandra had stood on her balcony and watched a man and a woman on the beach, walking toward one another—her long, brown hair cascading out of her sun hat onto her shoulders, his shirt hanging open and catching the wind. Arturo had arrived just then with the luggage so she'd not had a chance to see if the two people had come together, if they knew one another. She somehow felt they had, but there were other late afternoon beach-goers who could have belonged to each of them. In her painting it was morning and they had the beach to themselves, their expressions hidden by her sun hat and his down-turned face. In the sea Sandra had captured that particular blue of tropical waters, the azure of Cortez, and in the sky drifted salmon-toned clouds, coloured by the rising sun.

"It's very good."

Sandra dropped her brush, sending it clattering to the concrete floor.

"Sorry. I didn't mean to startle you."

She picked up the brush, leaving a splotch of blue paint on the white-washed floor, and turned to see who belonged to the voice.

He was tall, over six feet, and stood at the top of the stairs with his hands in his pockets. He looked like he'd slept in his clothes, and his hair was an unkempt mass of brown curls above a face overgrown with many days, or likely weeks, of untended beard. If he was a guest here at the hotel perhaps the airline had lost his luggage? The man's appearance was in stark contrast to his very proper English accent.

"It's not a problem. It's acrylic and will clean off." Sandra wiped up the smear of paint with her rag. "I didn't hear you come up. I was ... absorbed in my work."

"It's very good—your painting." He inclined his head toward her canvas. "Is it for sale?"

"Sorry, I don't sell my work."

"Oh. So what do you do with it then? Isn't selling rather the point?"

She shook her head. "No, not for me. It's more about the process, the learning. Mostly I keep my paintings—some I hang, the others are stored." Sandra glanced at the painting and then down at her feet. She was feeling a bit awkward at this line of questioning by a complete stranger. "A few I give away to friends or family."

"I see. So you wouldn't make an exception; just this once? I've recently moved into a house in the village and the walls are unbearably dull."

Something behind the mat of facial hair seemed familiar. Did she know this guy? Maybe he'd stayed at the hotel before.

Paul frequently had British guests. Her mind rolled back over her previous four visits but no one came to mind that fit the man before her.

"Have I offended you?" he asked.

"No, not at all. I'm flattered. Really. It's just that I'm not sure what I'd even charge … if I were to sell it to you. And, it's not finished …" She gestured toward the canvas with her paintbrush.

"I can come back. Paul is a friend so I'm here often." He pronounced it of-ten, rather than the North American version of the word that dropped the "t". "As for price, I would be willing to offer you $1,500 American, if you think that's fair."

Sandra was stunned; $1,500 sounded like a generous price for an unknown artist's work, from a man who looked like he might have to scrounge up the change for his next cup of coffee. Although, he did say he'd recently acquired a house, and his sunglasses looked expensive. Maybe the scruffy dude thing was just a look … and a smell. Nothing quite like the odour of last night's alcohol coming out through a man's pores.

"That sounds like a lot of money for an unfinished piece. I'm not sure I'm comfortable—"

"I've purchased a lot of original art, and for a piece this size, $1,500 is quite fair. But, if $1,400 would ease your conscience …" His head bowed forward and he peered at her over the tops of his sunglasses.

Again the familiarity, those wide brown eyes. She took a breath and her eyes went to her painting. The sale would cover over two weeks of her stay at Mar Azul. "Okay then … why not. $1,400. But on one condition."

"Which is?"

"The sale isn't final until you've seen the finished work, in case you don't like it."

"Fair enough." The man stepped forward and held out his hand. "It's a deal."

Sandra accepted his outstretched hand. "Well, thank you, Mister …?

"Jeffery. Mark Jeffery. Sorry, I didn't introduce myself."

Oh God. That's why he was familiar. This was Mark Jeffery, the British actor Mark Jeffery, the very famous, very handsome British actor Mark Jeffery. Yes indeed, she could see it now, those pearly whites peeking out from behind the beard when he spoke, the wavy mane. Men could disguise themselves so easily by growing some facial hair. And he was a bit bulkier than he appeared in his films.

"And you are?" he asked. Sandra realized her mouth had fallen slightly open and she was still gripping his palm.

"Sorry." She dropped his hand. "It's just that I didn't recognize you. I've seen your movies. You look … different than on-screen."

Mark's eyes dropped to his rumpled attire and he ran a hand through his greying brown beard. "Ah, yes, my hiding-out-in-Mexico disguise. Clearly it's working. But I still don't know your name."

"Of course. Sandra, Sandra Lyall." She reached out to shake his hand—again.

He politely accepted it. "A pleasure, Ms. Lyall."

"Yes. Absolutely. Mine too." *Really? Mine too? Shut up, Sandra!*

"Canadian?" he asked.

"Me? Canadian. Yes. I am. Is it that obvious?"

"It might have been northern America, but when you've studied dialects and accents as part of your job, the little things make the difference." He paused. "So, back to the business at hand; when do you think the painting will be finished so we can finalize the sale? And I'm not in a hurry so whatever suits you."

*Right, business, thank God.* "When I get started on a piece I usually dive in and work until it's finished. I'm a bit of an all or nothing painter. So, a couple of days. Tuesday?"

"Tuesday it is. How about I come by early? I like Paul's coffee."

"Early Tuesday would be fine." Should she shake his hand again? No, they'd done that—twice. *Just smile, Sandra. Smile and go back to your work.*

"See you Tuesday then. Enjoy your day." He gave a nod, turned and descended the stairs.

She was such an idiot around anyone remotely celebrity. Mark Jeffery. Wow. Paul hadn't mentioned he had such a famous friend—probably worried his female guests would be clamouring for an introduction. Sandra had first seen him in a period TV drama twenty years before. He had every woman who watched it falling for those dark eyes and unruly locks. Admittedly, he looked a bit different today, more vagrant than movie star. She couldn't recall what she'd seen him in last. It had been a few years.

But, right now, a painting to finish, and a pre-sold one at that. She dabbed her brush into the blue-green paint she'd mixed earlier and held it up to the canvas. "I wonder if he'd prefer the water more dramatic or kept as a backdrop?" Sandra mumbled to herself. The brush hovered over the sea, not sure where to touch down.

As the brush continued to hang in mid-air, she was reminded why she didn't sell her work.

*Maybe a swim.*


"Mark Jeffery? Are you serious?" Trisha's face looked up at Sandra from the screen of the laptop. She was Sandra's neighbour and closest friend, and a big fan of video Skype.

"Quite. He walked right up behind me and offered to buy the painting I was working on. I didn't recognize him at first, but yes, Mark Jeffery."

"What did you say? What did you do?" Trisha's grey eyes

were large as she leaned closer to the camera.

"Well, let's see, I blurted out a few stupid words, forgot to let go of his hand when I'd finished shaking it, and I think my jaw may have dropped. So, all in all, I made quite an impression."

"I'm sure you did fine. You're always so hard on yourself."

"You weren't there, and just because you would have handled the situation flawlessly doesn't mean a normal person would."

Trisha seemed fearless in even the most daunting of situations. She claimed that growing up in a household with four older brothers was the source of her feistiness.

"And so, did you sell it to him?"

"It isn't finished, so he's coming back on Tuesday to see the final product and decide."

"Clever ..." Trisha's digitized face nodded with raised eyebrows, her curly mane bouncing. "... getting him to come back."

"I was far from clever during that exchange, simply not finished. I'm not even sure I want to sell it to him, to be honest."

"Okay, I understand your reluctance to hold a full show in my gallery, but a rich and famous man wants to buy a painting you haven't even finished and you're not sure? I don't get you, Sandi." Trisha was one of those people who gave everyone a nickname. She'd never gone by her full name and didn't seem to think anyone should.

"He's offered me $1,400 US. Is that a fair price?"

"Fair? For an unfinished piece by an unknown artist? Unless it's the size of a bus I'd say he's being more than generous. So, enough about art, tell me about *him*? Is he as gorgeous as he is in his films?"

"That's the thing, not really, at least he wasn't today. If I'd passed him on the street I might have thought he was an old rummy. His clothes looked like they'd been pulled out of a hamper and there was wine spilled down the front of his shirt ... at least I think it was wine since he smelled like he'd been soaking in the stuff. And, I hate to say it but he's a bit ... well ... heavy."

"Fat? Oh lord, don't tell me that, not my Mr. Rochester!" Trisha had loved him in a BBC mini-series of *Jane Eyre*.

"Well, not *fat* exactly, but a bit … you know … thick around the middle. His voice and smile were all I recognized, and the smile was largely hidden behind this scruffy hedge of a beard. He said it was his hiding-out-in-Mexico look but the booze smell makes me think it's more than that. It wouldn't be the first time a famous person hit the skids and turned to alcohol or drugs."

"Come on now Sandi, I think you're jumping to conclusions. Maybe it was the morning after a good party."

"Possibly. I'll let you know how he looks on Tuesday."

"And what are *you* going to wear? How about that dress I gave you for the trip?" Trisha winked.

"On a Tuesday morning to show someone a painting? I'd look ridiculous! I promise to wear it at the first *appropriate* opportunity." Trisha had given her a short, red evening dress with a bibbed front and spaghetti straps that wrapped her neck and tied in the back. It looked pretty good, but it was a party dress, not a Tuesday morning on the deck outfit. "Besides, he's coming to look at my painting, not at me."

"Ah, but there's nothing wrong with being noticed."

Trisha had been noticed at least three times in her life, with two ex-husbands and her current groom to show for it. She changed her name with each successive marriage, liking the variety it provided to an otherwise dull aspect of life. Sandra had once heard her say, "Why wouldn't a woman want to change her name when she has the chance? A different handbag for every day of the week but one name to carry a lifetime?" She'd started off life as a Boyle, which she wore like an ill-fitting sweater, and was all too happy to change her name to Lang when the opportunity arose. Husband two was a Flanagan, which she thought suited her auburn hair and fair skin. Trisha Flanagan—it did have a nice ring to it. Sandra thought Trisha would leave it there, especially once she'd opened the gallery and created a bit of a name for herself in the art world, but no, Tim came along, and Delaroche had a poetic flair that Trisha felt was a good fit for her now fifty-year-old self. Sandra wondered what Trisha would have done if Tim's surname had been Butt or Gooch or Schmittendorf.

"I promise to wash my face and comb my hair before I show him the painting. Oh, and change out of my PJs."

"Very funny. Make an effort. Please? For me?" Trisha had her hands in prayer position at her chin.

"For you … but plain Jane is about as good as it gets."

"Humility is such an unattractive quality in a woman, particularly at our age. You look great for almost fifty, and somewhere deep down, you know it. Admit it!"

"I feel great. I'll admit to that. But nothing more. How's Tim?"

"Tim's good, I'm good, and Rufus has settled in fine with Molly and Maxwell. He's such a little thief. Molly's so smitten she's apt to drop her food at his feet as soon as he looks her way with those lost puppy eyes." Trisha's Molly and Maxwell were siblings, two purebred dachshunds. "She's nothing like you, I tell you that. A guy would have to do a lot more than look to get your attention. "

"I just prefer genuine lost puppies to the human variety." Sandra had found Rufus five years before, hanging around her back alley, scrounging whatever he could find next to the garbage bins. It was November, and the poor guy looked like he hadn't had a good feed in months. She eventually lured him into her back porch, and then into the rest of the house. By mid-winter he'd pretty much taken over the place. He slept wherever he chose, ate home-cooked food, and rode around with Sandra in her SUV—in the front seat, of course. Rufus was likely a cross between some kind of terrier and a beagle—beagle size and beagle shape but with wiry hair and a beard.

"Have you seen your friend Ian yet?"

"Now why would you think of him during a conversation about lost puppies? He's far from being a stray."

"I don't know, he reminds me a little of your Rufie with his bed-head and whiskers. So, have you?"

"Not yet, but I'm sure I'll see him soon. I've plenty of time and my first priority is to paint."

"And, when you do see him, what *then*?"

"Ian is a great listener, fun to be with, and a *friend*. Besides, you know I'm not interested in meeting anyone or dating." Trisha was constantly trying to set Sandra up with someone or imagining more to her friendships than was there. She did it because she cared, but Sandra still found it annoying.

"Maybe I should come down there and see what I can conjure up for you."

"Oh, really? How many times have I invited you to join me for part of my stay? Let's see, my second time down I recall inviting you at least twice before I even booked the hotel, another couple of times before I started packing, and multiple times while I was here. By the next year's trip, I was starting to get the hint but I still asked once or twice. Last year, I think I alluded to the idea just once, and you pretended not to notice." As long as Sandra had known Trisha, she'd not been further than Banff, about a two-hour drive from her front door. She'd visited every art gallery, eclectic shop, fine dining establishment and theatre in a two-hour radius of home, but not ventured beyond it.

"Some people go for the hundred-mile diet, I'm inclined to hundred-mile travel. It's environmentally friendly."

"And that's why you do it … right."

"There's just so much here in my own backyard, why go to all the trouble of packing a suitcase or getting on a plane. I don't get what all the fuss is about."

"The fuss is about summer weather in February. Shorts. Flip-flops. Suntanning. Dining on a patio without the need for a parka—"

"And … and," Trisha pointed her finger at the camera, "… sleeping on a mattress other than my Kingsdown, not having access to my closet, leaving behind Molly and Maxwell, entrusting my gallery to *Felix*. Not to mention jamming myself into a flying sardine can with a hundred different kinds of viruses. If I want warm temperatures and skimpy clothes I'll go to the spa, thank you. And afterward, I'll pick up a gourmet lunch-to-go from Sunterra Market and eat it in the Devonian Gardens in downtown Calgary!"

"And is there a beach with white sand and rolling surf in your Devonian Gardens?"

"No, but there are over five hundred palm trees."

"I'm sure there are. I get it. You don't like to travel."

"I disagree. I just don't like to travel long distances. But, if I did, San Leandro would be the first place I'd visit."

"Well, thank you for that. You're always welcome, even if you can only come for a few days. The La Paz airport is less than an hour away and I'd be happy to come and pick you up."

"I know you would, and I appreciate it. But, right now I should be getting back to the gallery. I've left Felix on his own for three hours and my palms are starting to sweat. Don't sell all of your Baja paintings because I'm determined to have a few hanging in my gallery … or maybe a full showing?" Trisha panned her hand across the screen. "'*Images of Baja*, by local artist Sandra Lyall.' I can see the posters now."

"I'm sure you can, as clearly as you see me getting together with Ian LeRoy. I hope you're enjoying the imaginary life you're creating for me, but I prefer my real world. I'm all right, you know. Quite content."

"I know you are, sweetie. Good to talk to you. I'll be checking in Tuesday night after your *rendezvous* with Mr. Jeffery."

"He's buying a painting!"

"Of course he is." She winked. "Bye now!" Trisha's face disappeared from the screen.

"You can be such a pain in the ass!" Sandra said to the Skype logo in the middle of her monitor. "… but in a good way." She smiled and headed for the shower to remove the salty remnants of the Sea of Cortez.

# *Four*

It was after sunset by the time Sandra wandered downstairs to the restaurant. She hadn't been able to tear herself away from the sky's end-of-day drama any sooner. She'd have to remember to thank Paul for the perfect room location.

Pablo's Grill and Lounge was situated on the ground level of Mar Azul and was open to the beach—one of the things Sandra loved most about Mexican architecture, the inclusion of the outdoors. Back home, restaurants had seasonal patios with doors or windows that opened out in good weather, but in Mexico, eating establishments were often as much outdoors as in, with courtyards, glassless windows and absent walls. Pablo's had been a large stone deck before Paul decided to turn it into a restaurant/lounge and the rough stone flooring and beds of vegetation remained. There were walls on three sides with the fourth open to the sea and the white plaster was adorned with art that Paul had collected during his years in Mexico, most of it from artisans in the area—metal geckos, ceramic suns, brightly coloured paintings.

Each table for two or four housed a small brass lantern which provided most of the light in the restaurant and those who had trouble reading the menu in the low light were given additional lanterns. Sandra had once seen a couple with four lanterns on their table, and still the man was using a flashlight, just to make a point, it seemed. Most of Paul's guests appreciated the warm but basic feel of Mar Azul. The bar was Paul's own work of art, a simple wooden structure on the south side of the lounge covered with treasures from the sea, all gathered by Paul and his guests on beach walks—shells, coral, bits of glass, driftwood and dried starfish.

Although two kilometres outside the village of San Leandro and forty-five minutes from La Paz, Pablo's had become a popular place for vacationers and locals to dine and share a few drinks. With space for only thirty or so guests in the hotel, the outside customers made Pablo's a profitable addition to Paul's business, and tonight was a perfect example. The hotel was quiet but the restaurant was more than half full. Paul had originally planned to call the place something more sophisticated, but with the locals referring to him as Pablo, the Spanish version of his name, it seemed a simple and natural fit. Now Pablo's was known for miles around for its eclectic menu, live music and warm atmosphere, and was full most nights of the week.

"Table for one?" Paul came from behind the bar to greet her.

"Unless you know a tall, dark stranger who would like a dinner companion."

"Well, he's not particularly tall and he's quite fair—but your friend Ian should be here sometime soon. He's playing tonight."

She clasped her hands together. "I was hoping to see him. He hasn't been in touch for a few months and I wondered if he'd run off with a band of minstrels, or maybe a Mexican señorita."

"That's unlikely. I think our Ian is quite settled in San Leandro and has left his wandering ways behind." Paul gestured to the main part of the restaurant and then to the row of empty bar stools. "What's your pleasure?"

"You know, I think I'd rather talk to Arturo than myself tonight, so how about a seat at the bar."

"It's also close to the stage." Paul smiled and pulled a high, cane-seated stool from under the bar. "Arturo has gone to fetch up some more wine. He'll be back any minute to fix you a margarita. Plenty of salt?"

"Absolutely. You remember!"

Paul chuckled as he stepped back and draped a napkin over his arm, his tone suddenly formal. "The special tonight is a Pescado a la Veracruzana—catch of the day in tomato sauce with jalapeños, capers and olives—served with an asparagus salad, and hearts of palm risotto." He placed a menu in Sandra's hands. "I'll send Elena over to take your order when you're ready."

He bowed his head and left through a door behind the bar that led to the kitchen. Chief cook and bottle washer, that was Paul's title. And desk clerk, maître d', bellboy, maintenance man, and holder of any other job that needed doing. Mar Azul was successful enough that he could hire out some of his tasks, but the hotel was a labour of love for Paul and he liked to be involved in everything. Fortunately, he did have help in the Flores family, who made up the bulk of the staff.

Paul had originally hired Carmelita Flores as a maid when he purchased the hotel ten years before and in the past five years, since the restaurant opened, she'd been working in the kitchen as well. At sixteen, her daughter Elena was hired to serve during the dinner hours. A year later, Carmelita's son Arturo came on board to help with luggage and other assorted chores around the place. When Sandra had first seen Arturo behind the bar last winter, following his eighteenth birthday, he'd been glowing with pride.

"Señora Lyall. Welcome back to Baja." Elena held a tray in her left hand and extended her right to Sandra.

"Elena!" Sandra stood and, ignoring the outstretched hand, gave Elena a hug. "I didn't think it possible but you are even lovelier than you were last year." It was true. She was a remarkably beautiful girl. If she wasn't tucked away in the small village of San Leandro, some modelling or movie scout would have undoubtedly scooped her up by now. She was a smidgen taller than Sandra, around five foot seven, and had the body of a dancer—long legs, graceful movement, a slender figure. Her enormous brown eyes were set into a flawless complexion, and her near-black hair swept across her forehead and cascaded over her shoulders.

"And you are looking very beautiful also, Ms. Lyall."

"It must be the dim lighting in here because I looked a bit like a raccoon when I left my room—too many miles and too many restless sleeps in strange beds since I left home."

"No, I don't think it is the lights …"

"I'm kidding, Elena. Thank you for the compliment."

Arturo had returned and was at the other end of the bar pulling bottles of white wine from a crate. His black hair was cut so it stood up on top, and his upper lip and chin were darkened by the beginnings of a beard. Sandra nodded her head sideways in the young man's direction. "Perhaps you can ask your brother for that margarita he and I talked about earlier?"

"Sí señora, and do you know your dinner or do you need more time to select?"

"I haven't looked at the menu yet but I'm sure I'll order the special anyway. It's always delicious."

"The fish special, then," she smiled, her face lighting up, "and I will ask Arturo for your margarita."

Elena walked toward Arturo, raising her voice to be heard over the noise in the restaurant. "Arturo—*una margarita para* Ms. Lyall."

"Coming right up. I have already prepared your extra-salty glass." He raised a pale blue stemmed bowl in Sandra's direction, the salt on the rim looking like the inside of a geode.

"You'd think I liked a box of salt with each drink! Is it really that much more than the average?" Before Arturo could answer, a voice came from behind Sandra.

"Sandra Lyall. I heard you were coming."

She turned on her stool. "Ian! So good to see you." He walked toward her with a guitar case in one hand and the other arm outstretched. She hopped off her seat and greeted him with a hug.

"And you're looking as ravishing as ever," he said.

"Oh please, Elena and I were just discussing my resemblance to a racoon." Sandra climbed back onto her stool.

He leaned in, inspecting her face. "Ah yes, I see the resemblance now … cute."

"And I'm told you're entertaining us on the stage this evening as well as here at the bar?"

"Well, I'm playing music. Whether or not you are entertained is entirely up to you."

"Yes, yes, I know. We're only as happy as we make up our minds to be. I remember."

"And have you made up your mind to be happy?"

"Indeed I have. Why else would I be here at Mar Azul?"

"Escape perhaps?" His eyebrows raised.

It wasn't the first time Ian had questioned her reasons for coming to Mexico. "No, not this year. This year I've come to paint!" She swung her hand in a flourish to the right, almost knocking the margarita from Arturo's hand. He managed to hang on but not without sloshing lime-green liquid on the bar and the floor. "Oh, Arturo, I'm so sorry. We who speak with our hands are at risk of half empty drinks—old Canadian proverb."

Arturo's brows knit together in confusion. "I will bring a cloth to wipe up, and this drink is on the house."

"No, it will not be on the house. It was my theatrics that spilled the drink. A cloth will do, and I'll wipe it up myself."

Ian was grinning at her. "What?" she said, mocking annoyance.

"Nothing. It's just good to see you. I'm going to get set up but maybe I can join you for a drink before I go on. Have you eaten already?"

"I gather you won't be eating until after your first set?"

"Am I so predictable?"

"Charmingly so. I've ordered, so if you don't mind watching me eat I'm happy to watch you drink while I eat."

"I'll be sure to keep my drink at a safe distance from those theatrical hands of yours."

Sandra gave him a shove. "Go get your musical gizmos sorted and leave me here to enjoy what's left of my marg."

Ian picked up his guitar case and made his way to the small stage at the front corner of the restaurant. Paul hosted live music as often as he could—some of the musicians were local, some travelling through, and some impromptu performers were guests of the hotel. A short wall behind the stage offered the beach and sea as the musician's backdrop and meant that patrons could enjoy the view without looking away from the show. Half a dozen palapas each had a string of tiny solar-powered lights around its thatched roof and the pathway leading to the restaurant was lined with solar lanterns hanging on pegs in the ground. Even after dark there was always enough light to see the white foam of the breaking waves beyond the beach. After being here the first time, Sandra had decorated her back and front yards with all manner of solar-powered fixtures, reluctant to return to the darkness of winter.

Ian glanced up and saw her watching him. He struck a rock star pose and winked at her. He was such a flirt—and he wasn't hard to look at. Ian was a youthful fifty-four. He wore his red-blonde hair, which showed only a dusting of grey at the temples, tousled on top and long in the back. He often wore a hat when he was performing—a straw fedora with a Guatemalan fabric band—but tonight he'd left his head unadorned, his hair animated by the breeze coming in off the water.

On stage and off, Ian's dress was casually tropical: khaki pants or bermudas and a cotton print shirt left untucked. He always wore a small silver stud in his left ear, two or three strings of beads or woven leather chokers around his neck, and an old Rolex wristwatch his uncle had left him. Just once had Sandra seen him dressed up, which amounted to tucking in his shirt and putting on a belt. Ian was the epitome of the Mexican ex-pat, his clothing incorporating the three Cs: comfortable, casual and cotton.

Ian double-checked his cables and gadgets, placed his guitar in its stand, and stepped off the stage. He walked over and pulled up a stool next to Sandra's. "So, you're back again. Sooner or later you'll be shopping for Baja property."

"I don't see that happening. I'm much more fervently Canadian than you are."

"Now what does that mean? I'm about as Canadian as you get—I speak both official languages, can skate almost as well as I can walk, can't eat oatmeal without maple syrup *and* I own a box of toques. Top that ... eh."

Sandra laughed. "Right, and your childhood pet was a beaver. So tell me then, super-Canuck, when was it you last lived in Canada?"

"I have a house there now, the same house I grew up in."

"Yes I know you own a house, but when did you last *live* there?"

"All right. I admit it's been a few years, but I do have a box of toques." Ian took a swig from the bottle of Corona that Arturo had set on the bar. "Not that I have much opportunity to wear them down here."

"Now, let's be honest. You've been in Mexico more than a few years. And I seem to recall you lived in the US before that and wasn't there a stint in the UK? So, I rest my case. I am much more Canadian than you are." She held her glass toward him in a toast.

"Fine. I proclaim you queen of the frozen north!" He clinked his bottle to her glass.

Elena arrived with Sandra's meal, placing it on the bar in front of her. Sandra leaned over the plate and inhaled, taking in the blend of tantalizing aromas. "If it tastes as good as it smells … mmm." She draped a white linen napkin on her lap and picked up her fork.

"Looks delicious. Fish?" Ian asked.

"Pescado a la Veracruzana was what Paul called it, I believe." She flaked off a bite-sized piece from the filet, scooped up some of the sauce and put it in her mouth. "Oh my, heavenly," she said as she chewed, the fish seeming to melt in her mouth. Ian was watching her. "Would you like a taste?"

"No, simply enjoying your enjoyment of it." He turned himself on his stool to face her. "So, how do you like my new face art?" He showed one profile and then the other. He used his face like a canvas, one week sporting a full beard, then maybe a goatee or a mustache, or combining the two for a Van Dyke. At present, a small chin beard connected to a moustache, forming an oblong shape of reddish-blonde hair.

"It looks good, but I'm sure I've seen this one before."

"Not exactly, but maybe something close to it. I don't expect most people to notice the intricacies of my work, but you? You're an artist. Speaking of, how's the painting coming?"

Sandra considered telling Ian of the movie star offering to buy her first painting of the trip, but decided she'd hold off until it was a done deal. "Picking up, but still slow-going when I'm home. It's why I'm staying here longer this year. I'm much more inspired painting outdoors next to the ocean. Photos are limited to what the camera captured. Outdoors, especially in such a fantastic setting, I get the smells, the sounds, the feel of the day." Her hand was painting the air in front of her as she spoke. "The painting becomes much richer."

Arturo approached from the other end of the bar. "Would you like another margarita Señora Lyall?"

"Yes please. Half a glass is not nearly enough. And please stop calling me señora. Sandra will do fine."

Arturo reddened. "And Ian? *Otra cerveza?*"

"No, thanks. I have to play in …" Ian looked down at his

watch, "three minutes. You're staying?" he asked, looking at Sandra.

"Of course. I haven't heard you sing in almost a year, at least not live. I have your CD but it's not the same."

"Charmer. I'll be back to reclaim this stool during my break." Ian patted the bar stool and turned toward the stage, winking to her over his shoulder as he ambled away.

He turned on the microphone and leaned in to it. "Welcome to Pablo's, ladies and gentlemen. I'm Ian LeRoy and I'll be keeping you company this evening. I'm happy to take requests. Just place a slip of paper in the bucket on the side of the stage, along with a twenty dollar bill." He was joking of course, unless you wanted to hear "Margaritaville". He started off his set with an instrumental piece, the notes uniting with the sound of the sea to create a bewitching blend of music and nature. Sandra adored Spanish guitar and Ian was becoming quite accomplished. *Impressive.* She must remember to tell him.

Ian had been kind of a big deal back in the day, at least on the folk music scene, touring with a number of groups and single performers, playing guitar, singing backup. In the '90s he had as many album credits to his name as any other artist in the country. By the time he inherited his childhood home and a hundred thousand dollars from his father, he was mostly doing solo gigs in restaurants and bars in Vancouver, where he'd been living for two years. He decided if he was going to be a bar musician, he might as well do it in a warmer climate. He loaded his '98 Dodge van, sold everything that didn't fit, and drove as far south as he could on the west coast of the continent—Cabo San Lucas.

He played in the tourist bars and lounges, made a name in the area, and threw himself in with the throngs of vacationers, many from Canada. From Ian's stories, it sounded like quite a party for a few years. When he turned fifty he decided he wanted to settle somewhere quieter and get back to writing music. As

Ian put it, when the crowd only wants to hear "Margaritaville" *one more time*, why bother writing? San Leandro was his quieter place.

He still played in Cabo and La Paz from time to time, and regularly at Casa del Mar Azul, enough to pay the bills, and the house in Montreal provided a steady stream of rental income during the slow months. The instrumental piece was over and he was singing something Sandra hadn't heard before. Ian didn't have the smooth voice of a crooner like Frank Sinatra, but his singing had a unique dusky quality that buffed the rough edges from whatever kind of day you'd had.

"How was your meal?" Paul hoisted himself onto the stool next to Sandra.

"Exceptional, as always. Where did you learn to cook like that anyway?"

"As an under-employed actor, a chap has plenty of time to tail after other interests, and my ex-wife was an appreciative diner. I was quite successful on that particular stage."

"Speaking of your acting days … I can't believe you are friends with Mark Jeffery and have never mentioned it." She leaned forward and gave him a gentle punch on the shoulder.

"Ah yes, my famous mate. Where did you meet him?"

"Up on the deck this morning when I was painting. He's actually offered to buy the piece I was working on."

"That's great! Good for you, Sandra."

"I hate to ask, but he was looking a bit, ah … rough. Is he all right?"

"This morning …" Paul pursed his lips and tapped them with the first two fingers of his hand. "Right, he was here for coffee, rather urgently as I recall. Yes, he's fine. He's just been having some trouble recently."

"So do you know him from your acting days, did the two of you perform in something?"

"We did, more than once, but we knew each other from

before that. We went to public school together, were great chums. I was actually the one who convinced him he should join the drama club. I don't know that he had much intention of acting, but when Mr. Dewhurst asked who was keen to play the romantic lead next to Mary Templeton's character, his hand was in the air, along with five other guys', including mine. As it turned out, she was why he'd agreed to join in the first place. I should have known." Paul looked away from Sandra, his eyes on Ian for a moment. "He got the part, was raved about in the school paper, and from that experience was prompted to follow me to the London Academy of Music and Dramatic Art." His eyes returned to Sandra. "Oh, and he got the girl. Mark always seems to get the girl."

"That doesn't surprise me."

"I was thrilled, at first, going to LAMDA with my best mate, but it got tricky after a bit, him getting the leads and me playing supporting roles. It turned out he was a natural, and much better looking of course. And the rest, as they say, is history."

"That must have been hard."

"It was, but he was a good friend to me. He got me auditions I wouldn't have had otherwise, introduced me to people who could help me with my career. But it just didn't happen. I never wanted to be a celebrity and carry all the baggage that goes with it, but I did want to make a good living at the work I loved. My security became my wife's job. And we both know how that turned out." His eyes travelled back to the stage.

Paul's ex-wife was a lawyer, and when his career hadn't met her expectations, she'd found herself another lawyer. At least that was the short version of the story.

"And how is it now between you and Mark, with you out of the business?"

"It's easier in many ways. I can be interested in his career without feeling badly about my own. I've made my choice. I love my life here and I don't envy him. It's not easy, you know, being famous for the work you do. It brings some huge expectations."

"I can imagine. Precisely why I don't sell my art!" Sandra laughed.

"But you have sold a piece. Best beware or you'll lose your obscurity, and then where will you be?"

"Hiding out in a small town in southern Alberta, like I am now. And he hasn't actually bought it yet. I insisted he see it finished before making a final commitment."

"He'll like it, I've no doubt. He has good taste. You had a chance to catch up with Ian?"

"Briefly, and he'll be back during his break to claim that stool you're sitting on."

"Ah yes, the most popular seat in a bar, right next to the attractive single woman—or married works just as well for some of us rotters." His eyebrows bounced with mischief. Paul stood. "I'd better get back to the kitchen. I've left Carmelita alone to finish up the dinner orders."

"Isn't that the boss's prerogative?"

"Not around here. That's what happens when you empower your employees. Damn that Stephen Covey!"

# Five

The endless blue skies and warm weather didn't help Mark's mood. In fact, they seemed to emphasize how lousy he felt. At least in London he could commiserate with people about the unending fog or drizzle, revelling in the shared wretchedness. Here in Mexico there were all these northern tourists grinning and bleating about the fabulous weather, as though it were unexpected to have a warm winter in Baja. He wished it would rain and send them all scurrying indoors.

The square was busy today with locals and tourists, all shopping, visiting, or wandering. The streets of San Leandro were scarce in number, but showed a pride of place in architecture and cleanliness. San Leandro was yet to become a full-fledged tourist town but those keen to find a place off the beaten path returned again and again. Mark had initially come here because of his friend Paul and found the place rather dull on those first two visits, but this time it was perfect, the ideal place to escape from the world—other than the idyllic weather.

"Señor!" A man called from behind the fish counter at the main street market. "Fresh fish, amigo?"

"No. Thank you. *Vaca*." Mark answered.

The fish vendor pointed down the aisle to his left with an enthusiastic smile.

"*Gracias*." Mark walked to the centre of the village each day for the ingredients for that night's meal. If he didn't, it was too easy to eat cheese and crackers washed down with a bottle of red wine.

With just over five hundred people, San Leandro was small, but the surrounding population and visitors made for a solid enough base of consumers to support a decent Sunday market and a few permanent shops. The variety wasn't huge but everything was fresh, sometimes caught or picked that very morning. The local beef was tougher than he was used to, and Pablo's was a better option for a steak, but there were always too many of those weather-worshipping tourists there. He preferred to dine on his verandah with his feathered friends, despite their constant chatter and squabbles over bits of food.

The farmer's stall had a wooden cut-out of a cow's head on one side and a pig's on the other, each hanging from the rough corner post that held the front of a blue tarpaulin. The market was a mosaic of orange, blue, and white poly tarps, to keep the sun at bay, held up with long sticks and guy-lines of twine. When he'd first seen it, Mark thought the market resembled a refugee camp. It was not at all like the weekly markets at home with their uniform pop-up structures.

"Do you have any steaks?" Mark asked. The woman stared at him. "Vaca?" he tried again.

"Si, vaca." The woman stood and smiled up at him. Her black hair was pulled back into a long pony tail that nearly reached the waistband of her apron. There was a regular butcher shop in the village but Paul told him the meat from the weekend vendor was a bit more tender. He should have asked Paul what to order; requesting porterhouse or New York cut was not going to get him far with the farmer's wife.

"Steak?" Mark put his index fingers and thumbs together to form an "O" with his hands.

The woman nodded and reached into the large cooler on wheels that formed one side of the stall. She pulled out a small roast.

"No, señora. Steak. Like …" he held one hand over the

other in an attempt to show something slimmer.

"Ah, sí!" She put the roast back and dug around in the cooler, producing a bag containing a two-inch thick slab of red meat.

It looked like a steak. Worth a try.

An electronic chirping cut through the sounds of the market. Mark pulled his cell phone from his pocket and looked at the display. "Sorry. I have to answer this. I'll come back."

"Hello Nate … Yes, I read it. … Truthfully? I hate it. … I don't think I need to read it again, unless the goal is to hate it more. … You're actually going to ask that question. No! Of course I don't want the role! What part of *hate it* isn't clear? Did *you* actually read that piece of rubbish? … Sure Nate, if giving a second thought to how much I hate it will make you happy, I'll do it, for you. Call it for old time's sake, when you used to give a shit about my career." Mark had wandered into the middle of the market, people flowing past him on both sides. "Yes Nate, I heard you the first time, and the second!" He smacked the red box on the small screen with his index finger. There was just no satisfying way to slam down a smart phone.

He pressed the heels of his hands into his forehead, slowly turning in a circle. He stopped when his eyes fell on the coffee vendor's cart parked at the end of the row of low, makeshift tents. Thank God. Lorenzo was here. Mark had met Lorenzo the week before and was impressed by the quality of the coffee he dispensed from the sidecar of an old motorcycle. The bean grinder rested on the carrier at the back of the bike and the sidecar held a steel counter with the coffee machine and condiments. A small trailer carried a cooler for the dairy products and other supplies. It was quite a clever set up, and Lorenzo was doing well at the many markets frequented by American and Canadian tourists accustomed to a gourmet coffee shop on every corner. All that was missing was a Starbucks logo on his gas tank.

Mark covered the length of the marketplace like a man

abandoned in the desert who's spotted water. "Lorenzo. You're a life saver. I'll have the largest cup of your strongest coffee."

"Sí, amigo. Latte?"

"No thanks, straight up please—no foam, no cow, no sweet."

Lorenzo smiled and nodded. "Coming right up. It is a beautiful day, no?"

"But when isn't it a beautiful day here?" Mark spat back.

"Señor?"

"Sorry Lorenzo, I'm just not having a great morning. Yes, it's a beautiful day."

Mark carried his double-layered paper cup of steaming black coffee to the fountain that sat in the middle of the village square and sat down on the concrete wall containing the fountain's pool. His head was pounding. Hopefully the caffeine would help. It was getting hot and he should have worn a hat. Mark stared down into his cup, his face floating on the surface reflected back at him. *Old. That's how you look, Jeffery. Old.*

"Mark!"

Paul was walking toward him across the uneven stones of the cobbled street. "Here you are. I thought we were meeting at the hotel?"

Mark dropped his head and exhaled with a sigh. "I'm sorry, I completely forgot."

"I've been waiting in the café. I saw you sitting over here."

Mark glanced at his watch. "Right, we were meeting at noon. I got distracted …"

"Not in a good way, by the look of things. Let's go get some lunch and you can tell me about it."

The San Leandro Hotel was the hub of the village, with a restaurant, bar and small store on its ground level. The rooms were basic and mostly occupied by budget travellers; the majority of area visitors staying at resorts and hotels nearby like Casa del Mar Azul. The restaurant took up the front corner of the building's main floor, its windows looking out on the square. The yellow adobe walls were sparsely decorated with colourful plates and copper light fixtures hung low over tables draped with green squares of vinyl.

"I'm over here by the window." Paul gestured to a table with a half full bottle of Coke set to one side. "Are you hungry? You don't look so good. How long have you been sitting out in the sun?"

"It's not the sun, although I do have a headache. Nate, my agent, called."

"Does he have something for you?"

"Yes. And no. He sent me a script a few days ago. This piece of trash." Mark pulled a pile of papers from his shoulder bag and slapped it down on the table.

Paul raised his eyebrows. The pages of the manuscript were warped and dog-eared with red stains along one end. "How did he send it, by carrier pigeon?"

"No, it … fell, in my kitchen, and there may have been some wine on the floor."

"Fell? You mean you threw it."

Mark shrugged. "He's trying to appease me with this … this … one hundred pages of crap!"

"I've heard you say that before, about scripts that were quite decent. You're picky, admit it."

"I admit I can be particular, but this one is complete drivel and the part they're offering is not even the lead. Read it. I don't see how you could possibly disagree." Mark pushed the manuscript over to Paul's side of the table.

"All right, I'll have a look. But first, let's order some food. I'm famished."

# Six

Paul looked up from his desk. "You're here early. And I see you found your iron." He nodded his head in the direction of Mark's slacks.

"Funny. Perhaps you should have gone into comedy. And good morning, by the way."

"Can I get you a coffee? I assume that's why you're here, a little jolt to get your day started."

"I'd love a coffee, but I'm actually here to buy a painting."

"Right. Yes. Sandra mentioned you'd be by to look at that piece. It's turned out very well."

"I've no doubt. She's talented."

"She is, although she doesn't seem to know it. Canadian humility, I guess." Paul wagged his finger at Mark. "And don't you be taking advantage of that."

"Of course not. I've offered her what I think is quite a fair price."

Paul glanced at the clock on the wall. "She's normally up on the roof about now. I'll go tell her you're here."

"No, you carry on. I'll wander up."

"Well, she might not appreciate that. She's up there at this time of the morning because no one else is."

"I'm sure it will be fine. I'll just let her know I'm here and come back down for a coffee. She can take her time getting the painting."

"The thing is ..." but Mark didn't hear the rest. He was out the lobby door and on his way to the stairs.

As he climbed to the roof, first to come into view were Sandra's feet with toes pointed and reaching up into the yellow-blue of dawn. He stopped, questioning whether or not he should proceed. Curiosity got the better of him. Each step brought her more completely into view—straight legs wrapped in short white tights, a pale green cotton tee falling away from her midsection, shoulders squared and arms framing the back of her head with hands gripping below her blonde ponytail. He stopped on the last step, waiting. The minutes ticked by and Mark wondered if he should go quietly back down the stairs or say something. He chose the latter.

"Hello."

Sandra's legs veered right before bending and forming a landing pad for the rest of her.

"I'm sorry, I seem to have startled you again."

"You do have a way of sneaking up on people." She smoothed the hair away from her face. "I didn't expect you so early."

"Yoga. That's a healthy way to start the day." He was suddenly conscious of how his belly pushed out the front of his shirt. He sucked it in.

"It helps to balance the margaritas and Paul's cooking when I'm here." She pulled her feet underneath her and stood, adjusting clothing as she went.

"Do you practice every day?"

Her t-shirt had ridden up her torso during the headstand and she gave it a few quick tugs to draw it down over her slim waistline. "Most days, but sometimes it's too tempting to lie in bed and listen to the surf." She was smoothing her hair again, and pulling at the legs of her tights. "I never seem to be able to get to it later in the day. It's a morning-or-not-at-all kind of thing." Her eyes met his and her cheeks flushed.

He dropped his right foot down one stair. "I don't mean

to interrupt. Paul said you were up here, he didn't tell me what you'd be doing." *Although he may have tried.* "I can go have a coffee while you finish."

"I am finished. I like to end with a headstand. It gives me a little rush to launch me into the day. And it's supposed to help me stay young looking." She smiled for the first time and patted her cheeks with both hands.

"I'll have to get you to teach me then. Looking in the mirror can be a rather shocking event these days."

"Give me a minute to put away my things and grab the painting. Meet you in the lobby?"

"Have you eaten breakfast?" Mark asked.

"No, not yet. A full stomach makes yoga more difficult, bending around the extra bulk."

"I can imagine." Mark placed a hand on his belly. "Paul makes a delicious omelette. Join me?"

"You know ... I ..."

"At home I typically dine with the gulls but Paul chases them off his patio and I hate to eat alone."

She met his eyes and then slowly nodded her head. "Okay ... but none of those addictive omelettes. What sort of crack does he put in there anyway?"

Mark laughed. "No one's sure. We don't want to ask in case it's something illegal."

"I'll stick with my fruit and granola."

"Of course you will. Bloody health fanatics—bastards! Always making the rest of us feel like schleppers."

"That is why we do it."

"I knew it! At last one of you is willing to confess. I'll leave you to pack away your mat of torture and see you downstairs."

# Seven

With the tube of her yoga mat tucked under one arm and water bottle in hand, Sandra headed for her room to put things away and retrieve the painting. *At least I didn't make a complete ass of myself this time but I'm sure I look a mess. What's with stopping by so early in the morning? Doesn't he know women, especially older women, need prep time before seeing other members of the human race?* Sandra stepped into her room and threw her yoga things on the bed before turning to look in the full length mirror. *Okay, not completely hideous, but maybe a bit of make-up would help, and a long shirt to cover up my backside in these tights. Breakfast? Why on earth did I agree to breakfast? Is it remotely possible that I can function like a normal person with Mark Jeffery watching me eat?*

Sandra dusted a bit of powder on her face and added some bronzer to the tops of her cheekbones. Her ponytail had released wavy strands from its binding, leaving them to dangle around the sides of her face. *Hmmm ... tidy or leave it be? It looks natural, leave it alone.* She pulled a button-up cotton shirt from the closet and slipped it on over her t-shirt and tights. "Better," she said aloud, forcing a smile at her reflection. "I look like I'm on vacation, which I am." The smile left her face and was replaced with a furrowed brow. *Buck up, girl. He's just a guy.* She turned to leave, the hotel room door swinging closed behind her before she remembered the painting. *Right, he's here to purchase art.*

The breakfast patio was situated on the south side of the

hotel with beautiful views of the sea, the beach, and the mountains in behind. It didn't offer the rooftop's 360-degree view, but was one of Sandra's favourite spots in the building. The side against the wall of the lobby was filled with flowering plants in bright pots, and ceramic art in the shape of starfish and other sea creatures swam on the white wall, all pointed toward Cortez. Once Pablo's was open in the afternoon, the half-dozen tables and chairs were stacked in the corner and sunbathers dozed on canvas loungers, working on their take-home tans.

Mark was sitting with his back to her looking out at the water. She walked toward him, keeping the painting facing her body. The flutter in her belly and the moisture on her palms reminded her this was not *just a guy* she was meeting. Like it wasn't nerve-wracking enough putting her work out there for scrutiny—really, Mark fricking Jeffery? She inhaled deeply, willing the nervousness to subside.

"Are you ready for the big unveiling?" she asked as she approached his table.

He turned in his seat. "Ready. Do we need a drum roll?"

"No, but I might need a drink. I'm remembering why I don't sell my paintings."

Mark crossed his legs and placed his hands around the top knee. He smiled, probably trying to look reassuring, but the Mark Jeffery smile was anything but comforting under the circumstances.

"Okay, here goes." Sandra turned the painting and held it in front of her, a flat hand pressed into each side of the canvas. She closed her eyes. Silence. She opened one eye and then the other.

Mark was looking at the painting but she couldn't read his expression. "It's splendid. You've done a superb job of finishing it, and it's ideal for the spot I have in mind." He raised his eyes to her face.

"Well … good … I'm glad," she said.

"Do you still need that drink?"

"It's actually a bit early for me, even in Mexico." She set the painting on one of the extra chairs, her shaking hands rattling it against the wicker. Taking the seat opposite Mark, she jammed her hands underneath her thighs. *Stay still, damn it!*

Sandra watched him, his eyes travelling over the painting.

Mark turned toward her and slapped his hands on the table top. "So, to business. Will a cheque do? If not, I don't have enough cash in-pocket but can certainly get it when I next go to La Paz."

"A cheque won't do, I'm afraid." Mark's eyebrows lifted. She continued, "But neither will your cash. It's a gift, for your new house."

"No-no-no, that's not what we agreed to."

"I know, but, I've given it some thought and, since I've had the pleasure of viewing your work on the screen, you should enjoy mine on canvas. It's a fair exchange."

"But you probably paid the going rate to go to the cinema?"

"Truthfully, I'm not much of a theatre-goer. I enjoy most of my movies on DVD or television, so I'm not a great contributor to your industry. Sorry."

"Oh, no need to apologize to me. Neither am I." Mark leaned back in his chair and put his hands behind his head. "You know, I'm kind of surprised that you've seen my work. You strike me as more of a film festival person than a fan of romantic comedies or period dramas."

Sandra pulled her now steady hands out from under her legs. The conversation was helping her to relax. "I think people generally take art too seriously. If it's not for enjoyment, then for what? Serious or complex movies can be enlightening, but there's nothing quite like a good romantic story. It's kind of like appreciating a gourmet meal and fine wine but also liking a good hamburger with an ice cold beer."

Mark chuckled. "You have a point. Although I'm not sure

how I feel about my life's work being compared to a burger and a beer."

"I don't mean that romantic comedies and period pieces don't have impact. I think they do, if they're done well."

"Well, that's a relief, although I'm not sure I agree with you." Mark seemed to be contemplating his hands, now interlaced and resting on the table top.

"Have I interrupted the negotiations?" Paul asked as he walked toward them from the lobby.

"You have in fact," Mark said. "I'm just in the process of refusing the rather ridiculous offer made by Ms. Lyall."

"She's asking too much, is she? Good girl, Sandra. Old money bags here can afford it."

"On the contrary, she's trying to *give* me the painting, the one I've offered fourteen hundred dollars for."

Paul shook his head at Sandra. "Oh no, you don't want to do that. I've heard the stories about him negotiating movie contracts. He deserves the same lack of mercy."

"I see …" Sandra lowered her eyes across the table at Mark. "But I haven't changed my mind. I told him at the beginning that I don't typically sell my paintings—how many have I given you now, Paul?—so gift it I will. That's my final offer. Take it or leave it."

"But I am just a poor *hotelero* … no comparison."

"Take it or leave it." Sandra looked back at Mark.

"You drive a hard bargain, my Canadian friend, and I see no choice but to accept your terms. But … on one condition. I owe you dinner, here at Pablo's, or in the village if you prefer."

"Make him cook." Paul interjected.

"He's a good cook?"

"Quite. He's responsible for a couple of the favourites on Pablo's menu, and he should have to work harder than simply paying the tab."

"All right, dinner then, home cooked, nothing out of a

package, and I do enjoy a nice red wine." Sandra extended her hand across the table to Mark. When he took her hand she felt her face flush with warmth as their eyes met. Right. She'd almost forgotten who she was talking to.

"Glad I could help broker the deal." Paul pulled out his pad and pen. "Now, what can I get you for breakfast?"

"I'll have your Florentine omelette and I believe the lady will have something intended to make me feel terribly guilty about every delicious bite."

"Ah, the usual then. One breakfast sundae coming up. And to drink?" Mark ordered black coffee and Sandra, the caramel macchiato.

"And so the lady does have a weakness," said Mark.

"Oh yes, more than one, I'm afraid," said Sandra.

"Don't tell him that, you'll just send him digging for the others." Paul left them for the kitchen.

Sandra's eyes went to her hands clenched in a ball on her lap, wondering what on earth they could talk about until they had food to put in their mouths. The only business they had in common, her painting, had been settled. She could feel his eyes on her. She met his gaze, those brown eyes making her breath shorten for a second; they reminded her of when her father took her gold panning, dark saucers with flecks of gold. "S-so ... Paul tells me you've been friends a long time, since high school?"

"We have. He's a good chap. I still feel badly that things didn't work out for him."

"You don't think they did? He seems happy here and business is good."

"True, but he didn't have the success in films that he would have liked."

"Maybe life had a different path in mind for him. I know I'm glad he's here. Mar Azul has been a haven for me."

"Do you honestly believe that, that life has a plan for each of us?" Mark asked, his tone changing.

"Ah …" Sandra hesitated. "I don't know. I guess it helps sometimes, when life dishes out events that don't make any other kind of sense." Even four years later, just a few words could bring thoughts of Nick flooding in. She spotted a sail on the horizon, making its way south through the waves.

"I think we choose our own path, we just don't always like where it leads. And other people get in our way or sabotage our progress." Bitterness had crept into his voice.

"Is that what you think happened to Paul? Other people got in his way?"

"Not specific people, but the way the industry is structured, who it favours, who it doesn't, the fact that there are many more actors wanting jobs than jobs wanting actors. I think good people fall victim to it, like Paul."

"He thinks he wasn't good looking enough, or lucky."

"Looks and luck are part of the equation, and fitting into one of the boxes they need filled. It happened the box he best suited wasn't in abundance."

"So I take it you fit into a box that is more in demand."

"I did, as in past tense. Age is yet another factor in the equation, and another we have no control over. You see, that's the wretchedness of it. I can do the best job of playing a particular part, but if I wasn't given the right looks or I don't speak with the right accent or I'm at the wrong age, that's it. When I was in my twenties and thirties and even forties, there were more boxes I could fill. Now there are only a few, but still a mob of us old guys lining up to fill them."

The darkness that clung to Mark was starting to take shape in Sandra's mind. She was quite familiar with the challenges of having a career that wasn't meeting one's needs or expectations.

"What drew you to acting in the first place?" Sandra asked, already knowing Paul's version of the story.

"Well, ironically, Paul did. I'm not sure I'd be here if it weren't for him … and my mother."

"Your mother wanted you to be an actor?"

"No, my mother wanted me to be like my older brother. I was determined to be a physician with Doctors Without Borders, travel the world helping people. Then my brother Matthew decided to go into medicine. I'd competed with him in academics, in sport, and every other damn thing throughout my youth, I wasn't going to compete with him in my career. When Paul said he was going to the drama academy, I thought 'what the hell' and went with him. I knew Matthew would never choose such a thing. It was safe territory."

"And you succeeded—quite nicely it would seem. Was your mother pleased?"

"Funny thing is, she died not long before my first major movie role. She'd seen me on the telly, and she'd always mention it, but still she'd go on about Matthew and his practice and some miracle he'd performed, some life he'd saved. He could do no wrong." Mark inspected the fingernails of his right hand, smoothing his thumb over each one. "Never make your life choices based on another person's expectations of you, the moral of my sad story." Mark drummed his fingers on the table and looked over his shoulder to the kitchen door. "Where is that man with the blasted coffee?"

"The omelette is delicious. How goes the granola sundae? Getting through it?" Mark asked, making yummy noises as he chewed the final piece.

"It's quite tasty, thank you. And there's no *getting through it*. You should try it sometime. You might surprise yourself."

"At my age I'm well beyond surprising myself." He took a mouthful of coffee.

"Well isn't that a sad state to be in, and at such a young age."

"Young? If I were young I wouldn't be *here*." He flung his arm in a half circle.

Oops, she'd managed to prod another of his prickly spots. Oh well, have to talk about something and bold seemed a better strategy than bashful. Trisha and Nick would both be proud. "Yes, young. And what on earth is wrong with *here?* The sun, the sea, the palm trees swaying in the breeze—to most people this is paradise."

"Paradise is entirely relative. One person's paradise is another person's *hell.*" The word hell seemed spat out.

*He's just a man, Sandra, don't be intimidated.* "So … why are you choosing to be here, if this is *hell?*"

"And how is that any of your bloody business?" He jumped to his feet, throwing his light wicker chair onto its back. He stared at her, his fists clenching and unclenching at his sides.

She didn't know how to respond. She dropped her eyes to the table and picked up her ceramic coffee mug, sipping the warm liquid, the sweetness of caramel blending with the bite of coffee bean on her tongue. She could feel his stare like two burning points on the top of her head. Maybe if she closed her eyes, there would be an empty chair across from her when she opened them, an upright chair, and her morning would be normal, and peaceful.

"Mark! Are you leaving already, mate?" *Paul to the rescue. Thank God.* "You haven't had your second cup of coffee yet, or your third." Paul spoke as one might to a hostage taker—*everyone stay calm and we'll all get out of this alive.*

Mark's hands relaxed and he leaned over to pick up the chair. "I'm sorry. I … I … didn't sleep very well last night."

"More coffee, Sandra?" Paul asked.

"You know, I should get going." Sandra pulled the napkin from her lap and laid it on the table. Breakfast had gone from awkward to excruciating and she had no wish to stay any longer. "I'd like to get started on another piece today, since I'm going to La Paz tomorrow."

"No. Stay for another cup. Please." Mark's tone had softened.

She didn't want to—but his eyes—like the pain of the world rested in them at that moment. Her mouth wouldn't form the word no. "All right." Sandra turned from Mark to Paul. "Another macchiatto then, this time the hazelnut, please." If she was staying she was going to need something pleasurable to distract her.

"Great." Mark said with an audible out breath. "I'll have one of those as well."

"Well, that was quite delightful." Mark said, looking down at the bit of foam resting in the bottom of his empty cup.

"I can't believe you've not tried one before. Paul makes some incredible specialty coffees. He's got about six different lattes on his menu, three macchiatos, a cappuccino, and all of them addictive." The conversation had remained superficial and pleasant for the twenty minutes it took to drink their second cups.

"I'm rather a 'give it to me black and strong' guy in the mornings. It's more of a drug than a beverage."

"I see. Well, I'd best get to that empty canvas." Sandra slid her chair back and stood up. "Thank you for breakfast, and enjoy the painting."

"Perhaps you'd like to come by at some point to see it in its new home? I do owe you a dinner."

"Sure, maybe." Sandra nodded and turned to go.

"Can I give you a ride to La Paz tomorrow?" he blurted.

Forty-five minutes in a car each way—she wasn't sure she was up for that. She turned back to face him. "Thank you, but I'm just going to hop on the bus. I wouldn't want to mess with your day. I'm only running a couple of errands, shopping things."

"Me as well. And my day is generally unplanned so, you see, you can't mess it up."

She met his eyes, unsure of what to say, how to politely

say no. She couldn't believe she was being invited on a road trip with Mark Jeffery and did not want to go. Trisha would kill her. But she had a stiff neck and sore head after an hour-long breakfast with a rich and famous companion. A full day? She couldn't imagine.

"I should be glad to have your company." He was standing now, looking into her face.

Damn those sad, over-sized eyes. It was a trick of nature, the same one used by puppies and babies. So much for her puppy dog weakness only applying to actual dogs. And how did he cover the distance between ogre and charmer so quickly? Again she found the word "no" eluding her. "Okay. If you're sure it would be no trouble, a ride would be … nice."

"Great." Mark's smile lifted the corners of his mouth, pushing his cheeks into two round pouches just below those girl-swallowing eyes. "Then I'll swing by around ten to pick you up? Does that give you enough time in the morning?"

"Ten-thirty would be better. You see, I'm already messing with your plans."

"If delaying me by half an hour is the worst you can do …"

"See you tomorrow then."

Sandra turned and made her way from the patio to the guest room hallway. She knew that thousands of women would give their right arm, possibly the left too, for a day in La Paz with Mark Jeffery, but she would honestly prefer a day to herself. La Paz—peace. It wouldn't live up to its name tomorrow.

# *Eight*

The wave travelled halfway up Sandra's calves as it made its way to shore. She stopped for a moment and closed her eyes, breathing in the moist, salt air. February. Her fifth time in Mexico for part of the winter and still it seemed unreal that this could be a February evening. Four years ago Baja had melted the ice she felt in her veins, like the winter had moved into them and could only be evicted by such a place as this. A tear ran down her cheek without any advance notice—no tightening in the throat, no burning eyes. The pain was less and yet the tears still came easily, like the trail had been blazed by so many before them that they could come without warning, without hindrance. She opened her eyes and pulled a tissue from the pocket of her capris, drying her face. The lights of Mar Azul were starting to come on in the distance as the sky darkened. Its warmth beckoned and yet she didn't feel ready to be with people.

The breakfast with Mark Jeffery had rattled her and the feeling had stayed with her through the day. Was it his celebrity, his outburst or simply the fact that he was an attractive man? She wasn't sure, but she knew she didn't want to travel to La Paz with him tomorrow. Trisha would say she was just nervous, but this didn't feel like a case of nerves, this stone in the pit of her stomach. She walked further out into the surf, the warm water now reaching her knees, soaking the bottoms of her pants. Turning her face to the sky she raised her arms in the air, placed her right foot to the inside of her left thigh in tree pose and waited for the calm to wash over her.

"So, what do you think of my famous friend?" Paul asked from behind the bar. Sandra licked some salt from the rim of her glass and let the tart, icy beverage follow it onto her tongue. "You're getting almost as good as Arturo at mixing a marg. Where is Arturo anyway?"

"He's in the kitchen, and you didn't answer my question."

"Well … he's a bit on the moody side I'd have to say. It's like dancing with a porcupine, all charm until you bump into him. Is he always like that?"

"He's always been impetuous, but the short fuse to anger is new. He's going through something of a rough patch right now. Career and ex-wife both giving him grief."

"He didn't mention his ex-wife but I gathered he's less than thrilled with his career at the moment. Wasn't he married to Serena Rhodes?" Sandra held her hand at chest height. "Legs up to here?" Paul reached over and slid her hand up closer to her neck. "Oh, thanks." She laughed. "I think I saw something about her in some magazine or other recently. I never buy them but I do indulge my curiosity when I'm in line at the grocery store."

"Serena, that's her, the ice queen. And what you probably saw is that she recently remarried."

"Why would that upset him? Aren't they many years divorced?" She leaned forward as if in confidence. "You know, it's strange to know so much about someone I've just met."

"Definitely a downside of fame, everyone knowing your business." Paul was slicing lemons, placing them in a blue and yellow flowered bowl on the top of the bar. "They have been divorced for quite a few years now but when every move you make is followed by the press, you appreciate a little heads-up when something's going to happen. He found out about her marriage from an entertainment news show on the telly, and right after that the reporters were ringing for his reaction." He took another lemon from the bag and sliced into it. "I always thought she was a bit of a bint, like every other woman he gets involved with. I'm one of his closest friends but I don't recall her ever making a point to talk to me." Paul leaned forward and opened his eyes wide. "Self-centered cow."

"Paul Hutchings! I've never heard you trash talk someone before. There's another side to our *friendly* hotelero."

"Only when it comes to Mark's girlfriends."

"I see. He's invited me along to La Paz tomorrow. I'm afraid I said yes."

"Just keep the conversation away from ex-wives and work and I'm sure he'll be as charming as I am."

"Maybe half ... *if* he works at it." Sandra took another drink from her over-sized margarita glass.

Paul's gaze jumped to the bar entrance. "Ian, welcome!" Sandra turned in her stool and waved as Ian approached. He was dressed in floral board shorts and flip flops. "I'm guessing by your attire you won't be taking the stage tonight."

"Not tonight, no. Just dropping by for a beer and some en-chanting conversation." He ordered a Dos Equis and hopped onto the stool beside Sandra, turning toward her. "And you're looking very nice this evening."

Sandra glanced down at her wet-bottomed capri pants and pink v-necked shirt. "I thought you had a better sense of fashion than that, being a Montrealer. I just came back from a beach walk."

"Exactly my point—colour in your cheeks, windblown hair, sand between your toes—what could be more attractive?"

"You'd compliment me if I were wearing a burlap sack and hadn't washed my hair for two weeks."

"Ooh, fetching. You might be right." He really could be quite enchanting, which is why he often had a lovely woman on his arm. "So how's the painting coming along?"

"Very good, actually. I'm well into a second piece and, get this, sold the first one."

"Sold one? I thought you didn't do that."

"Okay, well technically I gave it away, but to someone who was willing to pay me for it, and pay well I might add."

"And who, may I ask, was this person with impeccable taste in art?"

"A friend of Paul's, Mark Jeffery. Have you met him?" asked Sandra.

"Briefly, here at the hotel a few weeks ago. Is he still here?"

"Not here at the hotel but in the village. I think he bought a house."

"In San Leandro? Now why would he do that? Doesn't a big shot like him want a fortress closer to civilization?"

"Apparently not," said Sandra. Paul set down a brown bottle with two red Xs on its label. "Paul, did Mark *buy* the house in San Leandro?"

"I think he's leasing, not sure for how long."

"There you have it. I didn't think there were any movie-star-worthy properties in the area." Ian poured the amber beer into his glass.

"I think he's here because Paul's here."

"Maybe," Paul said, "but more likely because it was a convenient place to camp for a while. Excuse me." He left the bar to attend to a couple standing at the *please wait to be seated* sign.

"So anyway, Mr. Jeffery was here one morning, saw my painting, and offered to buy it to hang in his new house. Exciting, don't you think?"

"Absolutely. Good for you. Now," he tilted his head and raised his brows, "can you tell me why you gave it away when he offered to buy it?"

"It's a long story that has to do with Jane Eyre." Sandra waved her hand dismissively. "How are things going with your song writing?"

"Quite well. But don't think I didn't notice that quick change of subject. We'll come back to Ms. Eyre. There is a rather well-known artist looking at recording one of my songs on his next album."

Sandra clapped her hands together and extended them to Ian. "That's great!" He took her outstretched hands in his. "And who is this *rather well-known artist*? Someone I listen to?"

"I doubt it, but you've likely heard of him. Chet Morgan."

"Country! Since when do you write country music?"

"I don't, technically, but country is a much wider genre than it once was, and Chet cuts it wider than most."

"Can I hear the song?" Sandra sat back on her stool and pulled her hands onto her lap.

"When I'm here on Friday I'll play it for you. It won't sound like the version Chet will release, but I like it."

"And when will you know if he's putting it on his album?"

"He and his producer should be making those decisions now. It's been recorded. Now it's just a matter of whether or not it makes the cut."

"Well that is exciting news. Congratulations, Ian." Sandra lifted her glass toward him.

"It's what I've been working toward." He clinked his glass to hers. "Seems we both have something to celebrate. Paul—bring our artist another margarita!"


Sandra set her empty glass on the bar. "Okay, I need to go to bed. Three margaritas is one more than my limit and two more than my usual. If they weren't so darned big."

"Can I walk you home?" Ian lowered himself from the stool and extended his arm.

"You can, but only after I stick my toes in the ocean."

"You want to go to the beach? Now?"

"I do, just ankle-deep. It's such a gorgeous night."

"You know that ankle-deep can become thigh deep when the waves are right."

"And so I'll get wet. C'est la vie!" Okay, she was a little drunk, but she felt good tonight. The stone in her stomach was reduced to a pebble, there was no sign of a tear ambush and Ian was here. She threw a fist in the air. "To the beach!" Paul looked up from where he was sitting with one of the other guests.

"Oops," Sandra leaned in and whispered to Ian, "that came out a bit louder than I intended."

"Okay Margarita Mary, let's go before you get us *thrown* out. You can shout all you want outside."

The sand was still holding some of the day's heat and the water felt warm on her feet. Sandra stopped and turned her face up to a half-moon surrounded by a spray of stars. "I love it here. I feel so liberated." She let go of Ian's arm and extended her hands to the night sky. "Do you feel that way about this place?"

"It's why I stayed. Have you ever thought about it? Staying in Mexico?"

"That's the second time you've brought that up. Are you selling real estate these days?" They'd started walking again, the waves pulling sand from under her feet, taking it to the sea.

"Me? Certainly not. Just curious. From what you've said you haven't been happy, back in Alberta."

"I wasn't. You're right. But that's changed now." She linked her arm with his. "Things are good. I'm good."

"Well, glad to hear it. So, what's changed? New man in your life?"

"No! No man—new or old. What's changed is me. It just took some time."

"Ah yes, time heals all wounds—whatever they might be." Ian paused as if waiting for Sandra to reveal more. She remained quiet. "But so can the Sea of Cortez ..." Ian fanned his arm toward the open water and gave Sandra a look of invitation.

"All right, you're on!" Sandra released his arm and began walking into the waves.

"I meant healing to be near, not in!"

"Come on super-Canuck! The water's warmer than any Canadian lake in mid-August!" She was hip deep in the dark water, the waves splashing up around the bottoms of her shoulder blades.

"You have been drinking, Ms. Liberated, and should not be swimming in the dark," he called over the sound of the surf.

"Oh don't be such an old curmudgeon, come join—." A large wave swept over Sandra's shoulders, drowning out her last word. She laughed and spluttered, "—me."

"Okay, you win. I'm coming out to get you before you drown."

As Ian began wading toward her, Sandra moved further out into the water. "Sandra. I mean it. You need to stop there."

"You sound like my father, and I rarely listened to him."

He stretched his hand toward her even though she was still twenty feet away. "I know you can swim but tequila has a way of hampering athleticism ... and dulling common sense."

"I heard that!" Sandra got the words out just before a wave crested her shoulders and swallowed her head. When it passed, she was underwater, imagining Ian scanning the surface for her, calling her name. She could feel the surge of the sea pushing her toward the beach and then pulling her into its depths. Four years ago she would lie in the water and let the current pull at her, tempted to let it take her out, lacking the will to drag her weighted body back to land. It seemed the years had changed that, she no longer wanted to drift away, the shore had won out. She swam underwater in Ian's direction, knowing he'd be moving to where he last saw her. She guessed at the distance and launched herself to the surface right next to him, sending salty spray into his face. "Gotcha!"

He stood there waist deep in the rolling water, glaring at her, water dripping from his nose and chin. "What the hell, Sandra? You scared the crap out of me!"

"You *are* a curmudgeon. When did that happen? I'm sure you weren't like this last year when I was here."

They stood in the dark water, the surf continuing to roll by at shoulder height. Ian's back was to the beach, his face shadowed and grave. She flashed him her best "come play with me" grin. And then he started to chuckle, his chin dropping to his chest, shoulders bouncing. Sandra laughed with him, accepted his outstretched hands and turned a circle there in the sea. She wished she could wrap this moment up and tuck it away so its joy could be pulled out to light up her darkest thoughts. He held her hand firmly in his as they left the water and ambled back to the hotel, a trail of salt water drops behind them on the sand, the echoes of their laughter blending with the crashing of the waves.

# Nine

Sandra sat in Sukhasana, her hands resting on folded knees, palms facing up into the faint orange of the morning sky. She closed her eyes and still saw the glowing horizon on the backs of her eyelids. She was the only one on the rooftop and couldn't believe she alone was taking advantage of this perfect time of day. Even the gulls were silenced by the morning's blissful tranquility.

She stood and brought her feet together and reached up into the growing light, raising her eyes to the coloured canopy. Peace. *I will maintain peace through this day. I will maintain peace through this day.* Her arms panned wide as she swan-dived into a forward bend, fingers touching the bumpy green surface of her yoga mat. *I am an island of calm. I am an island of calm.* Her hands dropped onto the mat and she stepped back into Downward Dog. She smiled as she thought of Rufus mirroring her position, his tail wagging in an invitation to play. Despite the freedom it afforded, she missed his constant presence in her day. Maybe she'd talk to Paul about bringing him again next year. He loved the beach.

She lowered her forearms to the floor and kicked her feet up into a headstand. Mark would be here in a few hours. Was there any chance of maintaining peace through this day? She thought of the ease and fun of last night with Ian. Why did it have to be different spending the day with someone like Mark Jeffery? Why couldn't she just be herself? Because he was famous? She supposed that was the reason. And there was that porcupine thing he had going on. Tiptoeing around someone never made for relaxing conversation. She brought her feet and shins back down to earth and pushed her arms forward into Child's Pose. If only she could stay here all day.

Sandra heard a knock on the door as she was putting on her make-up, and then Paul's voice. "Sandra, Mark is here for you. He's waiting outside."

"Thank you. Tell him I'll be right there." *Okay, here goes nothing.* She'd Skyped with Trisha over breakfast and, between that and a lengthy yoga session, was feeling better prepared for her road trip with Mr. Rich and Famous. She just wanted to get through it with her self-esteem intact. Of course, Trisha had placed a whole other level of significance on the day.

"You lucky thing, spending the day with Mr. Rochester."

"He's not Mr. Rochester, Trish. He's an aging actor with a tendency to bite heads off."

"Oh, you'll cheer him up. You always do that for me when I'm in the dumps."

"Yes, but I feel comfortable with you. With him I'm worried I'll say exactly the thing that will set him off."

"Well set him off then. Maybe he needs a good rant to get it out of his system."

"I'd rather not, thanks. I thought he was going to come at me from across the table yesterday morning."

"Just don't get him all riled up when he's behind the wheel. Wait until you're sitting somewhere."

"Oh, I don't plan to be sitting anywhere with him. We're driving in together and when we get to La Paz I'll be going my own way until it's time to head home."

"If only I could inhabit your body for a few hours." Trisha closed her eyes and let out a sigh through her upturned nose. "What a different day it would be."

Having Trisha inhabit her body for the day wasn't a terrible idea. But, with the laws of nature against that happening, Sandra inhaled deeply, grabbed her bag, and regretfully left the serenity of her room behind.

"*Hola*, Señorita." Mark was leaning on the hood of a cobalt blue BMW convertible. "Your chariot awaits."

Although still bearded, today he was looking more like Mark Jeffery from the big screen, which wasn't necessarily a good thing. "Isn't this a little fancy for Baja roads?" she asked.

"Admittedly, yes, I have discovered it's not entirely practical for dirt roads, but it's got great suspension and it's only five miles to the pavement." He went around the car and opened the passenger door. "Hop in and I'll show you how a BMW handles these goat trails they call roads down here."

She couldn't deny it was a gorgeous vehicle. She slid into the soft leather bucket and pulled the seat belt over her shoulder. As he climbed in beside her his cologne met her nostrils, something spicy and very masculine. *Oh boy.*

"Are you okay with the top down?"

"Sure, why not. Curly hair doesn't look much different when it's windblown." *And maybe the noise will make for a conversation-free journey.*

Mark started the engine and she could feel its power as soon as he put it into gear, very different from her hybrid SUV. She wondered how much fuel it burned.

"I'll put the windows up for more quiet; that way we can chat." Mark grinned at her as he pressed the button and the small tinted sheets of glass rose up out of the doors.

They were nearing the sea again; she could feel the change in the air and taste the salt on her lips. Forty minutes had passed quickly. Mark seemed to be in a particularly good mood, or at least on good behaviour, and Sandra was trying to keep the conversation light. Weather, San Leandro, Paul—they all seemed to be safe topics.

"So where is it you need to go?" he glanced toward her, his hair dancing across his forehead and the tops of his Ray-Bans. It was the same face that had appeared behind her at Mar Azul on the weekend, still unshaven, still in sunglasses, but it seemed to have benefited from a few good nights of sleep.

"If you can drop me off near the cathedral, I should be able to get to everything I need from there."

"Catedral de La Paz, next stop." Mark stepped on the gas for the final straight stretch of highway before entering the city limits.


"If you stop there it'll be fine." Sandra pointed. "I'll meet you back here in a few hours?"

"I need to do a bit of shopping as well so we might as well find parking." He pulled the BMW into a spot along Revolucion and shut off the engine.

"Great. So we'll meet here at the car then, say two o'clock?" She opened the door and stepped out onto the sidewalk. No way, no way, she was not going shopping with Mark Jeffery. She would face the wrath of Trisha later.

"I'm a first-rate shopper. Maybe I can tag along and give you a hand."

Did that mean he didn't have anything to do but follow her around? She knew this was a bad idea. Why hadn't she taken the bus like she'd planned?

He came around the car and onto the sidewalk. "Where do you need to go? I've been to La Paz a few times and I'm happy to be your guide." He was smiling at her.

*No, no, no, no. I can't, simply can't.* He stood, waiting for her to answer, his expression bright. *He's making an effort to be pleasant, Sandra. Try to pretend he's just a fellow tourist and go with it.* "Okay ... well ... I need some art supplies and there's a shop on the next block."

The art supply store was sandwiched between two larger stores, one a clothing shop, the other a pharmacy. As they entered, Mark leaned toward her, "I speak enough Spanish to get by so if you need to ask for anything, I'm happy to translate."

"Thanks, but I think I'll be able to find everything I need."

"Señora Lyall! *Hola. Bienvenido!*" A small man came from behind a shelf of sketch books and canvas boards. He was wearing a loose shirt covered in random splotches of paint, looking somewhat like a Mexican version of Rembrandt with his hair curling out from under his red beret. "I was thinking it was time for you to come back to Baja."

"I see you don't need any help communicating," Mark said in a low voice, putting on a smile.

"Pascual. So good to see you. This is my ... friend ... Mark."

Pascual came forward and shook Mark's hand. "But you are Señor Rochester, no?" Pascual's gaze went from Mark to Sandra and back again, his eyes wide.

"Yes, Mark Jeffery. You've seen *Jane Eyre?*" Sandra was surprised.

"Oh yes, many times. It is Antonia's favourite."

"I didn't know Antonia spoke English."

"She doesn't, well, very little, but the picture has the voices en Español."

"Now that I haven't seen. How do I sound in Spanish?" Mark asked.

"Well, you sound ... very much like a Mexican."

Mark and Pascual both laughed.

Pascual looked to Sandra. "Will you be coming to the art

show, amiga? It is starting in one week."

"Art show? What art show?" Mark asked.

Every year the art council in La Paz put on a show at the end of February for area and visiting artists. Paul had tried to convince Sandra to put a painting in the exhibit for the past couple of years but she had declined.

"Perhaps this year you will allow us to include one of your pieces? Paul tells me they are very good."

Mark leaned toward Pascual. "I can attest to that. I own one of Ms. Lyall's paintings, purchased it yesterday, and I understand she's got another underway."

"Perfecto!" Pascual clapped his hands together. "You can enter that one."

"*That one,*" she lowered her eyebrows at Mark, "is barely started and I'm not sure it will be good enough to put on display."

"Are you involved with the art show?" Mark asked.

"*Sí,* I am a member of the committee, as is my wife."

"Well consider Ms. Lyall a participant then, with at least one piece. Mine is not for sale but I'd be happy to include it for display."

Pascual turned to Sandra. "Even better! With two pieces I can include you in the Visiting Artists tent. And maybe by one week you will have a third?"

"She just might."

"Excuse me," she said looking at Mark. "I haven't agreed to one piece and you've got me down for three?"

"Simply trying to be helpful. Put her down for three, Pascual."

"Don't put me down for anything. Mr. Jeffery is overstepping his bounds."

"Please, Sandra. I would be delighted to show the work of a talented Canadian artist. Please reconsider."

"You're breaking the man's heart, señora." Mark mocked a sad face. "Do you know Pascual, that Ms. Lyall here never sells her art, only hoards it in her cellar?"

"No, *que lastima*! Art is to be enjoyed."

"You hear that? He says it's a shame."

"The two of you are ganging up on me."

"If that's what it takes ..." Now Mark was grinning.

"All right! *One* piece." She pressed her lips together to keep from smiling.

"Plus mine makes two. The beach scene is no longer yours so I will enter it myself if I have to."

"Don't you have a rule about that, Mr. Jeffery entering a piece that he didn't paint but simply owns?"

"We have very few rules—"

"One of the things I like about Mexico," Mark cut in.

"—but we do have a rule that all art must have been created here in the La Paz area."

"There you have it. My painting qualifies," Mark said. "I saw her painting it on the rooftop at Casa del Mar Azul."

"Okay then, I will contribute two paintings," she turned to Mark, "under duress!"

"Duress, señora?"

"It means she's thrilled, and will very likely bring a third piece."

"*Muy bueno*! You have—what do you English say?—made my day."


It was difficult to get out of Pascual's shop but Sandra finally gathered together the supplies she needed and they returned to the street. It was quiet, which suited Sandra just fine. She was not one for crowds, particularly when she was on a shopping mission. She never had fit the shopping-loving stereotype imposed on her gender.

"So, what's next on your list?" Mark asked, eyeing her handbag.

"The list is actually up here," she tapped a finger to the side of her head, "and don't you have a list of your own?"

"We'll get to that. Didn't you mention something about shoes?"

Right, that had slipped out on the drive in. "Sandals, yes." Sandra stopped walking and looked down at her feet in a pair of faded blue canvas shoes, her baby toes starting to escape through the sides. "As you can see, I'm in need of a new pair of summer footwear."

"Mmm ... indeed."

"I didn't even bother to bring what's left of my sandals." She thought of the Mexican sandals she'd bought four years ago on that first trip to Baja. She hadn't packed any summer things that year and had had to buy everything when she arrived. The sandals were barely holding together these days but she couldn't part with them, not yet. They'd taken her on such a journey.

"And do you always wait until things fall apart before replacing them?"

"I don't like buying shoes. I have an unusual foot shape; shoes either pinch or slip. Boots are even worse. When I find something I like, I buy two pair and wear them out."

"How very practical."

"Thank you. I think so." Sandra started walking again.

"But rather dull. You'll be glad of my help today. I know just the place." Mark picked up his pace and stepped into the cross-walk.

"I'm sure there's a shoe store around the corner by the cathedral." Sandra hung back.

"There is, but they sell Mexican-made shoes only, and I think you may need something European."

"But I like the Mexican sandals, and I like the price."

"The shop I'm thinking of has local as well as imported. It will give you a wider variety to choose from. Come on then." Mark motioned for her to catch up.

Zapatos de La Paz was a block off the waterfront, tucked in between a women's clothing shop and a store selling Mexican ceramics. How perfect—three interesting shops in one location. Sandra's kind of shopping. Her mother had been particular about every purchase she made and was willing to travel all over Toronto for the right plums, the best coffee beans, or her favourite kind of underwear. Sandra was more the "one stop and get me out of here" variety of shopper.

The store's windowed front was floor-to-ceiling shoes displayed on glass shelves with clear plastic stands to raise their heels. Mark held the door open for her. "I bought a pair of shoes here only last week. I'm certain we'll find something you like."

*Now Mark Jeffery is helping me buy shoes for my oddly shaped feet. Isn't this a treat.*

Like its face, the inside of the store was all glass, a huge aquarium with multi-coloured "shoe fish" swimming in the many full height tanks. A path travelled through the various displays and a small bench sat at the back of the store for trying things on.

"*Buenos días. Bienvenido.* How may we help you today?" The shopkeeper's English was very good. Her accent sounded as though she'd learned the language abroad.

"The lady is looking for some new sandals, something comfortable ... and fashionable I'm guessing?"

"Yes, and how about I take it from here." Sandra accompanied her near whisper with a stern look, not wanting the same runaway experience of the art supply store. Next thing he'd have her modelling shoes in the La Paz fashion show, if they had such a thing.

He raised his hands and bowed his head. "Of course. I'm only here if you need a second opinion."

"We have a nice selection of ladies' sandals over on this side, all of which are very well made and, I assure you, very comfortable."

Sandra perused the display of summer footwear in various designs, some with heels, some flat, some adorned with jewels or shells or bits of metal, and others plain. Variety—the blessing and the curse of modern-day consumerism.

"How about these?" Mark pointed over her shoulder to a strappy sandal with a heel.

"I thought you were just a *second* opinion? And really, you think I'd want to run around San Leandro in high-heeled sandals?" But, they were pretty, and the red would go with the dress Trisha had bought her. "These are more my style." She pointed to a flat-soled shoe with three half-inch leather straps over the instep. Two of the straps were brown, the middle one red, and a vertical strap was decorated with two copper medallions and a red bead.

"Can I try these in a size nine?" Sandra placed a finger on the glass next to the sandal.

"Nine?" Mark raised his eyebrows.

"Yes, size nine. You have an opinion about that too?"

Mark made a zipping motion from one side of his lips to the other.

The sandals were made in Mexico, a selling point, and they were comfortable. She loved the red accents and, even without any kind of heel strap, the shoes clung to her feet, making a day of walking feasible. She checked the sticker on the end of the box and smiled at the low price. "I'll take two pair please."

"And she'll try on a pair of these … in a nine I believe it was." Mark was pointing to the red one with a heel. "What? I could tell you liked them. I'm just offering my *second* opinion."

He was right, as much as she hated to give in. "All right. I'll try them on. But if they're not comfortable I'm not buying them."

"Fine. Fine." He raised his hands and took a step back.

The shopkeeper brought out a white box and from it produced the larger version of the red display shoe. They were never quite as cute in her size. "These are made in Italy and are very comfortable for a heeled shoe. I have a pair myself."

Sandra sat down and slid her foot into the curve of the sole. It had arch support, unusual for a shoe with a higher heel. The width was exactly that of her foot and the four connected red straps somehow made her foot look daintier, smaller than its number nine measurement. And, they would go perfectly with her red dress. She buckled the ankle straps and walked one of the store's narrow aisles toward a mirror. And walkable!

"Well, what do you think?" She turned to Mark who'd taken a seat on the bench.

"I have been relegated to second opinions only. I'll need to hear yours first."

"So well-behaved all of a sudden. Well, I like them, and they're comfortable, and I can't often say that about dressy shoes."

"They're quite lovely. I think you should buy at least two pair." He was trying to look serious but she could see the mischief in his expression.

She checked the price on the box before turning to the shopkeeper. "I'll take these as well, please. But just one pair."

With Mark holding the bags of art supplies and shoes, Sandra browsed the ceramics shop, making notes on possible gifts for friends at home and a few new pieces for her own growing collection.

"Why not buy them today since you have your very own Sherpa," Mark pretended to bow under the weight of the parcels he was holding, "not to mention chauffeur?"

"If you're trying to make me feel guilty, it won't work. I

gave you an out when we first got here. You could be sitting on a patio drinking a latte about now."

"I chose my own fate, you are correct. So, while I am at your service, take advantage. It's what I would do."

"I'm sure you would." He was different today, less edgy, and quite charming, in a pushy way. She was finding it easy to forget she was spending the day with a movie star.

"All right then, English Sherpa, I will take you up on your offer. How much do you think you can carry?"

They stepped out onto the bright street, Mark's arms loaded with two boxes of well-wrapped ceramics, the shopping bags of shoes and art supplies dangling from his hands.

"Are you sure you don't want me to carry something? Let me take the bags."

"Absolutely not. I'd be the laughing stock of my Sherpa order if I let you carry your own parcels. It's only two blocks to the car." He set off down the street.

"All right then. Suit yourself. Anyway, that's it for my list. Should we tackle yours?"

"My list. Right. I guess it's lunch then!"

"Lunch? That's your list?"

"It's the first item on my list. Better to have a go at the rest on a full stomach."

Sandra recalled her words to Trisha that morning, "I don't plan to be sitting *anywhere* with him." But now it didn't seem like an unpleasant prospect.

# *Ten*

La Paz's waterfront featured the five kilometre long el Malecón, with its wide sidewalk, beaches, benches and tourist pier. The iconic Hotel Perla faced the sea. Its lower level, which housed the restaurant and nightclub, open on the street-side. Mark pulled the car into a space half a block past the hotel. Free parking—that was something Sandra seldom found at home. The City of Calgary was always trying to encourage people to come downtown, but without offering anywhere inexpensive to park.

"Have you been to Hotel Perla?" Mark asked as he hopped out of the car.

"I have. I stayed here for a few days on another trip down when I was feeling like being closer to civilization. Great view, but then it's pretty spectacular at Mar Azul, with less traffic."

They took the two steps up into the almost street level restaurant. As Sandra wound her way to a table at the front, she could feel Mark's presence behind her, making her conscious of every step. She settled into a chair that sat sideways to the view and turned her head to look out at the waterfront. The shopping had gone better than expected. She'd been able to relax and enjoy herself. She had to give Mark some of the credit for that, putting her at ease, making it fun. But having lunch with *Mark Jeffery* immediately brought the butterflies to her belly and clams to her palms. What had Trisha said? Be herself? Okay, it was worth a try. She closed her eyes and breathed deeply through her nose, drinking in the moist air scented with sea life. "You know what two things I love most about Mexico?"

Mark pulled out the chair opposite and sat down. "I can't imagine."

"You just don't like it here do you? I love the air, and the colours."

"Funny, I somehow envisioned Canada as being rather … airy."

"Oh, there's plenty of air in Alberta, often coming at you with enthusiasm, but this soft, warm breeze is completely different. It's what I miss most when I go home. And the colours." She ran her hands over the smooth yellow finish on the arms of her chair. Each chair at the table was painted a different colour—blue, green, purple, turquoise. "Where do you ever see beige in Mexico? The rest of North America is obsessed with beige."

Mark was smiling at her. "Spoken like a true artist."

A young waiter arrived at their table holding menus in one hand and a notebook in the other. "*Buenas tardes. El menus?*" His name tag read Juan Manuel.

"Sí," Mark responded, "and una cerveza. Pacifico por favor."

Sandra held up two fingers, "Dos Pacifico. Gracias." Juan Manuel placed the menus on the table and moved on to a group of four seated nearby.

"You drink beer. I'm surprised," Mark said.

"Shouldn't be. Beer is a big part of my Canadian culture."

"I just haven't met many women who drink beer. It's typically wine or cocktails, or tea in the case of my mother."

"Until I met my first margarita, I wasn't much for hard liquor, and with beer and rye usually the only drinks at university parties, beer was the lesser of two evils. I guess I acquired a taste for it." Sandra glanced toward the bar where Juan Manuel was talking to the bartender. "I'm not a very dedicated beer drinker. I like a few—the fairly light, not bitter variety. Most of the Mexican beers are quite drinkable." She paused. "I would have pegged you for a wine drinker."

"I am. In fact that's one of my errands today, picking up a case of my favourite wine. The selection in San Leandro is rather dismal."

"I didn't realize there was a selection at all."

"The hotel will sell wine by the bottle."

Mark's eyes went to the traffic rolling by on Alvaro Obregon, which ran the length of el Malecón. It was a busy street, day or night, with the local and tourist traffic interspersed with police and military, undoubtedly to put the tourists at ease. "I owe you an apology," Mark said, looking back at Sandra, "for my very rude behaviour yesterday."

"It's okay—"

"No, it isn't. You asked me a question and I *threw a wobbly*, as my dear mother was fond of saying."

"Wobbly … sounds much cuter than it is … but really, it was none of my business."

Juan Manuel returned to the table with two bottles of pale gold beer covered in droplets of water. "You are ready now?" he asked in stilted English.

They hadn't looked at the menus. "We'll need a few more minutes to decide," Mark said.

When the waiter had moved away Mark continued, "You asked me why I was choosing to be here in hell, if hell is what this is for me. Fair question, since I'm a man of means and free to leave any time. I'd like to explain, if you'll let me."

"Okay."

Mark stared out at the street. "Well, in a nutshell, my career has hit the skids, my ex-wife is a secretive bitch and I don't have anything better to do but hang out in fucking Mexico drinking cerveza." Mark lifted his bottle as if to toast and took a big swig.

*There* was the guy she'd had breakfast with yesterday. Sandra had been wondering if he'd show up. She studied the label on her beer bottle, her thumbs sliding up and down its wet sides. Lunch wasn't ordered yet, she could still make a getaway.

"Right, that didn't come out quite like I intended. Perhaps I should give you a standing apology for everything unpleasant that escapes my lips since my internal censor seems to have gone on holiday." He took another long drink of Pacifico. "Please say something, before I spit out some other vile bit of verbiage."

Sandra smiled at his effort to be civil and rein in what was obviously wanting to break out of the gate. "Well, I'm a pretty good listener, or so I've been told. How about I ask you some questions and you try to answer them. You don't need to censor everything for my benefit, but I do have two requests: one, that you remember I'm trying to help, and two, keep in mind we're in a public place."

"Fair requests. Ask away." He leaned back in his chair.

She wasn't sure where to start now that she was venturing from the safe zones of weather, shoes and beer. She let her mind wander back to her idyllic morning yoga session and tried to regenerate that feeling of calm. Nope. That wasn't going to happen. Maybe she'd try Trisha's approach. What would she ask him if he were "just a guy" sitting across the table from her? "So, is it the career or the ex giving you the most grief?"

Mark peered into the neck of his beer bottle. "That's easy. The work. Serena pissed me off, but that's nothing new. If it hadn't been on the backside of being sacked it wouldn't have been a big deal."

She leaned forward with her forearms on the table top, her eyes fixed on Mark. "Okay, that's a good start. So, you were fired?"

He stared at his beer for a moment before meeting Sandra's gaze. "I was offered a lead role in a movie with a very big British director, a role that could have changed the course of my career. I agreed, enthusiastically, and came to Baja to see Paul and go over the script. A week after I arrived, I found out another actor had been signed for the role, without even so much as a phone call or email from my agent or the director. I read about it online in Star Power. I flew to London to try to salvage things but it was done. I'd been dropped. They wanted someone with more *Oscar potential*," Mark made bunny ear symbols with his fingers.

"Ouch."

"Indeed. My agent has assured me he'll find me something as good or better but his most recent suggestion is an absolute piece of tripe."

"Maybe it's time for a new agent."

"I've thought about that, almost fired his sorry ass on the spot, but Nate's been good to me, until now, and he has a lot of connections. At my age I'm not itching to hit the pavement looking for someone new to represent me. I'm comfortable with Nate, even when he pisses me off. If he'd only got them to sign the bleeding contract ..." He took another drink.

"So you think it was his fault they gave the role to someone else?"

"No, not really. I'd merely like to blame him rather than admit my career is turning to crap." Mark glanced at the menus resting at the end of the table. "I guess we should think about ordering." He opened his menu.

Sandra opened hers but continued to look at Mark. With his head bowed toward her, she could see the grey strands of hair around his crown, and the angle of his face revealed little pouches under his eyes. She'd always thought aging must be so much easier for men. Maybe not, particularly for someone famous.

Juan Manuel returned to take their food orders—two catch of the day specials, another Pacifico for Mark, and a glass of water for Sandra.

"So what is this new course you'd like your career to take?" Sandra asked when the waiter was on his way back to the kitchen.

"Playing the romantic lead was fine twenty years ago but those opportunities start drying up as the years go by, much like we do. Like it or not, we live in a society that values youth."

"Don't I know it. Try being a fifty-year-old woman in a beauty-obsessed culture."

"Try being that fifty-year-old and having your wrinkles and flabby bits show up on the cover of a tabloid. That's the life of an aging celebrity, male or female. Admittedly, you ladies do seem to get the worst of the lot."

"But don't you think we also gain credibility as we age?" Sandra asked.

"That's true in many types of work. Unfortunately, acting is more than skill and experience; it's also a game of looks, type and age. One of my instructors at the academy cautioned me on taking advantage of what he called my 'matinee idol' looks. He said I might not enjoy being typecast. I didn't listen at the time, because the roles I was being offered were leads, the goal of every acting school graduate. At first, the BBC dramas were a miracle—a chance to be in films—and playing in *Jane Eyre* got me noticed by the Americans, something else I'd set my sights on."

"I know I've seen you in American movies so it seems that worked out for you?" The direction of the conversation reminded Sandra just who was sitting across the table. She leaned back in her chair, rubbing her hands on her thighs. *I am an island of calm.*

"It did. But the roles in America were all romantic comedies, some good, some dreadful. I never turned one down, thinking I was working my way up the ranks in Hollywood and would earn the opportunity to play roles with more substance. But, I continued to be called when they needed someone with a posh British accent to play in a romcom. I was *the good-looking Brit* when they needed one. I'd been typecast, precisely like I was warned I'd be, and now I'm mostly too old to fit the type.

So what's left? Apparently, pathetic bit parts in second-rate movies." Mark took a drink from the fresh beer Juan Manuel had delivered.

"So the period dramas and romances were a means to an end? They didn't have value in and of themselves?"

"Value in financial terms, absolutely. You can't continue to act unless it puts bread on the table and my career has always been lucrative. So many actors, like Paul for example, find themselves doing things on the side to fund their acting. I never had to do that. I was lucky. But romantic stories don't alter people's lives or make a difference in the world." He took another drink.

"You don't think so? You don't think the stories by Jane Austen and Charlotte Brontë affect people?"

"Other than people who work in tissue manufacturing? Not likely."

"Such a cynic! You know, I had an English prof in university who said that real people will forever remain a mystery, no matter how well we think we know them. We only truly get to know people in stories, and from knowing them we learn to understand real people, and ourselves. So, what if your Mr. Rochester inspired someone to express love or abandon prejudice. Wouldn't that be of value?"

"And what if all my Mr. Rochester did was inspire thousands of women to swoon ridiculously over an imaginary man played by someone they knew absolutely balls about?" He picked up his beer bottle again, taking another long drink. Sandra was starting to see the pattern: touch on something uncomfortable, the man takes a drink. Not a coping mechanism she admired or had much tolerance for.

"I think that would be a sorry statement on all womankind, one that I don't believe. Falling in love with an on-screen or on-page character doesn't make someone ridiculous, only vulnerable, and a bit of a romantic. And you have no idea where stirred emotions may lead a person. What if it awakened someone's creativity and caused them to discover a passion they didn't know they had? Point is, when you put art out there, you have to trust it will find its way into the hearts of the people who can benefit from it. You don't get a say in how people will be affected or not."

"Wise words from a woman who keeps her art in the cellar." He smirked.

Sandra knew she'd been caught. "For starters, I don't keep my work in a cellar …"

Juan Manuel arrived with two bright yellow plates piled with food and a basket of tortillas. *"Dos especialidades de pescado fresco."*

When he'd gone Sandra continued. "I used to work in galleries, as a curator. I watched people's reactions to art and I watched the artists' responses. A few artists, a handful, felt they'd made their statement and were satisfied. They didn't seem to care if their pieces sold or were even appreciated. This one artist, Byron James, painted these magnificent landscapes. They were so vivid and alive with colour you wanted to step right into them. He sold out every single show, won a bunch of awards, but he'd never show up to receive the recognition, unless someone brought him to the gallery at gunpoint. He just kept painting. Until I can be that removed from what people think of my work it will stay *in my cellar*. I don't want to paint for someone else; it needs to be my gift, not something I expect praise and payment for."

"That's a high bar you've set."

"I get that from my father, in a roundabout way. Everything he did in life was to impress someone or garner some kind of attention. I don't think it made him happy." Sandra dug into her plate of fish and refried beans. The fish flaked apart with the lightest touch of her fork.

"Was he an artist?"

"No." She paused to chew the mouthful of fish, her tongue sorting out the various seasonings used in the grilling.

"An archaeologist. A successful one—published, respected. He was an incredibly clever man, but arrogant. It's because of him I was a curator instead of a painter. Once he realized my interest lay in art, curator was the only career choice that suited him. It was never very important what suited me. But anyway, we were talking about you. Another question …"

"I think I'd prefer to hear more about your relationship with your father." Mark placed a forkful of the Yellowtail in his mouth.

"I'm sure you would. But you don't get off that easy." Sandra dabbed her napkin to her mouth, preparing for the next question. "So, what was so different about this part you didn't get? Different from the other roles you've played."

"It wasn't a romance for starters, a complete rarity in my career. When have you heard about an actor in a romantic comedy winning an Oscar for best actor?"

Sandra smiled. "Jack Nicholson, *As Good As It Gets*."

"Well done," Mark nodded as he chewed, "but try a second."

She thought for a moment. "Richard Dreyfuss, *The Goodbye Girl*."

"I'm impressed. Remind me to choose you as a partner if we're ever faced with a game of Trivial Pursuit."

"But I get your point, there haven't been many. Was that the difference with this movie then, potential for awards?"

"Partially, and credibility with the right people."

"The *right* people?"

"The people that make award-winning movies, I suppose."

"So it's all about the awards?"

"No, not really … they're just a way of measuring what's … valuable."

"And so we're back to what adds value to people's lives."

"It would seem so, unfortunately. You've tricked me!" Mark pointed his fork at Sandra.

She was starting to enjoy the conversation. When she could

forget he was famous and that he might bristle at a wrong turn of phrase, he was fun to talk to. "I believe you stepped into this trap all by yourself. So, would you say that all Academy-or-other-award-winning movies add value to people's lives, in the way that you want to add value?"

"No, probably not, but there's more potential for it."

"Okay," Sandra thought for a moment, "so if you were to look back over your career, what role gave you the greatest satisfaction, as an actor?"

"It would have to be Rochester. I won a BAFTA for that one."

"So was it the role or the award that made it satisfying?"

"I refuse to answer that question on the grounds that it may incriminate me." Mark responded in his best American accent.

"Very good." Sandra clapped her hands. "But what's your answer?"

"I enjoyed the challenge of the role. I enjoyed the accolades. I enjoyed the money. Did I feel I had given something of value to the world? Not really."

"So, would this new role, the one given to the other actor, would it have added value in the way you think is important?"

"Are you sure you're not some kind of therapist, masquerading as an artist?"

"Answer the question."

"No, wait, perhaps a barrister."

Sandra stared at him.

"All right then—no, probably not. It had the potential to make the award lists. The subject matter was not of much interest to me and I doubt it would have changed the world. But what movie ever does?"

"So if movies don't change the world, what does? Who does?"

He began counting on the fingers of his left hand, tapping the pinky as it rose from his fist. "My brother does. He's a surgeon; saves lives nearly every day." His ring finger stood next, empty of any ring. He smacked them both with the index finger of his other hand. "My father does. He's a history professor at Newcastle; builds young minds." His middle finger joined the other two and Mark thrust his hand toward Sandra. "My friend Norman definitely does. He's an old school chum who runs a humanitarian organization that's brought aid to a dozen different countries, horrid situations most of us aren't even aware of." Mark looked out to the sea. "He called me last week, asked me to narrate a documentary for him, on the high rates of child mortality in Mali and a couple of other African countries." Mark's gaze came back to Sandra's expression. "Don't feel bad. I hadn't heard of it either."

"Well doesn't that fit with your definition of work with value?"

"A low-budget documentary that will be shown by film societies and universities? My agent was horrified. I believe he called it *euthanasia* for my film career."

"Perhaps it would be, but maybe it's time." As soon as the words passed her lips she wished she could pull them back.

"Time to put my sorry career out of its misery?" Mark slammed his hand on the table top hard enough to make the cutlery jump. "Is that what you think?" Heads turned toward them from the surrounding tables.

Sandra glanced toward the exit, wondering if leaving would be more or less uncomfortable than staying. She leaned forward and spoke in a hushed tone, "Number one—trying to help; number two—public place." She was surprised at her own boldness.

"Right. Sorry." Mark signalled the waiter and ordered another beer.

"What I meant to say was that if your career is no longer satisfying, why not venture out into something different?"

"Because I'm not ready to give up yet. I'm not ready to call time." The edge was still there. "I've invested more than thirty years of my life in this business. I can't just throw that away."

"Fair enough." Sandra leaned into the back of her chair and took the last swallow of beer from her bottle. It seemed the fun part of the conversation was over.

"That's it?" he asked.

"That's it. I rest my case."

Sandra followed Mark down the steps to the sidewalk in front of La Perla. She pulled her sunglasses from the top of her head to the bridge of her nose.

"The marina is a short walk down this way. Care for a stroll?" Mark asked. "I'm rather an admirer of the floating craft."

The remainder of lunch had passed without incident. She'd gone back to Paul's recommendation and kept the conversation away from career and ex-wife. Twice they'd sat across a table from one another, twice he'd had some excessive display of anger. Driving was fine, shopping went well. Maybe the key was to keep him moving. A walk sounded like a reasonable idea and she was wearing her new and comfy sandals. What the hell. "Sure. I haven't seen the marina."

The two-lane roadway running in front of La Perla had parking on one side and La Paz's famous Malecón with its wide sidewalk on the sea side. They ambled southwest on the paving stone walkway, red stones flowing through the grey ones in bands, the palm trees like sentries every fifty feet. White wrought iron benches placed at regular intervals seemed more befitting of a Victorian garden than a Mexican resort town, but they provided great stopping places for tourists wanting to enjoy the view or rest their feet. Mark seemed content to walk without conversation, whether out of discomfort or lack of anything to say Sandra didn't know or care. Between his stardom and his temper it was fatiguing spending the day with him, and the walk along the Malecón was a refreshing reprieve. She loved the waterfront here, and being outdoors always helped to ground her.

Mark broke the silence. "The marina is beyond the end of the walkway, but we can take the street the last bit."

Masts came into view as they rounded the corner past a large condo complex. "Sticks," Sandra said, more to herself than to Mark.

"I'm sorry?"

"*Sticks*, it's what my ... friend used to call them—sailboat masts. He thought they looked like a bunch of sticks all in a group like this." Nick had had a unique way of seeing many things, often amusing, always interesting. She still missed him so much. She felt the slight burning in her eyes that came right before they filled with tears and she dropped her gaze to the new sandals making their way along the pavement.

"I don't suppose you've sailed, given your landlocked location."

"I have actually. I sailed some with my husband's family, back in Toronto, on Lake Ontario."

"Husband? I didn't realize you were married."

"I'm not, anymore. That was a *very* long time ago. It almost feels like something I saw in a movie rather than lived through. Have you ever felt that way about a part of your life?" They'd stopped at the entrance to the marina near a large flowering shrub. Its pale pink flowers gave off a heady scent similar to lilac.

"I feel that way about many parts of my life, but in my case, it's often true." Mark laughed.

Sandra blushed. "Of course. I should have thought of that. Is that the case, can real life and acted life get confused?"

"Not really, at least not beyond filming. When you're in a character's head all the time the line between yourself and your role can become blurry, but it goes quickly once filming is wrapped. Should we go in?" Mark nodded his head toward the open gate.

"Can we? It's not for members only?"

"Some of the members offer boat charters so I'm sure they're happy to have us poking about."

They walked past the marina office and down to the docks. Each pier had a gate at its end, preventing access to anyone without a code, but many of the boats were viewable from the shoreline boardwalk.

"And you? Have you sailed?" Sandra asked him.

"I have, as a boy, in London—my brother and I took lessons—and then again about ten years ago when I was working on a movie. I enjoyed it so much I certified with the *Royal Yachting Association*." He'd made his accent even more posh than normal. "I know enough to charter a boat and generally keep myself out of trouble." Mark stopped and turned to Sandra. "Would you like to go?"

"Go?"

"Sailing. I'm sure someone must charter sailboats for the day."

Sailing. Now did that qualify as a moving activity or was it more of the sitting and talking variety that had proven problematic? It might depend on the weather and water conditions.

"Um … so … where would we go?"

"I'm not sure. I've not sailed here before. But I'm certain there are a number of day sails in the area." His brown eyes were locked on her face. "Well?"

Sandra felt immediately claustrophobic at the idea of being on a boat all day with Mark and yet the words came out of her mouth. "Okay then. Let's do that." *What? Who said that?*

"We'll need to bring the paintings in for the art show next week. Maybe we drop them off early and go sailing the rest of the day?"

*We? Now we're a we?* "Sure, that seems like a good plan." *Or not!*

If her words sounded as unconvincing as they felt, it didn't show in Mark's reaction. "Splendid! It's a date then. I'll look into getting a boat organized and plotting our destination."

Her head was starting to throb. *Splendid. Indeed. A date?* She turned back in the direction they'd come. It was time to go home. Her balcony at Mar Azul was calling. "Shall we go and get your case of wine then?"

"Good idea. And following that I have somewhere I'd like to show you."

# *Eleven*

"You lucky thing!" Trisha squealed from the laptop screen.

"But I don't feel that way, Trish. I feel like I want to relax and paint and swim and he keeps … inviting me places." Sandra plopped herself down on the bed, her face toward the monitor.

"Oh you poor doll. A rich and famous gentleman—oh, and did I mention incredibly handsome?—is ruining your alone time with his invitations. Forgive me if I'm having a hard time feeling sympathetic."

"From your perspective, I'm sure it's difficult to understand, but it's so hard to relax around him. When I'm not focused on the fact that his face has been on the big screen and the entertainment news, I'm scrambling out of the way of his temper. I have these fleeting moments of enjoying his company, because he can be quite charming, but it's too much stress for me. I come here for the tranquility of the place!"

"Well, I can't believe I'm actually saying this, but tell him to go away then. Say no when he asks you to spend time with him."

Sandra let out a sigh and dropped her face into her hands. "I've already agreed to go sailing with him next week, and I'm living here at his friend's hotel. What are the chances of avoiding him without appearing rude?"

"So I guess you have a decision to make, endure his company or endure the discomfort of being rude."

"Ohhh …" Sandra flopped over on her back, her arms landing on the pillows above her head.

"So tell me about the charming part, those moments when you forget he's *MARK JEFFERY* and just enjoy yourself." She spoke his name like Vincent Price may have narrated it in a horror film.

"Ha ha. Well, most of today he was on good behaviour. We went shopping and he was helpful … fun even—"

"Ooh, sounds terrible."

"But then, over lunch, he apologized for that little outburst at breakfast yesterday, the one I told you about—"

"Apologized? The cad!"

"Just listen, would you? I can mute you." Sandra poised her hand over the touch pad on the laptop's keyboard.

"Go on then." Trisha rolled her eyes.

"He went from pleasant to spitting mad as soon as he started talking about what's going on in his life and I was ready to head for the nearest bus stop. Although … he did get some control and we managed to have a decent conversation about what's bothering him. That is, until he pounded his fist on the table hard enough to make the silverware jump. He had the whole restaurant staring at us."

"So what's got him so riled up?"

"He got dumped from a role, a good one, apparently."

"Well that's got to hurt. You have to cut him some slack Sandi. He's got a high profile life for getting fired."

"I know, and I'm trying. But then he's off on some chair-tossing, fist-pounding hissy fit and I want to crawl under the table."

"So what set him off, when the conversation was going well?"

"I suppose I did, with a comment I made … that I probably should have worded a bit less … bluntly. BUT, his response was still over the top. He apologized, again, but the tension didn't leave his voice until I changed the subject."

"So stay off the subject."

"That's what Paul said, and what I did for the rest of the day. But I don't like tiptoeing around people. You know that."

"I know, love, and you're good at talking people through things, but maybe not in this case." Trisha's hand went out of the camera's view and returned with a coffee mug, a green ceramic with leaves circling its rim, undoubtedly the work of one of her gallery potters. She took a drink from the steaming mug. "So, the rest of the day in La Paz was ...?"

"It was nice."

"Nice? Really? Can you come up with a less descriptive word?"

"Okay, fine, we had a lovely walk along the waterfront down to the marina, which is where he came up with the idea to go sailing." Sandra closed her eyes and dropped her head back. "A whole day on a boat, Trish. How will I manage it? What will we talk about?"

"I'm sure you'll think of something. Or, you could always leave town."

"I hadn't thought of that."

"I'm kidding, you ninny! You can't leave town. He'll be there when you get back, unless you come home. Is that what you'd like to do? Let this man chase you home?"

"No. I don't want to go home. I want to paint!"

"Well paint then, and go sailing with the actor hunk next Tuesday and try to enjoy yourself. If you can't do it for you, do it for me!"

"I will channel you as best I can."

Trisha lifted her coffee mug and held it between her two hands. "So then what, after the marina?" She took a sip.

"We went to a liquor seller where he picked up a case of wine—"

"A case? What, is he throwing a party?"

"No, he just likes wine, among other intoxicants. He went through three beers to my one over lunch."

She set the mug down. "Okay, now that concerns me more than the temper. You know I went down that road with Jack, and my father before him."

"I know. You see? You see why I'm not easy with this?" Sandra sat up and pulled the computer onto her lap. "Anyway, after the wine pick-up he drove me to this lookout, this absolutely amazing spot that looks down over La Paz and across the Gulf. We had the place to ourselves."

Trisha leaned in, her face filling more of the screen. "Now the story's getting interesting."

"Don't get too excited. It was just a hike up a steep trail. But there was this one moment—"

"M-hmm?"

"Well, I wasn't wearing great shoes for climbing so he took my hand to help me over the steepest part. He looked back and smiled at me with his hair blowing around his face and I felt like I was the heroine in one of his movies. And, I admit, my knees felt weak for a moment and I may have approached a swoon."

"A swoon! Well, that's a great deal more than *nice!*"

"But it's not real Trisha, it was purely a movie star crush kind of swoon."

"So? Who cares? You're on bloody vacation. Lap it up!"

"I'm trying but I'm just not—"

"Normal. I know. So then? Tell the rest."

"I took a few photos of the view and we went back to the car. The drive home was pleasant enough; he talked about his family, his house in San Leandro … normal stuff. It was one of those times when I forget he's anyone other than an average Joe."

"We're all average Joes on some level Sandi, even Mark Jeffery."

# Twelve

Mark awoke to the familiar sound of gulls and rolled over to look at his bedside clock. Seven. Time to get moving. It was Thursday, the day of his weekly tennis game with Paul. Through Paul's connections in the hospitality industry, they had an arrangement with Baja Waters Resort to use the courts once a week. Neither of them was a very good tennis player, but they were matched well enough to enjoy a game.

The smell of coffee drifted to his nostrils. A cuppa with the morning news on the verandah—the daily ritual. He swung his legs over the side of the bed and stretched his arms over his head. He pulled on a pair of white shorts and a yellow t-shirt, smiling as he thought of Paul's certain annoyance at his wearing a shirt the same colour as the ball. Like it made a difference at their level of play.

Coffee cup full and toast on a plate, Mark settled himself at the outdoor table and hit the power button on his iPad. His first stop was always the BBC World News and then on to things more personal, like the U.K. entertainment news. There was more about Patrick Janzen and his exciting new movie role, but the story didn't seem to have the same sting as on previous mornings. Mark hummed to himself as he continued to flip through the digital pages, alternating between sips of coffee and bites of toast.

A large white gull landed on the railing a few feet from where Mark sat. "Ah, good morning Geoff. You're here early.

You must have caught the scent of toast." Geoff was larger than most of the gulls that frequented this part of the beach and he had a black band around his yellow beak that set him apart from the others. "Do you like marmalade?" Mark tossed a small piece of crust toward the bird who hopped down to the deck to retrieve it. Geoff pointed his head skyward and gulped down the bit of bread. "It's not biscuits but it seems it will do. Smart man, take what's offered in case it's all there is." He paused. "Unless of course you'll choke on it. Then I'd advise against." He stared at the bird without seeing him for a moment. "Right." Mark stood and gathered his dishes and iPad. "Well old chap, there's a tennis court with my name on it. I'll see you back here for biscuits this afternoon."

"Are you ready, mate?" Mark asked as he walked into the lobby of Mar Azul. Paul was where he often found him in the mornings, at his desk behind the front reception counter.

"I am ... just ... give me ... a ...," Paul said, not looking up from the pile of paper in front of him.

"A minute?" There was no response from Paul. "I'll go ramble the decks." Mark left through the side door, stepping out onto the breakfast patio where two couples were seated at tables. They glanced up as he entered their space and he gave a quick nod of acknowledgment. He crossed the patio and took the stairs to the rooftop. It was empty this morning, its white floor gleaming, a few deck chairs stacked over to one side. At the edge of the roof he looked down onto the beach; it was quiet at this hour. A man wearing a bright orange shirt sat at one of the palapas reading a newspaper, a woman jogged by at the edge of the surf, her ponytail bouncing with each stride, and far down the beach a couple walked hand in hand, pointed in the direction of San Leandro.

Back in the lobby, Paul was still at his desk but this time he looked up and smiled as Mark returned. "Good morning!"

"You realize I was here a few moments ago?"

"Oh, was that you?" Paul said as he put away his papers and notebook. "I was trying to balance things from yesterday's receipts. Why did I not pay more attention in math class?"

"Because you were too busy thinking about girls … and drama."

"I think it was more like drama and then girls for me. I was always realistic about my options. And, at the end of the day, I succeeded with neither." Paul laughed. "Just let me grab my bag and off to the courts!" He made a dramatic flourish with his arm in the air.

"You do know that those kinds of hand gestures are possibly why the girl thing hasn't worked out for you?" Mark called after him.

A few minutes later, Paul returned through the door that led from the lobby to his private quarters. "You're in a good mood this morning. It will be nice to play tennis without that dark cloud hanging over our court. I guess I'll need my sunglasses."

"Since when am I a gloomy tennis player?"

"Seriously? You're going to pretend you haven't been a dismal Jimmy these past few weeks?"

"No, I suppose not."

"So, did something happen? Did your agent come through for you?"

"No, nothing's changed. I'm still pissed off about losing a good role and being offered total crap in its place. It just seems to be feeling less oppressive today."

"Well, I'm happy to hear it. I'll let Arturo know I'm headed out." Paul leaned through the side door and waved to an unseen person. "Arturo. I'm off."

"*Hasta luego*. Enjoy the tennis." Mark heard Arturo's voice from outside.

The two men followed the stone pathway to the parking

area, the intoxicating scent of the bougainvillea thick in the air. The woody vines climbed the walls at the entrance to Mar Azul, their pink flowers hanging in clumps.

"So your Canadian guest doesn't seem to be around this morning."

"Which Canadian? Oh, Sandra Lyall?"

"Yes, Sandra. When I've been here in the mornings lately she's been painting or up on the roof standing on her head."

Paul smiled. "I saw her go down to the beach about half an hour ago, with her easel and painter's bag."

"Hm, I didn't see her there either."

Paul stopped and turned to Mark. "You were looking for her?"

"Well no—not exactly. I was wandering around the decks while I waited for you and I didn't see her about."

Paul grinned at him and nodded. "I see."

"You see nothing."

"I saw that you took her to La Paz yesterday, although I didn't hear how it went. You didn't throw any more furniture did you?"

"I didn't *throw* my chair that morning. I stood up quickly and the blasted thing fell over. It's like they're made of feathers, those chairs of yours. A decent wind would carry them all out into the sea." He threw his arms in the air and toward the beach.

Paul dropped his duffel bag into the back seat of the BMW. "So it was the chair at fault."

"I didn't say that. I said they're light. And, to answer your earlier question, no, I didn't throw any furniture in La Paz."

"Well, good. I'd rather you refrained from frightening my guests."

"Although ..."

"Oh sod. What *did* you do?"

"I may have lost my temper and rather ... banged my hand on the table, a bit harder than I planned to."

"Mark …" Paul shook his head as he settled himself in the passenger seat.

"But I apologized, as I did for my breakfast outburst. She doesn't strike me as the delicate type."

"She isn't, but she's a good soul who probably doesn't want to spend her holiday hanging out under your dark cloud."

"I will endeavor to not frighten her but I enjoy her company." Mark put the car in gear and started up the long driveway to the road.

"So you're telling me you're interested in Sandra?" Paul asked. "She doesn't strike me as your type."

"Not *interested*, no, and she's not my type. I'm simply enjoying her company at the moment. She's a bit like … vanilla ice cream—not terribly exciting but predictable and rather refreshing."

"Not sure I like the sound of that."

Mark stopped at the top of the driveway and regarded Paul over the top of his sunglasses. "Look, my life has been rubbish this past month and I've found a bright spot amid the crap. Is that so bad?"

"Not bad for you, no, but she is a living, feeling person. I'm not sure she'd be happy knowing that you're using her."

"I'm not using her, I like her. I'm finding it pleasant to spend time with someone completely outside my normal circles."

"Okay, but if you hurt that lovely woman …" Paul leaned toward Mark and opened his eyes wide. "I'll have your guts for garters."

"Right." Mark chuckled. "I promise to do my best, but …" Mark grinned as he pulled onto the road toward San Leandro.

# Thirteen

"I know I'm predictable but I'll have the fish special again, Elena." Sandra closed her menu and handed it to the waitress.

"And I will have a plate of your fabulous fish tacos." Ian slid his menu on top of Sandra's.

"Such a beautiful girl," Sandra sighed as she watched Elena's retreating back, the burgundy highlights in her hair reflecting the lamp light. "If only I did portraits ..."

"So, you've been painting?" Ian asked.

"I have, and, you'll be shocked to learn, I'm exhibiting two, maybe even three pieces in La Paz next week."

"And just how did that little miracle come about? Has someone threatened you?"

"No, not threatened exactly, more ... convinced."

"Seriously? How many times have I tried to get you to exhibit in that show? Apparently, I need to take some lessons from—who was it, Paul?"

"No, Paul's friend, the one who bought my painting. Mark Jeffery."

"Ah, so that's the catch. I'm not famous enough to be convincing? Or maybe not sufficiently handsome?"

"No, nothing like that. He and Pascual ganged up on me at the art supply store in La Paz. They made it impossible for me to say no."

"Mm ... I see. Well, however it came about, I'm pleased. It's about time." Ian lifted his glass. "Here's to your success then."

Their wine glasses clinked together.

"So you went to La Paz with Mr. Jeffery?"

"I did—a couple of days ago. He offered me a ride and I found it hard to say no, even though I would have preferred to take the bus."

"I see a pattern developing. You realize that "no" is quite a short word, very easy to say. Let's try it—" Ian's eyes jumped to the beach entrance. "I believe your convincing friend just walked in the door. Careful, or he'll have you ordering a glass of Scotch and maybe the octopus appetizer."

Sandra gave Ian a gentle punch before glancing over her shoulder to see Mark walk up to the bar. "That's a first. I've never seen him in here."

"I have, but not for weeks."

"I thought it odd he never comes, since he and Paul are old friends," she said.

"So you've been watching for him."

"You don't have to watch for someone in a place this size to notice they're never here."

"Best practice that difficult two-letter word. He's coming this way."

Sandra turned to see a smiling Mark moving toward their table. "Sandra, hello." Mark held out a hand for her to shake. He turned to Ian. "And ... I'm sorry. I've forgotten your name."

"Ian. LeRoy." Ian extended his hand.

"Of course. I apologize. I'm terrible with names. May I join you?" He was already pulling out one of the two empty chairs.

"Be our guest," Ian said, the annoyance obvious in his voice. Sandra gave him her best *be nice* look.

Mark didn't seem to notice as he settled into his seat. "So, are you playing this evening?" he asked Ian.

"No, not tonight. There's a flamenco duo in from Cabo."

"Excellent. Nothing quite like live music. Rather lifts the

spirit, wouldn't you say?" Mark looked from Sandra to Ian and back again.

"Yes ... absolutely." Sandra said.

Elena approached the table and took Mark's order. When she left, the three sat in silence. Mark spoke first. "Soooo, Ian ... did Sandra tell you she's showing in the La Paz art show next week? It took some persuading but I think it's a good thing. What is the point of art if not for the enjoyment of others? It would be like you, playing music solely in the privacy of your own home, or me, reciting lines from Shakespeare in front of my bathroom mirror. What would be the point? We artists are destined to express ourselves for the enjoyment of others. Wouldn't you agree?"

Ian hesitated. "Well, yes, I suppose that's true, but there is also an aspect of creating art for one's own enjoyment and satisfaction. Wouldn't you agree, Sandra?"

Ian had a tone that Sandra recognized, that slightly mocking, ready-for-a-debate tone that was entertaining under the right circumstances, but unnerving in this situation.

"I'd say you're both right and it's just a matter of personal preference and comfort, and probably talent, that determine how much of our art is for ourselves and how much for public consumption. And yes, I did tell him how you and Pascual coerced me into showing three pieces in La Paz next week."

"Three? Aha," Mark pointed his finger at Sandra, "I knew you'd be keen once you were committed. She's a reluctant exhibitionist, this one."

"It's not really in her nature to show off."

"Show off? Is that what you think it is to display her work?"

"No, I just don't think there's anything wrong with not being an exhibitionist. Some of us are quieter about our talents."

*Well, isn't this shaping up to be a fine evening.* Sandra stood. "Ian, can I get you another glass? I'm headed to the bar." It probably wasn't a good idea to leave them alone at the table, but maybe she'd be lucky and they'd take it outside before she got back. She, for one, needed more wine.

Elena cleared away the empty plates. "Everything was very good?"

"Tell Paul that everything was delicious, Elena." Mark said as he placed his napkin on the plate.

"Excuse me." Ian rose from the table and headed toward the *baño* sign at the back of the restaurant.

Mark turned to Sandra as soon as Ian was out of earshot. "I have exciting news, and I have you to thank."

"Me? What did I do?"

"You inspired me, dear lady, to do something I should have done a long time ago."

"I did notice that you've pressed your slacks."

"You must be getting your material from Paul. I talked to my agent yesterday—"

"You took the documentary part."

"Oh God no, I'm not an idiot. But I did give him an earful, refused that piece of rubbish he sent me, and demanded he find something better or I'm taking my business elsewhere. This morning he called, and he's got something. I don't have the script yet but he assures me I'll love it and that it's in the bag if I want it."

"Well that is good news. Did he give you a sense of what kind of movie it is?"

"No, not really, but he guarantees I'll be pleased so I'm imagining it's something of the calibre of film that fell through." He leaned back in his chair and took a sip from his glass of burgundy wine. "He knows I won't be happy with much less."

"Well ... good."

"You don't sound convinced."

"I don't know your agent so I have no business passing judgement."

"Perhaps not, but tell me what you're thinking."

Sandra hesitated, not wanting to spoil his good mood, and not wanting a repeat of the last two times they'd dined together. "It's just that his idea of what suits you and yours seem to be travelling in different directions."

"That is true, but, I was *quite* clear."

"I'm sure you were." Sandra could see Ian making his way back to the table. He stopped half way to visit with two women he seemed to know. Although, with Ian, it was possible they were strangers soon to be friends. "I'm only suggesting you save the celebration until you see the script."

"Such a pessimist. I'm surprised."

"I'm not a pessimist, just inclined to caution."

# *Fourteen*

Saturday morning. Sandra had only been at Mar Azul for a week but it felt longer; so much had happened in such a short time. She took in the view of the water from her perch at the edge of the rooftop. The horizon glowed molten orange beneath a barge of grey cloud and the waves floated golden coins on their crests, gleaming in the sun and vanishing as they made landfall. The yoga sessions were helping to keep her grounded but she was losing some of the calm she'd come to associate with being in Mexico. It was Mark and she knew it, his attentions rattled her, left her feeling conflicted. Last night in Pablo's he'd hung around for the entire evening, much to Ian's disappointment. It was obvious Ian didn't like him. She'd have to find out why. Maybe something had happened between them before Sandra arrived or Ian knew something about Mark that she didn't. Mark seemed oblivious to Ian's uncharacteristic sharpness but Sandra knew Ian well enough to recognize his irritation at their uninvited third.

When she'd first come to Mar Azul four years ago she'd immersed herself in the peace of the place and had been resuscitated. She couldn't come here without remembering her excruciating sorrow but, more profoundly, the healing that succeeded it. Mar Azul had become like a magic elixir taken once every year to sustain that healing. This year she'd had one day of the elixir before Mark entered the picture. If she listened to Trisha's advice she'd be all over him, but she didn't trust the draw she felt. He was so not her type, so not Nick. The attraction was purely a movie idol crush and that just wasn't her style—it seemed a setup for embarrassment, or pain.

Last night he'd been so buoyant. They'd even had a dance while Ian fumed alone at the table. Despite his background in music, dancing was not one of Ian's ways of enjoying it. The duo had played some salsa numbers and, although she was apprehensive, Mark took her hand and led her to the small dance floor. She knew only the very basic back and forth steps of the footwork but Mark obviously had experience with Latin dancing and guided her through more complicated moves. It was exhilarating. For those two dances she let herself go and enjoyed being propelled around the floor by a good looking and accomplished dancer. His right hand felt strong pressing into her shoulder blade, and his left incredibly warm wrapped around hers—

"You look lost in thought."

Sandra started and turned to see Paul at the top of the stairs. "I suppose I was. Good morning."

"Can I interrupt?"

"Of course." She patted the empty bench beside her. "Come and sit."

"Everything okay?"

"Yes. Fine. Why do you ask?"

"I usually see you down for breakfast before now. Just checking in."

"Above and beyond the call of duty, that's our Paul. Nothing's wrong. I finished my yoga and got to staring out at the sea. It's a beautiful colour this morning. Sometimes the blue is so vivid and deep. I keep trying to capture it on canvas."

"So you were thinking about painting?" Paul asked, eyebrows raised.

"All right, what is it you really want to know?"

He sat down next to Sandra. "I saw you dancing with Mark last night. Another realm where he always showed me up—rotten bastard." Paul smiled.

"He does know how to bust a move. I'll give him that."

"And you're no slouch either." He nudged her with his elbow.

"Well thank you. But you didn't come up here to compliment my dancing."

"No, I didn't." Paul inspected his hands.

"Well, out with it. I've not known you to beat around the bush."

"Okay, this is none of my business but I'm going to butt in anyway. I'm concerned about you spending so much time with Mark, about your feelings for him."

"We're friends, that's all. When he's not brooding he can be fun."

"I know that. I've been his friend for almost forty years. And I also know that a lot of women fall for him and that he can be ..."

"A bit of a jerk?"

"Well yes, that too." Paul chuckled. "But what I was getting at is that he can be a bit oblivious to others' feelings. I wouldn't want you to be hurt, that's all. He's a great guy but he's only here sorting some things out and then he'll be back to his film star life and his celebrity girlfriends. San Leandro is far from his kind of place. He's usually good for a week before he starts whinging about how dull it is. I'm surprised how long he's stayed this time, and that he's leased a house, but I know it's just the funk he's in. It won't last."

Sandra put her hand on Paul's. "Thank you, but you don't have to worry. I'm quite aware that I am not his type and even more aware that he's not mine. I'd be happy if he'd find something else to occupy his time, to be quite honest. I consider myself pretty grounded, but hanging out with a movie star has been messing with my equanimity."

Paul was quiet for a moment, squinting out at the sparkling waters of Cortez. "You know, even though he's been down in the dumps recently, he's seemed more honest, more the Mark I knew before he became famous. He was a good guy, still is under all that obsession with getting the *right* roles, connecting with the *right* people, and looking good for the media. He didn't used to be so superficial."

"I think he's just torn between what he wants and what he thinks he needs in order to maintain this life he's created."

Paul looked at her, a soft smile touching his lips. "Very insightful, Ms. Lyall. You might be right."

"And so you'll cease to worry about me falling head over heels and having my heart tromped on by Mark Jeffery?"

"I'll do my best."

"So, how about that breakfast? I'm famished!" She rubbed her stomach and glanced down at her watch. "And, I'm late for a Skype session with Trisha."

"Where have you been?" Trisha asked. She was sitting at her kitchen table with her hands wrapped around a mug of coffee.

Sandra's laptop rested on the table, the umbrella overhead allowing her to see the screen with the brightness turned on high.

"Good morning to you too." Sandra responded as she settled herself in a chair facing the monitor and the sea. "I went a tad long in my yoga session this morning. Sorry about that."

"No prob, but I can't talk long. I have to get to the gallery. Where are you anyway? It looks like you're outdoors."

"I'm on the breakfast patio. I normally talk to you from my room but I needed breakfast and Paul only serves until ten. I'm afraid you'll have to watch me eat."

"Tell you what. I'll throw a couple of slices in the toaster and join you." Trisha disappeared from the screen and Sandra could hear her movements around the kitchen. "Go ahead. I can hear you. What's been happening?"

"I finished my second piece for La Paz, and today I'm starting my third."

Trisha's face leaned sideways into view. "That is fantastic. Are you going to the opening?" She disappeared again, the kitchen sounds resuming off-screen.

"I am. It's on Wednesday and Ian has agreed to come with me, for moral support. I'm nervous."

"Of course you are. You should be. The public can be ruthless."

"Oh thanks, that makes me feel a lot better."

Trisha returned to her chair. "I'm kidding. They'll love your work. Your style is unique but not out there far enough to turn people off. Which is why I've been trying to convince you to exhibit in my gallery for the past, oh, let me see now, eight years is it? I'm thrilled you're doing this but I may never forgive you."

"I promise I'll think about doing something at home. It's easier here where no one knows me."

"I understand that, but I still won't forgive you until I have a Sandra Lyall showing at my—" Trisha's eyes left Sandra's face and were directed over her shoulder. "Well, hello there, this must be your actor friend."

Sandra turned her head and looked up into Mark's cleanly shaven face.

"Good morning," he said.

On an impulse, she reached for the laptop to pull the lid down.

"Don't you dare, missy," Trisha said. "Aren't you going to introduce us?"

Sandra still hadn't said anything. "Right, of course. Trisha, this is Mark Jeffery. Mark, this is my friend, Trisha Delaroche." The words spilled out in rapid fire.

"Good morning, Ms. Delaroche, a pleasure to meet a friend of Sandra's. I'd shake your hand if it weren't for this blasted monitor." He extended his hand over Sandra's shoulder toward the computer.

Trisha's hand loomed large on the screen. "Consider it shaken."

"And you are speaking to us from …?" he asked.

"The lovely town of Okotoks, Alberta—the very frozen north, at least today. You're lucky you're in Mexico, Sandi. The temperature dropped to minus twenty last night and the wind chill this morning has brought it down into the minus thirties."

"Thirty degrees below? What is wrong with you Canadians? You do realize there are many more hospitable climates in the world."

Sandra opened her mouth to respond but Trisha cut in. "So, Mark, Sandi and I were just talking about her upcoming showing in La Paz and I hear you had a hand in bringing that about. I must know your secret since I've been trying to get her to show at my gallery for ages. Have a seat. Tell me the tale."

Sandra was hanging over the arm of her chair so that Mark could lean in toward the camera.

"It would be my pleasure." He looked down at Sandra. "Do you mind?"

"No, of course not, why should I mind?" Seemed he was going to hijack another visit with a friend. Mark set his coffee cup on the table and sat down in the closest chair. She angled the computer so that Trisha could see him instead of her.

"Too far," Trisha said. "Turn it so I can see you both."

Well that was a rather thinly disguised trick to get her and Mark to sit shoulder to shoulder. Sandra narrowed her eyes at Trisha and Trisha smiled back at her. Mark slid his chair until its arm was butted against Sandra's. "That's better," Trisha said with a light chuckle. "First of all I must tell you that I loved your Rochester. Of all of the versions of *Jane Eyre*, you captured Mr. Rochester like nobody else has. He was perfection. Bravo." Trisha clapped her hands where they could be seen on the monitor. Sandra marvelled at how comfortable Trisha was in the face of fame.

"Well, thank you. It's always a pleasure to meet a fan. I hope you haven't been too disappointed with everything I've done since."

"Definitely not," Trisha replied. "The one where you played the single father a few years back? What was the title? Sandra and I both loved you in that one. Didn't we, Sandi?"

Sandra nodded, trying to think of a way to change the subject to something less uncomfortable.

"The Michael Bridges film. I enjoyed that role."

"So Sandra, you told me Mr. Jeffery was looking a bit bushy but he looks quite freshly shaven this morning." Trisha's eyes danced with mischief.

*Oh God, where is a connection failure when you need one.* "He is, isn't he? A refreshing change from his impression of Tom Hanks in *Cast Away.*"

"So you've told your friend about me," he said, looking at Sandra. "How lovely. What else did she have to say?"

*So much for a less uncomfortable topic.*

"She hasn't told me much really, just that you bought one of her paintings and bullied her into showing her work in La Paz." *Thank heaven for that bit of uncharacteristic discretion on Trisha's part.*

"And good that I did or she'd have two more pieces to lock away in her cellar."

Trisha laughed. "You've gotten to know our Sandra well in a short period of time."

"In truth, I haven't. She's rather reclusive and I've had to push my way into every outing we've had."

"Including this one," Sandra added with a forced smile.

Mark continued, unfazed. "But, I have convinced her to come sailing with me on Tuesday. Did she mention that?"

"She did." Trisha's eyes went to Sandra's face. "But she didn't tell me much. Is this an overnight sailing voyage?" Trisha had a promiscuous lilt to her voice.

*Shoot me now.*

Mark flushed a little red and chuckled. "No, simply an afternoon sail with a picnic, and a bottle of wine perhaps." There was a question beneath Mark's words. They hadn't talked about plans except to confirm Mark would charter a boat for a few hours. At least Sandra could take some comfort in the fact that he also seemed embarrassed by Trisha's question.

"Didn't you tell me you had to get to the gallery, Trisha?" asked Sandra.

"I probably should be off to check on my Felix. He's a dear boy but not always on time, and the gallery should be opening ..." Her eyes went to her watch. "Right about now. It's been delightful to meet you Mark. I'll let you two enjoy what looks like a lovely Mexico morning."

"And a pleasure to meet you." Mark nodded his head toward the screen. "Perhaps we'll talk again."

"I certainly hope so. Bye now. Talk soon." Trisha blew a kiss to Sandra and disappeared from the screen.

Sandra closed the laptop and pushed it to the other side of the table. "Excuse me for a minute. I'm going to track down Paul or Arturo and see what's become of my breakfast. I think they may have forgotten me."

As if she hadn't felt awkward enough around Mark. *Ga! I could kill her!*

When she returned to the table with her breakfast sundae, Mark had taken the chair opposite hers, his back to the beach. He was looking up toward the hills, the sun catching the side of his face. His skin was pale where the beard had been and had that smooth, I-know-you-want-to-touch-me appearance that men's faces get when freshly shaven. He'd dropped his sandal to the tiled floor and his bare foot was across the opposite knee, his hands resting on his tanned calf. When he saw her he smiled, and there it was, that gorgeous mug she'd seen on the big screen, no longer partially concealed by a beard. She felt her knees wobble. He'd been easier to ignore with an untended beard and wrinkly clothes.

"You did come back. I thought your friend may have frightened you off. She's rather a forward one, isn't she?"

"Forward. That's one way to put it."

"She's delightful though, really."

"Yes, she is, but a bit of a handful at times." Sandra set her breakfast on the table and took her seat.

"You've known each other long?"

"About eight years. When I first moved to Okotoks, she ran an art collective that offered classes and I signed up. It turned out we lived on the same block and we've been close ever since. She's been a good friend. I wish I could convince her to come down here with me. She would love it."

"She won't come? Why ever not? Didn't she say it was thirty degrees below zero where you live?"

"She doesn't travel. I'm not sure why since she's adventurous in other ways. She claims to be a hundred-mile traveller, like the hundred-mile dieters, but I think there's something else to it. I don't fly, so I'd completely understand if that were the reason."

"You don't fly?"

"No. Never. I did when I was a kid but not since."

"Well how did you get here if you don't fly?"

"I drove."

"From Canada. Funny."

"No, really. I drove. My car is sitting out back. Look for yourself—a Toyota SUV with Alberta plates." She knew the smirk on her face was making her less than convincing.

"Right then. I'll bite." Mark got up from his chair and took the back stairs from the patio down to the parking lot. A few minutes later, he returned to his chair on the sundeck.

"You realize, statistically, it's much more dangerous to drive through Mexico than it is to fly over it?"

"I'm aware."

"So you do it because …?"

"I told you. I don't like to fly."

"And you like Mexican banditos?"

She laughed. "I've not had the chance to get to know one so it's hard to say. But I don't drive down alone. I meet up with others; RVers who are travelling here for the winter. It's a beautiful drive down the Baja Peninsula."

"I've no doubt it is. Beautiful *and* dangerous—like so many things."

That was a bit how Sandra was beginning to feel about Mr. Jeffery.

# Fifteen

Sandra placed a blank canvas on her easel, clipping it into place to keep the wind from throwing it onto the sand. Her third piece for the show was going to be a portrait of Mar Azul. She'd walked south along the shore to give a broader view of the surroundings. She wanted to capture the spirit of the place that so spoke to her own spirit.

"So, what are you painting?"

She'd tried to discourage him from tagging along but it seemed he was more determined to come than she was to stop him. He promised he would stay out of the way on the back side of the easel so as not to watch her work. He'd brought along a blue canvas chair from Paul's deck and was sitting in it now, facing the sea, a few magazines resting on his lap.

"Mar Azul."

"There's a very nice painting of the hotel hanging in the lobby. Is that one yours as well?" Mark said.

"It is." She'd once painted Mar Azul from one of the palapas and the hotel filled the canvas. "I gave that one to Paul two years ago. This one will take in more of the landscape."

"Well, let me know if you need a second opinion or any suggestions." He opened a magazine.

"I certainly will." She didn't mind the company as long as he didn't watch her paint. Nick used to accompany her on painting excursions and she enjoyed his quiet energy—there but not there. She wasn't sure Mark could be *not here*, although she didn't know if the problem was him or how she felt around him. *Nick*. In addition to his quiet presence, as an architect, he had been a welcome second opinion when she was painting any kind of structures. She would do her best to channel his excellent eye.

She looked down the beach to Mar Azul, its white walls rising up out of the desert. The definitive moment—where to place things and what percentage of the canvas to give each element. This was the only planning she did for her paintings. The remainder came through eye and feel. Sandra pulled a pencil from her bag and began to sketch in a rough outline of the image before her. Her paintings were often a combination of reality and imagination but this one she wanted to be a true capturing of the place, its colours, its peace. Mar Azul was taking shape on the canvas—its flat roof, its square pillars and angles, the stone wall that separated it from the surrounding desert. Sandra sketched in the palapas and where the sand met the sea before tucking her pencil behind her ear. She opened her paint kit and began placing blobs of various colours on her palette. Blue. Whenever she thought of Mar Azul she thought of the deepest, richest blues. She could close her eyes and see them on the backs of her lids, some vibrant, some dark, some shimmering, some cool. Shades of blue—maybe a good name for the painting, or shades of Mar Azul.

Sandra looked up past her canvas and realized Mark was watching her.

"Sorry," he said. "I enjoy watching people at work, especially when they find their work so absorbing."

"It's all right. I'm used to painting with other people around. Usually they're painting too, but I can make this work." Standing at her easel with her palette in hand, she felt grounded, more herself, even in the company of Mark Jeffery.

"Can I ask you a question?"

"As long as it isn't mathematical or otherwise drawing from

the left side of the brain, sure." Sandra was making the first strokes of colour around the pencil outlines.

"Have you always loved to paint, since you were a child?" he asked.

She continued to paint, not looking up. "I used to sit with my father in his library on Sunday mornings. He would read and smoke and I would do some kind of art. Each Sunday I'd try something different—paints, pencils, charcoal, pastels. At that time, pencil sketching was my favourite. I liked the simplicity of it, that I could take it anywhere." Sandra rinsed her brush in the jar of water at the base of the easel and selected a different brush with a larger, flatter bristle.

"I'd often sketch my father, trying to change and improve on my work each time. He always looked the same so he was a good subject, sitting in that wingback chair he loved, cigarette in one hand, book in the other. I don't know where he got that crazy chair, somewhere in South America I think, but the back was made of elaborately carved wood and twice his height when he was sitting. It towered behind him like some Brazilian throne. He'd sit there, smoking, which he did all the time." She stopped painting and looked over the canvas at Mark. "Do you know, I can't smell cigarette smoke and not think of him, or think of him and not smell cigarettes? Marlboroughs."

Sandra mixed a pearl of white paint into the side of one of the three blues on the palette. "Anyway, it was as if I could return each week and he'd be sitting there, waiting. I once did a detailed and complicated composition and, even though six days would pass between my sketching sessions, my father would be posing in exactly the same way, like he was doing it on purpose." She paused, looking over her canvas again. "I'm sorry, you were probably looking for a simple yes, I've always loved to paint or no, I took it up when I was forty, kind of answer."

He chuckled. "No, not at all. I assume your father was thrilled to be the subject of so many works of art?" He lay the magazines on the sand beside his chair.

"You'd think, wouldn't you? But no, he never saw any of them. Never showed an interest; and I was too afraid of his criticism to volunteer them. When I was twelve, my father planned an outing for the whole family to the National Gallery in Ottawa." Sandra stopped painting and stared at the canvas. "It was a life-changing experience. Each painting, each drawing, each sculpture was a complete fascination for me. The colours, the brush strokes, the faces, the landscapes, all blending in this ..." Sandra waved her paintbrush through the air over her head, "this wondrous place where art was celebrated. And my father, he asked questions about what I liked, what I didn't, and why. He asked why I thought the artist had used certain colours or media. My mother oohed and aahed over every piece I liked, finding something positive to say about each one. It was a beautiful day—maybe my best family memory." Her eyes returned to the work in front of her.

"So your father ended up being supportive of your interest in art?"

"He was that day, but only because he was trying to steer me in the *right* direction, his direction. He didn't see art the way I do. He thought it frivolous, simply ..." she deepened and stiffened her voice, "self-expression with a singular and selfish motive." Mark laughed. "The day in the gallery, I saw how it affected people, brought them together, showed them something of each other, and I knew how it felt for me to create it." Sandra continued to apply paint to her canvas, filling in the walls of Mar Azul, laying in the base colours of the sand, sky, and water.

"What was the *right* direction, according to your father?"

"A university degree in art history, focusing on the study of art and its forms rather than creating it. And that is how I ended up as a curator instead of a painter, at least for a while."

"And what does your father think now? Does he appreciate the work you do?"

"My father is dead. Has been for a very long time. He died in a plane crash in South America when I was in my early twenties." She hadn't spoken of her father for years and was surprised by how little emotion he brought up.

"I'm sorry," Mark said. "Is this the motivation for your choice of driving over flying?"

Sandra's eyes went to the waves rolling onto the beach and then back to Mark. "Initially it was. He and his team were on their way to a remote dig site when their plane went missing." She recalled the families of the three young people who'd travelled with her father, at the house every day, clinging together, hoping for some shred of good news. "It was a month before they found the plane, and the bodies. There was something about the horror of it, imagining over and over their final moments, knowing they were going to crash and die. For years I couldn't imagine getting on a plane. I don't think I'm afraid to fly anymore, I just don't relish the feeling of disorientation that comes with being transported thousands of kilometres in less than a day. And I discovered the joys of long distance driving, being gradually immersed in a new climate and culture over many days." Sandra returned to her painting. "My father lived to see me finish university and get my first gallery position. I'm sure he felt he'd done his job." Sandra tasted bitterness in the back of her throat but swallowed it. Her eyes rose to Mark's. "Five years after he died I left Toronto, left my position as curator of a rather swanky gallery, and started my life over— creating art rather than trading in it."

"And you didn't go back to working in galleries?"

"No, never, and I'm sure my experience there has been part of my reluctance to exhibit. I saw and heard what went on behind the scenes. Of course, Trisha's gallery is very different from the kinds of places I worked, much more down to earth and far less political."

"So what did you do, when you left Toronto?"

Sandra used a large round brush to put the base colours into the sky. "I headed west, as many easterners do. It has this magnetic pull for those of us who grew up in Canada's older, more established regions—the lure of the old west maybe. I bummed around for a bit and then settled in Calgary, got a perfect, low-stress job working for an architectural firm and painted in my spare time. I was a bit of a fixture along the Bow River with my easel and paint box. The runners and cyclists all knew me by name. It was a good time, very freeing."

As the afternoon wore on, Sandra stayed focused on her work, sometimes stepping back from the easel with her brush held out in front of her, her gaze travelling between the scene and the canvas. She wore a broad-brimmed hat in an effort to keep the freckles on the bridge of her nose and cheeks from becoming more pronounced. Wisps of hair no longer captured in her braid brushed her cheeks and had to be pushed back over her ears as she worked.

He'd been watching for a while now, maybe thinking she was too caught up in her work to notice. But, it felt okay, even good. She dropped her brush into a container of water and set her palette on the folding table beside her.

"Well? Can I see it?" Mark stood and put his magazines in the sling of blue canvas he'd been seated on. He'd been surprisingly well behaved. For the past hour he'd only interrupted her once to point out a group of four Brown Pelicans gliding above the crest of a wave like surfers.

Sandra closed her paint box and began rinsing her brushes. "I suppose. But keep in mind it's not finished."

Mark came around to her side of the easel and raised his sunglasses to his forehead. He took two steps back and then one forward, leaning in and then back again.

"Well …?" Sandra was trying to focus on her clean-up but his long silence was causing her to fidget.

"It's tremendous, finished or not. You have captured the

soul of Mar Azul. Paul will love it. I love it. Very well done." He turned to her with a broad smile.

"I haven't quite worked out the blues, over here, where the light hits the water ..." Sandra gestured to the bottom right corner of the painting.

"Spoken like a true artist. The work can *always* be better. You should try watching yourself on the screen. At least your work doesn't have you larger than life and talking."

"Do you really find it difficult, seeing yourself on the screen?" Sandra closed her paint box and placed her brushes in their roll-up bamboo carrier.

"Oh God yes, horribly, especially once the critics have had their say. I hear every awkward word, see every poorly executed movement. It's dreadful stuff."

"That surprises me."

"Really? Why?"

"I don't know. You just seem so, confident."

"Have you forgotten? I'm an actor." He grinned at her. "What can I carry for you?"

# Sixteen

Mark went straight to Lorenzo's sidecar coffee shop. He'd stayed up the night before to catch Nate in his London office and, after another fruitless conversation, hadn't slept well. A good jolt of caffeine might clear the fog. The Sunday market was extra busy today, and the two tour busses parked down the main street explained why. He pulled his hat further down onto his forehead and wished for the anonymity his beard had afforded. He hadn't been recognized often in San Leandro, but two bus-loads of tourists were bound to contain at least a few *Jane Eyre* fans. He dreaded that inevitable question: *So what will we see you in next?* He didn't yet have a name for the script he was waiting on, or even a description of the role, and this time he'd keep his mouth shut until there was something on paper. After Janzen grabbed that last part, the tabloids had been all over the story of his being passed over for another actor. Vultures—delighting in the misfortune of the same person they were in love with the week before.

"Lorenzo, my friend." Mark held out his hand to the coffee vendor who was leaning against the seat of his motorcycle.

"Amigo. So very good to see you. What can I get you this morning?"

"Let's go with the espresso. Make it a double."

"Would you like a swirl of caramel or chocolate on the top?"

"You know, a bit of sweet sounds good. I'll have the caramel."

Lorenzo drizzled syrup on top with a flourish. "There you go, one double espresso."

Mark took the paper cup and gazed at a caramel star floating on the surface of his coffee. "A star?"

"My sister Daniela tells me you are a movie star." Lorenzo gestured toward a young woman behind the counter of a nearby fruit stand. She was filling a bag with avocados and didn't notice she'd become the topic of conversation.

"She did, did she? Do you think I should go over and say hello?"

"She would like that very much. She and her friend Sofia are always going to the cinema. They know all the stars."

Mark took a sip from his cup and closed his eyes for a moment. "Mmmm, terrific coffee, Lorenzo. Gracias." He lifted the cup in a salute.

He walked over to Daniela's fruit stand. She had her back to him, rearranging the bins of lemons, limes, oranges, and grapefruit. She was tiny, less than five feet tall, and her black hair hung down her back in a braid that reached her waist.

"Buenos días, Señorita."

Daniela turned with a big smile, prepared to meet another of the day's customers. "Señor Jeffery!" Her eyes widened and went to her brother, sitting on his motorcycle, grinning at her. She looked back to Mark. "Buenos días."

"Do you speak English?" he asked.

"A little only."

"Lorenzo tells me you like movies. Ah ..." he dug for the word, "*la película?*"

"Sí, *muchísimo.*" Her olive face was developing a pink hue. She looked down at her hands that she'd twisted into her apron and quickly pulled them free, smoothing the fabric.

"And you've seen some of my movies?"

"Sí, I think ..." She held up three fingers. "*Está bien.*"

"Well, thank you. It's always a pleasure to meet a fan of my work." He held out his hand to shake hers.

She hesitated but then put her tiny hand into his, shaking it with enthusiasm.

"Those oranges look nice. Perhaps I'll have four, *cuatro naranja*, and a bunch of the grapes." He pointed, when her eyebrows scrunched at the word grapes.

"*Sí, sí.*" She pulled a pink, plastic bag from a box behind her and picked through the oranges for four of the best, adding the largest bunch of grapes to the top. She tied the bag closed and handed it to Mark.

"These look perfect." He placed the fruit in his canvas shopping bag.

Daniela stood looking up at him, continuing to smile.

"What do I owe you señorita? *Cuánto?*"

"Oh … sí." She blushed again. "*Cincuenta pesos, por favor.*"

Mark placed five coins in her outstretched hand. "Gracias."

He headed down the market, turning once to see her still watching him. She waved and smiled. It wasn't always bad running into fans. It helped when they didn't speak enough English to ask questions.

Next task, a picnic for a sailing excursion. His eyes scanned the row of vendors, looking for food items that would pack well but not feel like a brown bag lunch. He recognized her hat before he saw her face. He'd spent the better part of yesterday afternoon watching that hat. Her face had been only partially visible above the back of the canvas but the hat was always in full view, its brim tilting up, dropping down, turning to the side, stepping back. It was a simple straw hat with a wide brim, wide enough to shade fair skin from the sun, and it sported a leather band emblazoned with turquoise and silver.

She was down near the end of the row of stalls looking at leather bags and belts, speaking to the boy in the booth. The boy was smiling and talking, his hands as animated as his face. Mark wondered what Sandra had said to him. No doubt she'd asked him precisely the thing that would get him talking. She was wearing a long skirt today, its white folds hanging loose from her hips. The hem was intentionally uneven and showed off her new La Paz sandals. She'd been right, they were her style. Her arms were bare, a blue tank top tied halter-style behind her neck, and her pale skin was bright in the sunlight. Wasn't she worried about sunburn?

Sandra made a purchase from the boy, placing it in her shoulder bag and turned to continue down the market. Her eyes browsed the tables and tents as she walked, not noticing Mark standing in the middle of the laneway. He was enjoying watching her and wondered if he should find a less conspicuous location. Before he could move, she stopped four stalls down from where he stood, her eyes going to the jewelry on the table: bracelets, rings and necklaces in silver and turquoise.

The elderly woman in the stall got up from where she was working and greeted Sandra. He couldn't make out their words amid the sounds of the busy market but the Mexican woman was speaking and holding up various pieces for Sandra to examine. Sandra lifted a heavy silver chain with a long pendant from the table, letting it hang from her right hand as her left examined the stone set in silver. The vendor pulled a mirror from under the counter and held it in front of her as Sandra put the chain around her neck, fastening it behind.

The Mexican woman spoke, probably giving a price, and a high one by Sandra's reaction. She shook her head and started to remove the necklace. The woman reached her hand out to touch Sandra's arm and spoke again—the counter offer. Sandra shook her head a second time and lay the jewelry back on the table top. Now Mark could hear the vendor, raising her voice as Sandra moved away. "Wait, amiga. I give you good price. Señora!"

It was then that Sandra saw him, standing in the middle of the market, holding his shopping bag in one hand, his empty coffee cup in the other. He must have appeared a bit of a stooge, like a boulder in a stream, shoppers spilling around each side of him. She walked toward him, her head tilting back enough to allow the sun to touch her face below the brim of her hat. In spite of the shade offered by the wide brim, freckles trailed across the bridge of Sandra's nose and onto her cheeks, more visible today than they had been when he'd first met her a week ago. "Good morning," she called as she approached.

"Good morning. Looks like you weren't able to make a deal." Mark inclined his head toward the jewelry stand.

"You were watching me?"

"Just for a moment." He lied. "I heard her calling after you."

"Ah yes, she was ready to make a very good deal—for her—on her overpriced jewelry. It's nice, but not that nice. Paul warned me about this one. Wonderful craftsmanship, but too pricey. I can probably buy the same necklace in La Paz for half the money. At least I'm going to give it a try." She pointed to the empty cup in Mark's hand. "Getting your morning fix?"

"Indeed, and a very good one it was. Have you been to Lorenzo's motorcycle coffee bar?"

"Motorcycle?"

"I'll take that as a no. If you fancy a coffee I'll take you there now." Mark offered his arm to her.

"I've had my morning macchiato but the motorcycle part sounds intriguing."

She still hadn't taken his arm and he was beginning to feel awkward standing there with his elbow pointing at her. Force of habit really, to offer a woman his arm. When your life was filled with premieres, film festivals, and cocktail parties, it just went with the territory. Her eyes met his and he hoped his discomfort wasn't showing on his face.

"Sure, a coffee, why not," she said, as she took his arm.

"And after that you can help me choose some delectables for tomorrow's sailboat picnic."

# Seventeen

The sky was clearing when they pulled into the marina. The towering clouds to the northeast and their curtain of rain were now making their way south to the Pacific. They'd left Mar Azul around eight o'clock, Sandra's three completed paintings wrapped and lying in the back seat of Mark's convertible. Pascual had been thrilled with her contributions to the show. Of course, he was inclined to be complimentary, but his enthusiasm seemed genuine. He and his volunteers would be setting up the show all day and Sandra's work would be included in the *Visiting Artists* tent. She'd be in good company with another fifty-plus paintings sharing the space, each artist providing three to five pieces, depending on size. She didn't know the artists in the area but she hoped her work wouldn't look amateurish displayed next to theirs.

The charter boat owner was waiting for them at the marina and went over all of the rigging and equipment with Mark, showed him how to operate the radio and provided charts of the area. "So you are fine from here, amigo?"

"I think we should be. Gracias." Mark shook the man's hand and began loading their bags into the cockpit of the boat.

He looked up at the sky and then to Sandra standing on the dock. "You see, I told you the weather would be fine."

"It does look promising. And where are we headed Capitan?"

"To a lovely wee bay with pristine white sand beaches I'm told, and possibly dolphins."

"Dolphins. I like that." Sandra stepped onto the boat. She'd almost cancelled today's trip many times but, now that she was here, she was glad she'd come. In the end she'd taken Trisha's advice to stop worrying so much and enjoy the attention. And besides, she'd loved sailing back on Lake Ontario. "So, you said you haven't sailed here before."

"I have not. *But* ... I have spoken to someone who knows these waters very well, a fisherman in San Leandro. Locals are always the best source of information."

"But you have *sailed* before?"

"Yes." He eyed her over the tops of his sunglasses from his kneeling position at the back of the boat. "Skeptical bloody Canadian. Would you like to see my RYA card?"

She laughed. "No, I believe you, but my sailing experience is from the Mesozoic period so you won't be able to count on me for a lot of help."

"Do you remember how to pull on a line?"

"I might."

"Well that should be about all the help I need. You, fair lady, can sit back and enjoy the ride."

*Ode to Joy* was a Cal 34, an older boat but well-maintained, her rigging and sails recently upgraded. They untied and motored out of the harbour, the gulls squawking overhead and a gentle breeze off the nose of the boat. La Paz passed by them on the right, the waterfront pathway dotted with strolling tourists, each of them a different splotch of colour from Sandra's vantage point. She pulled her sketch book from her bag and did a quick drawing of el Malecón—its buildings, statues and palm trees, and the people wandering its pathway.

"The beginning of another painting?" Mark asked from behind the wheel.

Sandra continued to focus on her sketch. "Possibly. I like the colourful little tourists against the city backdrop. It was thoughtful of them to wear such a variety of colours ... not that I couldn't brighten them up a bit if they were all dressed in brown."

"Ah yes, the artist's prerogative."

Sandra flipped the page and started a second sketch. Her pencil moved rapidly, her eyes going from the page to the shore and back again. She could see masts up ahead, bright white against the hill behind them. She turned another page and began drawing the resort marina as it came into view.

"Now, I don't want to interrupt an artist at work, but I would like to put the sails up soon, now that we're out of the harbour."

"No problem ..." Sandra added shading to some areas of her sketch and closed the book, tucking it back into the pocket of her duffel. "Done! At your service, Skipper. What can I do?"

Mark switched on the autohelm and they set about raising the main sail and genoa, the crisp white triangles reaching up into the Baja blue sky. When the sails were set and Mark was back at the wheel, Sandra's sketch book was out again. This time she sat at the bow of the boat, her back pressed into the pulpit, the front of the foresail against her shoulder.

"I thought you didn't do people." Mark called from the back of the boat.

"I don't really. You'll just be a shell of a person, without features."

"Ah ... I'm the perfect subject then."

She returned to her drawing. It was an opportunity to look at him without noticeably staring—one benefit of being an artist. He looked so relaxed today. His white short-sleeved shirt was untucked and blowing in the breeze. He wore a pair of blue and white plaid shorts and his bare legs and feet were brown against the white deck of the boat. Sandra went back to her sketch and tried to capture him on the paper. His untameable hair was at its best this morning, the wind turning it into a moving mass of brown curls around his head. Every now and then he would pull his fingers through it to move it from his face, making it stand up all the taller above his forehead.

"Are you sure I'm just going to be a shell. It seems as though you're looking at me rather intently."

"It's the sunglasses that make it seem that way." She tapped the side of her glasses with her pencil. "Just a shell. Absolutely." Sandra looked down at the image evolving on her lap. She'd never been good at drawing or painting people but it was something she wanted to work on. A movie star seemed like a good place to start; with his square jaw and symmetrical features his face wasn't so different from architecture, and she'd drawn plenty of buildings. And then there were those broad shoulders, muscled arms, gorgeous hands—definitely not a tough subject to keep your eyes on. If Trisha were in her head right now she'd be so proud.

They travelled that way for an hour or more, Mark at the stern with his hands resting on the wheel, and Sandra at the front of the boat, sketching him, the boat, the sails, the changing landscape and the rolling waves of the sea.


They reached their destination two hours after setting sail. Without the chart and the directions from the fisherman, the bay would have been invisible with its narrow entrance between two fingers of land reaching out into Cortez. Once inside, the water went calm, like they'd dropped onto a quiet lake.

"It's beautiful," Sandra called back to Mark from her position at the bow. They'd taken the sails down before attempting the entrance. The water was deep and without rocks, according to the chart, but the width made Mark err on the side of caution. Steering accuracy was more easily achieved under power.

The dark hills of rock and acacia shrub rose up from the water all around the bay, with sandy expanses of the palest beige at their base. The water grew shallower as they motored further in, its colour changing from indigo to turquoise. Sandra let her eyes drink it all in, trying to capture the colours for her canvasses. "What a marvellous place to paint."

"Did you bring your paints?" Mark dropped the engine to an idle.

"No, only the sketch book. I'll have to try to remember the colours."

"Do you not own one of those new-fangled inventions—a camera, I believe they're calling it?"

"I do, but I didn't bring it. When I have it with me I tend to take photos instead of sketching, and I prefer to work from sketches."

"Well, I did bring a camera. So if you'd like some photos to back up your drawings, I can take some for you. Can you come and take the wheel while I get us anchored?"

Sandra took her place at the wheel, holding the boat steady while he pulled the anchor from the locker at the bow and dropped it overboard. "Okay, put it into reverse, but just idling." Sandra did as she was instructed. "And now into neutral." She felt the anchor catch and the boat begin to swing sideways. "Right. I think we're there. Lunch!" Mark brushed his hands together and returned to the cockpit.

"You really have done this before."

"Do you mean to tell me you agreed to go sailing on the open sea with someone you doubted had ever been on a boat?"

"Well, I figured you'd been on a boat but, you know, just acting. Crazy, eh?"

"Aha! There it is."

"There what is?"

"The 'eh'. I've been waiting to hear the 'eh' you Canadians are famous for. It hasn't shown up until now." He pointed a finger at her.

"That's because it's not nearly as common, or as uniquely Canadian, as its reputation."

"Ah yes, the idiosyncrasies of speech, often exaggerated by those of other cultures."

"I know, eh."

"You're going to do that all day now aren't you?"

"I might ..." Sandra smiled. "So, let's eat, eh? I'm starving. You got any back bacon in that icebox?"

Mark chuckled and opened the cooler that was tucked into the front of the cockpit. "I'm afraid not, but I do have some lovely smoked fish if that suits, as well as some cheese, which you selected from the market, some fresh bread, some olives, and ..." He opened the locker behind him and pulled out a dark green bottle. "A bottle of my favourite Italian red."

"Sounds yummy ... but it's been a long time since I've sailed so I'm hoping you won't need a designated helmsman."

"Has my friend Paul been telling tales? I promise to drink only one glass. Speaking of, can you go down below and find the wine glasses? Our friend back at the marina told me the boat had a fully stocked galley."

Sandra climbed down the steps of the companionway into the cabin of the boat. The blue trim of Ode to Joy's exterior was echoed inside by her navy upholstery; and the cupboards, the benches, the bunks were all a dark red shade of teak. When Sandra reached the bottom step she was in the kitchen and began her search for wine glasses, or something that would suffice. Aha—tucked in a drawer, two plastic glasses with, what else, blue stems. And beside them, plates. Those might be handy as well. Dishes in hand, she checked out the rest of the cabin, going through a small doorway into the front v-berth. Cozy, but certainly comfortable. She could imagine spending some time on a boat, falling asleep to the waves lapping at the hull. Ah, and the head, something she needed. She set the glasses and plates on the galley table and stepped inside the tiny room, locking the door behind her.

"Are you lost down there?" Mark called from the companionway just as Sandra exited the bathroom.

"I was but I think I see the way out now." She grabbed the dishes and climbed back up to the cockpit, handing them off to Mark as she hit the top stair. "Found the glasses, and some plates. It's quite nice down there. The boat I sailed on with my in-laws was more of a racing boat, so not well-equipped for living. You have to minimize weight if you want to win."

Mark had their picnic laid out on the port bench, a small, brightly coloured piece of fabric underneath it.

"I love the tablecloth. I've seen those in San Leandro at the market. Nice touch—for a boy." She took the glass of wine he offered.

He poured one for himself and held it toward her in a toast. "Cheers. To fine weather and fine friends."

The plastic glasses clicked together. Fine friends—oddly enough, they did seem to be growing into just that. He smiled at her, the whiteness of the face that had been hidden under his beard beginning to colour in the sun. He had the kind of skin that tanned rather than burned. How nice that must be.

"So, dig in. A little Italian-style picnic to go with the wine, or vice versa perhaps."

Mark sat next to the picnic and Sandra sat across from him on the open bench, loaded plates in their laps, wine glasses perched on the top side of the hull.

"How are you feeling about the art show, now that the pieces are finished and delivered?" Mark asked.

"Quite good, I think, but still nervous."

"Will you go, to the show?"

"I told Pascual I'd be there for the opening tomorrow. He'd like the artists there every day but I don't think I'll do that. I'd rather be painting and I don't want to paint in public."

"I was planning on going at some point. Can I give you a ride?"

"Thanks," Sandra examined the food on her plate, "but Ian has offered to take me. He has some things to do in La Paz, and he'd like to see the show."

"Right. Not a problem." Mark took a swallow from his glass

and began piling smoked fish onto a slice of bread.

They ate in silence for a few minutes, looking past one another at the surroundings.

Sandra spoke first. "So, have you received that script from your agent yet?"

"It's gone back to the writers for a few changes. Nate says it should be here within the week."

"And ... things are still looking promising?"

"According to Nate the directors *and* the executives want me in the role. Last time around, I was the director's pick but not a safe enough bet for the movie execs—and the men who hold the money have the power."

His features had darkened. Sandra wondered if she could ask the next question without getting tossed off the boat. "What do movie executives consider a 'safe bet'?"

"In this case an actor with Oscar potential, which I, apparently, am not." His plastic glass hit the boat surface hard enough to splash wine over the top. It ran down the inside of the cockpit, leaving a dark trail on the bright white gelcoat. He picked up the napkin from his lap and wiped up the spill before turning to Sandra. "Apologies. As you may have noticed in prior meetings, this is a subject that makes me rather snappish."

"If you don't want to talk about it, that's fine. I just find that problems sometimes lose their power when we get them out in the open, and I'm happy to listen if you'd like to talk." She hoped her voice carried more confidence than she felt. She'd decided to ignore Paul's advice and not stay on safe subjects today. It wasn't her style to avoid something that so obviously needed to be aired.

He looked at her across the boat, the thoughts visibly swimming behind his eyes. "You're still willing to listen, despite my behaviour—the chair tossing, the table slamming," he gestured to where the faint outline of red still showed on the white hull, "the wine spilling?"

"Maybe I'll hold your wine glass when I ask a question." She reached for his glass and he pulled it back.

"I think I can manage to be civil. I'll try to be more stereotypically British and keep my feelings under my hat."

"No, I think you need to express what you feel, but try using words instead of … gestures."

"Like I'm doing radio rather than telly."

She laughed. "If that works for you, sure."

"I've never been good at talking about how I feel, or knowing what it is, for that matter. I guess as a British male that shouldn't surprise me. It just seems that after thirty-plus years of expressing the feelings of dozens of characters, I should be better at it, and certainly better at keeping it from coming out sideways."

"I'm not an actor, so I can't say how it works for you, but for the rest of us, acting is precisely the way we hide what we feel. We pretend to be someone else—someone stronger, someone who doesn't care, someone … different."

"So you think the acting keeps me from knowing my own thoughts and feelings?"

"It might. If your introspective energy gets focused on getting inside the head of another person, what's left for you? But I'm speculating." Sandra popped a stuffed olive in her mouth.

Mark leaned back against the hull and faced her. It was difficult to tell what he was looking at behind the dark glasses but she felt his eyes on her. She shifted in her seat and rearranged the food remaining on her plate.

"You know, that rather makes sense. I feel different when I'm in character, more real, oddly enough. I found that especially true of acting on the stage."

Whew. Sandra exhaled and felt her courage building. "So you were in theatre?"

"I was, and I enjoyed it very much, that instant and spontaneous feedback from the audience, the possibility of bettering the performance with each night's presentation." Mark eyes were drawn to a gull circling overhead.

"And do you still perform on the stage?"

"Rarely. I miss it sometimes, but it's a lot of work, and less money. After a few years in the theatre, I started to get television and movie roles. The feel was quite different from the stage, not nearly the adrenalin, but I enjoyed the challenge of acting without an audience to perform for. Getting the part of Rochester in *Jane Eyre* was a huge boon for my career. The story is so well-known and loved that we had an instant audience, and Rochester was an interesting and complex character to portray, probably one of the favourites of my career."

"But didn't you say something about romances being a waste of time? I believe it was something to the effect of 'women swooning ridiculously over an imaginary man', if I'm not mistaken."

"Yes, I believe I did utter some such rubbish. But," he tapped his temple, "since then I've given it some thought—and have reconsidered my position. In truth, Rochester was an enormous opportunity, and quite a challenging role. Unfortunately, I made a shambles of the possibility it afforded me, and here I am, waiting for the phone to ring."

"How did you make a shambles of it? I've seen you in a number of movies since *Jane Eyre*, both British and American."

"If quantity is the important measure, I've done fine. The 'shambles' I'm speaking of is misjudging Hollywood. When the offers started coming from America, I jumped at them, no matter what they were. One of them," his eyes shot skyward, "a dreadful thing I agreed to without reading the script. That was a mistake, one I hope you didn't have the misfortune of seeing."

Sandra did recall one particularly bad movie she'd seen him in about ten years before but decided it was best to remain silent on the subject. She shook her head.

"I thought that once I had my foot in the door I'd be able to make my way on to better roles, away from the romantic comedies. But, it seems the only way I'm going to climb out of my typecasting is to grow old, which I'm doing a snorting good job of." Mark raised his glass as if to toast and then took a long drink.

"We're all doing that."

"We are, but the value of your painting doesn't diminish because you're a year older. In fact, it's likely your talent will grow over time and your paintings become more valuable. Is that not the case?"

"It's not quite that easy but, it's true, artists often improve over time."

"As do actors. The problem is that movie-goers want to see people their own age on the screen, or so the execs tell us, and people over fifty tend to spend their time at home."

"But we still watch movies."

"You're not over fifty." Mark pulled his sunglasses to the tip of his nose and peered over the top of them.

"I will be, in about six months. The big five-o, in October."

"Hm, well, you certainly don't look it."

Sandra felt heat rush to her face. It was the first time he'd said anything about her looks. "But, I believe we were talking about your career," she said.

Mark dropped his head back and moaned. "Oh, that tiresome subject. Must we go on? Is this some manner of Canadian torture?"

"I'm surprised it hasn't made the newspapers over in the UK—'Canadians develop most polite system of torture ever!'"

"Polite? Having me dig into my bad decisions and failures? I'd rather the rack!"

"I don't happen to have one of those in my bag and I believe I also left my thumbscrews back at the hotel, but I could come up with some kind of water torture." She inclined her head toward the back of the boat. "Care for a swim?"

———

Mark lounged at the stern of the boat, his head tilted back, face turned to the clouds drifting by overhead.

"Are you sure you won't join me?" Sandra asked as she emerged from the cabin.

"You've just eaten *and* had a glass of wine. Someone has to play lifeguard. Besides, I'm not much of a swimmer."

"Exactly the sort of lifeguard every woman wants, one who can't swim."

Sandra wore a loose white wrap over her swimsuit and was reluctant to take it off. The decision to buy one more bikini before she turned fifty now seemed a terrible idea and she was trying to sort out how to get in the water without him seeing her. It was an impossible feat on a boat and she'd look ridiculous peeling off her beach wrap once she was in the water. *Oh well, here goes.* She stepped near the bow of the boat, dropped her wrap to the deck and dove in. The water was cool enough to send a shock through her body as it enveloped her, such a contrast to the warm air above. She continued to dive until the water felt even colder before turning back toward the surface. Her eyes were closed but she could see the growing brightness as she kicked her feet and pulled the water down with sweeps of her arms. She burst onto the surface about twenty feet off the boat's starboard hull and smoothed her wet hair back from her face with both hands.

"It's lovely. You should come in." She called to Mark, still in his seat at the stern.

He shook his head. "Certainly not. I'll sit and watch, and keep one hand on the life preserver in case you start cramping up. Nice dive, by the way."

"Thanks." Sandra dove again, swimming just under the surface toward the back of the boat. The softness of the salt water caressed her torso and legs as she swam, and in this underwater haven, with all sound and sight blocked, she found herself again. Mark, the boat, even Nick, all washed away by the healing waters. She wished she could swim to Mar Azul, walk onto the beach and rewind her life to the day she arrived, carrying this sense of peace with her. But, she needed to breathe. She surfaced to find she was thirty feet from the stern and Mark was now standing with one hand shading his eyes, scanning the water around Ode to Joy.

He spotted her. "There you are! I was trying to recall the single episode of *Baywatch* I once saw."

There would be no rewinding; it was impossible to swim backward in water or in time. She waved to Mark and rolled onto her back, letting her arms trail out to the sides, moving her feet gently to keep her legs afloat. She closed her eyes and let the sun warm her face. She'd always been a buoyant person, able to float for hours if she wanted to. Maybe the current would take her to Mar Azul. She was enjoying the day, even the conversation seemed to be going well, but underneath it was that persistent discomfort at being out of her element. She wasn't sure she was capable of looking at Mark Jeffery as just this guy she knew and hung out with. It was all so surreal, chumming around in Mexico with a movie star. Whose life was this?

If she believed Trisha, it was oh so simple, just enjoy it! But that seemed easier said than done. And then there were Paul's words of warning about getting attached, and she couldn't deny an attraction to Mark, as much as she might try.

She opened her eyes and righted herself, treading water. He was still sitting at the stern, looking very much the movie star on his yacht—designer sunglasses, good looks and a glass of red wine in hand. He smiled and gave a low wave. He was her lifeguard so it was good he was keeping an eye, but she'd felt his eyes on her many times through the day and had to wonder what was going on behind those dark glasses. Surely he wasn't interested in her beyond a casual companion? A tingle ran up her arms to the base of her neck. No, it wasn't possible. A guy who dated models and movie stars twenty years his junior, attracted to her? Not likely. As she started swimming toward the boat, she realized she would need to climb aboard using the ladder at the stern—right past Mark. A few feet away she stopped, treading water again. "Would you be so kind as to get me a towel? I left it in my bag on the v-berth."

Mark set his wine glass down and went below, returning a few minutes later with her towel. He set the towel down on the rear bench, picked up his glass, and took a seat on the port side.

Sandra climbed up and over the stainless steel rail of the pushpit, aware of him looking in her direction and conscious of her low cut top as she bent to pick up the towel. She wound it around her torso and stepped down into the cockpit. He watched her without saying a word, his hand cradling his glass of wine.

# Eighteen

The sails filled as Mark steered the boat south toward La Paz. The wind was behind them now and still light.

"It won't be a quick trip back but we should make it by our five pm curfew," Mark said.

"Sounds good, Captain." Sandra's hair was nearly dry and she tucked it into a pony tail to keep it from blowing forward into her face. She sat near the stern, a few feet from Mark's position at the helm, looking in their direction of travel.

"You enjoyed, then?" Mark asked.

He was standing and she smiled up at him. "It was nice. Thank you for taking me." Her eyes explored the landscape as they passed by, the desert dark and colourless between the blue of the water and the blue of the sky.

"And you'd come again?" His hair blew across his cheek and forehead when he turned to face her.

Part of her wanted to say yes, but as soon as his invitation met her ears, that other feeling returned, the one that crawled up in her chest and tightened its grip. "Sure, if there's time … sometime." She turned her attention to the genoa, its white fabric pulled tight by the wind.

"Ha! Such enthusiasm."

"I only meant that I'm not here that long, and who knows how long you'll be here, and it's possible the boat won't be available—"

"I get it. I get it." He smiled and focused ahead beyond the bow that rose and fell with the waves. "We'll play it by ear is what you're saying."

"Yes, that's what I'm saying." What she was saying was that, as much as she'd enjoyed the day, she wasn't sure she wanted to continue spending time with him. The moments she felt at ease were fleeting, and being his hiding-out-in-Mexico entertainment, cast aside when he went back to his life, didn't suit her at all.

Sandra felt the wind freshen at the back of her neck and turned to look behind. Dark clouds were building over the headlands near the bay they'd been moored in.

"Should we be concerned about those?" she asked, pointing to the clouds.

Mark turned his head to look. "No. Thunderstorms are a summertime thing in this area. There were clouds this morning that departed without issue. I'm sure these will too."

Sandra continued to look at the darkening sky off the stern. "Fair enough, but if I were home on the prairie, I'd be thinking about battening down the hatches. These things can come up fast."

"We might get a bit more breeze and a scattering of rain but I venture that will be the worst of things."

"Okay, I'll trust you, but I'm going down below to grab my jacket all the same. Do you want one?"

"I didn't bring anything."

"Seriously, you didn't bring a sweater or a coat?"

"Indeed I did not."

"Foolish Englishman." She went below to get her jacket. She was half way across the cabin when the gust hit, sending the boat lurching on its nose and knocking her to the floor. Her head clipped the corner of the table on her way down. "Shit!" Sandra put her hand to her head and got back on her feet, holding the settee to maintain her balance. Jacket mission abandoned, she hurried to the cockpit and saw the cloud was building to a towering mass, its layers boiling one on top of the other. The waves were cresting all around them, the rolling sea transformed into a frothing mass.

"I'll need your help to drop the sails." Mark hit the start button and the diesel engine roared to life. He began turning the boat toward shore and into the direction of the wind. As the wind released the sails from its grip, the stiff fabric snaked back and forth, whipping the air. "Release the sheet on the jenny so I can furl the sail." Mark shouted over the fusion of roaring wind, snapping sails and diesel engine. Sandra released the line that held the back of the genoa and Mark hit the button for the roller furling. Nothing happened. He hit the button again, and again, then with more force. Nothing. He looked at Sandra, his mouth a grim line.

Her eyes went to the deck of the boat, searching for the halyard. She grabbed the red line marked genoa and pulled as hard she could. The line popped from the cleat and the top of the genoa went loose. The bow rose and fell dramatically as it dove into a trough and then shot up on the crest of another wave, each one bringing a cascade of salty water over the front of the boat. Sandra took a deep breath and climbed out of the cockpit onto the deck.

"Don't do that, Sandra!" Mark shouted.

She glanced back at Mark and then to the bow of the boat. There wasn't a choice. She made her way forward, clutching the lifeline as she went. By the time she got to the bow she was on her knees, gripping the rail of the pulpit. She let go with one hand and grabbed the front edge of the sail. Something was jammed, it wouldn't slide down the forestay to the deck. She looked up at the stubborn sail and her father-in-law's voice echoed in her head, '*Remember, one hand for the boat and one hand for you.*' *Sorry Dave, I'm going to have to break that rule.* Sandra let go of the pulpit and hauled down on the sail with both hands. It dropped, a few feet, and she reached up and pulled again. The sail was mostly on deck, its folds resting against the starboard stanchions and lifelines. She reached for a handhold just as a huge wave hit the bow and washed over the foredeck. Her knees slid across the wet surface and her legs went under the pulpit crossbar and over the side. The water pulled at her as the bow rose but she wrapped her arms around a pulpit post and held on. She could hear Mark yelling from the back of the boat but couldn't make out the words. Life jacket—why hadn't she put on her life jacket? Even on a calm day on Lake Ontario they always wore life jackets.

Again she felt the grip of the water on her lower body as the bow dipped into a trough. The next time the bow rose she swung her right leg toward the deck of the boat. Her ankle smacked into the rear post of the pulpit before dropping back over the side. She held tight through the next wave and tried again. This time when her leg swung upward it was grabbed between two strong hands that pulled her through the pulpit opening and back onto the deck. She lay there with her arms still encircling the post, soaked to the skin, her breath coming in gasps. As another large wave swept the bow, Mark dropped to the deck next to her and wrapped his arm around her torso. She could feel the warmth of his body through her wet clothing and she shuddered as the tightness eased and the fear left her. She turned her head toward him, her arm still wrapped around its anchor. His face was white and only inches from hers, his hair plastered to the sides of his face.

His eyes went to her forehead. "You're bleeding," he croaked.

"It's just a flesh wound." She tried to smile in an effort to relieve the tension she saw in his eyes. "Shouldn't you be driving the boat?"

"Autohelm's got it covered. I needed to rescue my crew."

"Well, your crew appreciates it." Her whispered words were lost in the roar of the wind but he answered by squeezing her tighter.

As they scrambled into crouching positions, Mark continued to hold Sandra's arm even though she was gripping the lifeline with both hands. She leaned toward him to be heard. "I promise to hold on, and you need to do the same." They inched their way from the bow, Mark looking back every few seconds to make sure she was still there.

"We need to drop the main," he said as he climbed down into the cockpit.

"Aye aye, Captain. You go take over for Otto and I'll get that done."

Mark returned to his place at the stern and took the boat off autopilot while Sandra sought out the halyard marked "main". There it was, right next to the genoa, and she hauled the heavy line from the jaws of the cleat with one swift pull. The mainsail dropped part way to the boom and Sandra pulled it with both hands again and again until it was flaked between the lazy jacks.

"Okay," she called to Mark, "turn this rig around."

Neither spoke as he turned the boat south. With their backs to the blow, *Ode to Joy* motored her way through the cresting surf on course for La Paz harbour.

Sandra hopped off the boat as they pulled up next to the dock, taking the bow and stern lines with her. Mark reversed into place and she tied the front of the boat to its dock cleat before doing the same at the rear. He killed the engine and stood in the quiet with his hands resting on the wheel. The wind had lessened as they made their way back to La Paz and was now returned to a friendly breeze.

"You okay?" Sandra asked.

"Just happy to be back in the marina. That's easily the heaviest weather I've been out in."

"Me too. But here we are, safe and sound."

"Well, for the most part, yes." He pointed to her head and

then her knees.

Sandra put her hand to her forehead and felt the dried blood. "I'll be fine. Once it's cleaned up you'll hardly see it. And my knees will be a bit colourful for a few days but nothing to worry about." Sliding across the deck and over the toe rail had removed some skin and banged up Sandra's knees.

"I shouldn't have angled the boat so high into the wind. I could have lessened the pitch of the bow." Mark stared at his hands on the wheel. "And I should have paid more attention to the weather to begin with … *and*, apparently, listened to the prairie girl."

"And I shouldn't have gone up on the deck without waiting for your instruction, and definitely should have followed the golden rule, 'one hand for you, one hand for the boat'. Should have, could have—it's okay, really. Let's pack up and head home."

"Drinks along the Malecón before we had back to San Leandro?"

"You know, thanks, but I think I could use a nice long bubble bath more than I could use a drink. Although, I might have one *in* the bubble bath."

"Maybe a drink later at Pablo's then?"

"Maybe, if I'm awake long enough. All of that sea water seems to have sucked the life out of me. I'm seeing a good book in my evening."

"Right." Mark nodded and cast his eyes downward.

She knew she'd hurt him, rejecting his invitations, but she was so tired. On more than one front, the day had left her confused and shaken and she needed some time alone.

Paul was at his desk when Sandra entered the lobby, the entrance chime pulling Paul's eyes from his work and immediately to her forehead. "What the bloody hell happened to you?"

She didn't think it was so noticeable now that she'd wiped

off the dried blood. "Just a little boating incident. I'll be fine once I wash off the sea water."

"You were caught in that storm, weren't you? Damn him. I told Mark the weather was unsettled and he shouldn't be going out. Let me have a look." Paul came around the front desk and inspected Sandra's forehead. "I'll get you a bandage. Was there no first aid kit on the boat? Does he not know how to do something as simple as put a plaster on a wound?"

"I do, but Ms. Lyall here insisted she didn't need one." Mark was standing in the doorway.

"And I'm still insisting I don't need one. What I need is a bath, a hot meal, and maybe a pot of tea. You two are like a couple of old hens."

Sandra went over to Mark and took her bag from his hand. "Thank you for bringing this in, oh and …," she turned to look at Paul for a moment before looking back to Mark, "and thank you again for saving me from drowning." She walked across the lobby, heading for the hallway to the guest rooms, smiling at Paul on her way by.


Sandra leaned back into the hot water, the bubbles pushing up around her ears. *Aahh* … that was better already. If only she could order food and drink from here, life would indeed be perfect. Okay, perfect was a stretch, a big one. Her head was throbbing, although she hadn't revealed that to Mark, and her knees stung when they hit the hot soapy water. But truly, the physical pain paled in comparison to what she was feeling inside. He'd been fun today, and kind, and concerned, and he might have even saved her life. So why did she feel compelled to run as fast and far from him as she could?

When she thought of spending more time with Mark she felt a tightening in her chest. Trisha would say it was love, with a wink, but that wasn't it. When she'd fallen in love with Nick she couldn't get enough of him. She wanted to wake up to his smile every morning and go to sleep to the sound of his breathing each night. She still missed him so much. His laugh, his blue eyes, the way he listened to her and was her greatest supporter in everything she did. Seventeen years wasn't nearly long enough. Was it even possible for her to fall in love again?

Her mind drifted to the warmth of Mark's body against hers, his arm wrapped around her holding her close as they lay on the deck of the boat, the sound of his voice so close to her ear. She slapped the water with the flat of her hand. Why had she not followed her own instincts and stayed away from him to begin with?

Sandra slid deeper into the tub, immersing her head in the warm water and shutting out all sound but the beating of her own heart. It felt safe under the water, except for that sting at her forehead. *Ouch.* She sat up and put her fingers to her head. Okay, maybe a Band-Aid wasn't an all-bad idea for a day or two.

There was a knock at the door to her room. "Sandra?" It was Mark's voice.

*Oh please, just go away.*

Another knock. "Sandra?"

"I'm in the bath," she called back.

"Paul sent me up to take your order. He'll have it brought to your room."

"That's kind of him. Tell him to send the special. It's always good. And some tea, please. Tell him thank you."

"Done. And Sandra?"

She didn't answer but instead slipped back underneath the water, ignoring the burning sensation above her eye.

# Nineteen

Despite her initial reluctance to participate, Sandra was delighted to see her three paintings hanging in the visiting artists' tent of the La Paz Art Festival. The festival stretched for three blocks on a street just back from the Malecón, the cobblestone lined with colourful tents of green, gold, and blue in varying sizes. The tent for visiting artists was actually three gold tents strung together to make a twelve by thirty-six foot space. Sandra's paintings were hung in a vertical column of three, Mark's beach scene at the top, Mar Azul in the middle, and her new painting of the headlands at the bottom.

"Nice job, artista." Ian nudged Sandra's arm with his elbow. He leaned in to her and whispered, "Yours are the best in the tent."

"Shh …" Sandra gave him a look. "Thanks, but they are not."

"Oh yes, they absolutely are, and I'm not the only one to say so." Ian inclined his head toward the check-out area where Pascual was speaking with some guests, his hands moving wildly as he talked. "Your little Mexican Van Gogh agrees with me."

"Pascual? He probably says that about every artist in here. He wants us all back next year."

"Okay, but how many paintings are displaying a sold sticker merely …," he looked at his watch, "forty-five minutes into the show? Hm?"

"That one was sold over a week ago. I don't think it counts."

"Ah right, Mr. Jeffery, I forgot he was a fan of yours."

"I wouldn't say he's a fan. He just happened to connect with that piece."

"And with you too, perhaps?"

"What does that mean?"

"I just heard you've been spending time with him."

"Who told you that?"

"I have my sources." Ian raised his eyebrows.

"The Mar Azul grapevine, I'm guessing. It's a small place."

"And so, it's true? You're being courted by Mr. Rich and Famous?"

"Courted? God, no!" Sandra glanced around to see if anyone had heard. She lowered her voice and continued. "We're friends. That's all."

"Friends ... I see. By the way, there's a Band-Aid sticking out from under your hat."

Sandra touched her forehead, her fingers going to the plastic bandage that could be felt below the straw brim.

"Why do I get the feeling it has something to do with your *friend?*" Ian asked.

She adjusted her hat forward. "Can you still see it?"

"No, and your secret is safe with me, whatever it is."

"There's no secret. We went sailing yesterday and got caught in a blow. I fell and hit my head. End of story."

"And the knees. What happened there?"

"So, what, you've been inspecting me?" Sandra's eyes went to her capri pants to see if they were covering her scraped knees.

"No, not inspecting, they were sticking out when you were sitting in the car and I happened to look over. Why are you being so sensitive?"

"And why are you being so meddlesome?"

Ian raised his hands and took a step back. "Okay, how about we dial it down and go for a walk. Meddlesome? Really?" He turned and left the tent, Sandra following.

When they were outside Sandra spoke first. "I'm sorry. You weren't being meddlesome. I'm just feeling a bit frustrated with the Mark situation."

"Ah, so he's a *situation*, is he?" They started down the row of tents.

"Well, yes, sort of. He keeps inviting me out and I keep going but I'm not sure why because … well, I'm here to paint and walk the beach. And besides that, he makes me uncomfortable a lot of the time."

"He's a bit of an arrogant prig so I can see why."

Sandra stopped and turned to Ian. "No he isn't—arrogant or priggish. Why would you say that?"

"He just strikes me that way. I don't like him—didn't before he started following you around, like him less now."

"He's not following me around. I think he's a bit out of his element here in Mexico and I'm kind of … convenient."

"Ah, that's what's bothering you. You think he's using you."

"I didn't say using. I said convenient."

"And there's a difference?"

"Well … yes … it's just … different … let's walk. I think better when I walk." They continued down the block. The street was closed to traffic but beginning to fill with art shoppers. "He's nice to me, and we have fun, so I wouldn't call it using. What I meant by convenient is that I'm not his typical kind of friend, but since we're not exactly in Hollywood here," Sandra scanned the crowd around her, "his kind of people aren't in great supply."

"I've met a lot of musicians in my days of playing, including some famous ones, and though they do like to spend time with other musicians, I wouldn't say they have a *kind of people*. You've helped me make my arrogant-and-priggish argument."

"I shouldn't wander too far. It's getting busy and Pascual wanted me around to meet with people." They turned and started back toward the tent. "I have to admit, now that I'm here, it's kind of exciting to be in a show. Pascual would like me to come every day, but that might be more than I can manage. Maybe I'll come back on the weekend for a bit."

"And what do you plan to do about your English stalker?"

"I don't know. I find myself wishing his agent or some girlfriend would call and he'd get on a plane back to London or L.A."

"He has a girlfriend and yet he's hanging all over you?"

Sandra stopped again. "He isn't hanging all over me, okay? No courting. No hanging." She continued walking. "As for girlfriends, I don't know. He and Paul were talking about someone in London named Roxanne." Sandra remembered walking in on that conversation in Pablo's and Mark had promptly changed the subject. Whoever Roxanne was, he hadn't been speaking very glowingly of her. Sandra had done some on-line research and found tabloid photos of Mark with an actress named Roxanne Murphy. It wasn't clear from the article who she was, just that she'd been spotted "around town" with actor Mark Jeffery. She was gorgeous, of course, with a perfect complexion, long dark hair, longer legs, and thirty-five at best.

"You okay?" Ian broke into her thoughts.

"Yes, sorry. What were we talking about?"

"You apparently need to get out of the sun. We were talking about—well, speak of the devil."

Sandra followed Ian's gaze and there was Mark entering her tent. "Really? Today? I'm just not up for it." She stopped walking.

"Do you want me to drive you back to San Leandro? I will." Ian put his hand on her arm.

"I would love that, but no I can't. I told Pascual I would be here for opening day."

"Well let's go find a coffee then." Ian put his hand on the small of Sandra's back to lead her across the street. "Maybe he'll be gone by the time we get back."

———

There was a line-up at the coffee shop and the barista had been slow so Sandra thought Mark would have moved on by the time they returned to the tent. She walked in and glanced around. Thank goodness. No Mark.

"There you are!" A British accent from behind her. She turned and there he was, coming through the entrance toward her.

She made an effort to smile. "Hey, good morning." He looked as if he was going to embrace her so she stepped forward and shook his hand. She looked to where Ian had been standing but he'd moved to the end of the tent, intentionally no doubt, and was talking with Pascual.

"How are you?" Mark's expression was serious as his eyes went to her forehead.

"I'm fine. Really. It's not a big deal. A good night's sleep worked its magic."

"And … things are going well here?"

"The first hour was quiet but it seems the tourists have gotten over their hangovers enough to get out of bed."

"Mm, I know how they feel. I stayed a little late at Pablo's last night. I didn't feel like going home, and Paul kept putting beer in front of me."

"That Paul, such a terrible influence." She shook her head.

"So, I guess I can't get you a coffee," he nodded toward her cup, "but I think I'm going to get myself one. Care for a stroll?"

"You know, Ian and I were just out walking. I should stay here for a bit."

"Right. Where is Mr. LeRoy?"

Sandra pointed as Ian looked up. He started walking toward them.

"Well, be back soon then." Mark turned and left the tent.

Great, now she had Mark and Ian facing off like a pair of

hockey players at centre ice. Sandra placed her fingers on the space between her eyebrows. The throb from last night was returning.

"Is he going to hang around all day?" Ian asked.

"I don't know. Why don't you go ask him?" Sandra said. Mark had returned with his coffee an hour before, studied all of the paintings in the tent and then taken up residence near the check-out counter, chatting with Pascual's friend Mario, who was helping out with sales. He would glance in Sandra's direction every now and then and smile with a lift of his chin, like he was trying to reassure her. "I think he's trying to be supportive."

"Supportive? What the hell for? You are quite capable— and, you have me."

"Yes I do, and I appreciate your being here, but I can't exactly ask him to leave now, can I?"

"You could try it." He grinned.

"I think I should lock the two of you in a room together and see what happens."

"Brits don't know how to fight. I'd absolutely win."

"And Canadians have such a reputation for being brawlers. He might surprise you; he's probably had fight training for his work. That's where he learned to sail."

Ian's eyes went to her forehead. "And I see how good he is at that."

"It wasn't his fault. The skipper doesn't control the weather."

Ian watched Mark for a minute and then put his arm around Sandra's shoulders, leaning in to whisper in her ear. "I think he's into you."

Sandra pulled away from under his arm. "Oh stop it. Just because you chase every skirt you see doesn't mean all men do."

"So that's what you think of me, a philanderer. I see. Well, I'm going to wander, maybe pick up a girl or two. Back in a bit." Sandra watched him go, his sandy hair catching the sun as he stepped outside. She looked back to Mark and saw he was watching her again.

Ian had his left hand on the wheel and his right resting on the gear shift of his VW bug. "I can see why you're getting frustrated with Mr. Jeffery. He's like a stray dog, hanging around all day, inviting himself along for lunch. He needs to get a life, or find where he left his and get back to it." They were on their way home to San Leandro, the sun setting behind the hills.

"Don't be so hard on him. He was pleasant enough," said Sandra.

"Sure, pleasant, but still irritating—*indeed, Mr. LeRoy, delightful, Sandra*—what a prig!"

Sandra couldn't help but laugh at his fairly accurate impersonation. "Now, now, be nice. It's the way he speaks. It doesn't make him a prig."

"On the contrary, Ms. Lyall, I do believe you are mistaken." He was still speaking with a posh British accent.

As they crested a hill, the Sea of Cortez came into view below. It was always startling to see the brilliant blue water appear in the midst of so much dry land. The air from the open window caressed her face, its coolness signalling the onset of evening.

It was dark by the time Sandra sat on her patio eating leftovers from lunch in La Paz and drinking a glass of wine from the bottle she'd purchased that afternoon. She was hiding and she knew it. Mark had mentioned he'd be in Pablo's tonight and she didn't have the energy for him. A day of constant people and questions about her work on top of the palpable tension between Ian and Mark had drained her dry.

The lights of Pablo's radiated from under its rooftop and

the solar lights lining the entrance looked like a small landing strip from above. There was just enough light to see the white of the foam on the waves as they ascended the beach, their rhythmic sound relaxing, almost hypnotic. She loved this place but she felt the need to get away. Pascual was pushing her to spend more time at the art festival, Ian was behaving like her over-protective big brother, and Mark felt like some great hovering bird of prey. After two weeks at Mar Azul she'd normally be well into *mañana* mode, but instead she was more wound up than when she'd arrived.

Sandra took a sip of the deep red wine, stretched her hands around the smooth bowl of the glass and closed her eyes, leaning back in her chair. There was the surf again, returning her to the peace she had found here and her memories of other visits. A tear escaped from under her eyelid and rolled down her cheek, its saltiness coming to rest on her lips. She set down her glass and wrapped her arms around herself, imagining she could feel Nick's warmth in the breeze and hear his voice in the waves.

# Twenty

Mark was smiling as he walked along the beach toward Mar Azul. In the time he'd been staying in San Leandro, he'd always driven the short distance to Paul's hotel but this morning he felt like walking. The sun was beginning its rise out of the sea as he left home and shorebirds were feasting on the morning buffet left behind by the tide. He was planning a dinner party and needed to extend an invitation to his guest of honour.

When Sandra hadn't shown up at Pablo's the night before, Mark resisted the urge to go knock on her door. At least he assumed she was in her room, if she hadn't stayed out with her friend Ian after the art show closed. *Friend. Hmm.* It was obvious the blonde bard was after more than friendship. For Mark, Sandra had started out as a pleasant distraction from his troubles but the day on the boat changed all that. When he saw her go over the side his heart nearly stopped, and the surge of emotion he experienced when he pulled her back on deck and held her close took him completely by surprise. Since then he'd wanted to be in her company, even when Ian was glaring at him, even when she seemed to be avoiding him.

Had she avoided him last night? She may have just been tired. He'd stayed at Pablo's until almost eleven o'clock, nursing two glasses of wine all evening, hoping she'd come in for a nightcap or a cup of tea. He and Paul had chatted about the art show and made plans to attend on Thursday morning. Paul hadn't seen the completed painting of Mar Azul and wanted to have a chance to buy it before the weekend crowd arrived.

Mark had driven home with the top down on the BMW, the trumpet bush filling the air with its musky perfume. Where the road ascended the headland, he could see the cluster of lights at San Leandro down below and the white froth of the surf shining as the moon climbed into the sky. He pulled over to enjoy the scene and imagined Sandra taking in the same view. It was tempting to go back to Mar Azul and bring her up here to share this with him, but he knew that was a bad idea. She could be long asleep or soaking in a bath or, yes, avoiding him. It was then he remembered he'd agreed to cook dinner, in payment for her painting. Perhaps it was time, time to invite her to his home, time to acknowledge she had become more than a pleasing distraction.

"She's gone? Where? I thought she was here until March ... or April." Mark realized he hadn't asked Sandra how long she was staying. It hadn't seemed important until now.

Paul looked at his friend with eyebrows raised. "She *is* staying until April, but she's gone off horseback riding for a few days. Why are you so concerned about her whereabouts?"

"I'm not. I was planning to invite her for that dinner I owe her, for the painting."

"Ah, I see, and that's it?"

"Yes, dinner."

"No, I mean that's all that's going on?"

"Yes. No. I don't know." Mark jammed his hands in his pockets and began circling the small lobby, glancing up at Paul every so often.

Paul stood behind the reception counter continuing to sort the guest cards into piles. "You're going to wear a path in my carpet," he said without looking up.

"Oh blast. I should have gone to see her last night."

Paul laughed. "Is that so? Maybe it's time you tell me what's going on. Hm?"

"There's nothing going on. I simply wanted to invite her for dinner."

"Mm. Well, she'll be back, in a few days I think. She spends some time at a ranch every year when she's here. I thought she was going there middle of March but I may have misunderstood. She left this morning around sunrise, riding hat in hand."

"Riding. So, horses."

"Yes, horses. You know, the big hairy creatures, with long legs and noses."

"This isn't funny," he shot back at Paul.

"I think maybe you need a coffee, or perhaps you've had one too many of those already. I have a lovely herbal tea called Chill."

"Go ahead, have your fun with me. I'm only surprised she didn't mention she was going. I just saw her yesterday."

Paul laughed again. "I'm sorry, but you've been telling me you have no interest in this woman—what was it you compared her to, vanilla ice cream?—yet here you are pacing my lobby and snapping at me because she's gone away without telling you."

"I owe her a dinner and am trying to make good on it. I may be called away to work any day and I don't want to leave owing a debt."

"Oh please. This has got to be the least convincing performance of your career."

Mark stopped his pacing and glared at Paul, who stood grinning. He could be so infuriating. "So, art show tomorrow then? Pick you up around nine?" Without waiting for Paul to answer, Mark stalked out of the lobby and hurried down the beach toward the village.

"So you're not going to tell me?" Mark asked. He and Paul were seated out front of a beverage tent at the art festival.

"I don't know. It's somewhere on or toward the East Cape I think. There's a guy there, a horse trainer, an American if I remember correctly."

"You're telling me she's run off to spend time with an American cowboy?"

"She's gone off to ride horses under the guidance of a trainer is how I would put it, but then I'm not a jealous pillock." Paul picked up his bottle of beer and took a drink. "We've been friends a long time, Mark. Why don't you tell me what's up?"

Mark stared at a painting being displayed out front of the neighboring tent. It was a Mexican village scene with small adobe buildings in a rainbow of earthy colours. Paul waited, his eyes on Mark's face.

"I'm just sorting that out myself. I've been having these—feelings—I can't quite explain."

"About Sandra Lyall."

"Yes, about Sandra." He looked back at Paul. "She's come to mean something to me, even though, as we've both pointed out, she's not exactly my type."

Paul leaned forward and placed his forearms on the table. "Now don't take this the wrong way, but is it possible it's a kind of rebound effect? You lost a big part, your ex-wife remarried, you're not satisfied in your relationship with Roxanne. It's like the rebound trifecta."

Mark studied the beer bottle between his hands. "I don't know. I feel like my whole fucking world has been turned up-side-down and for some reason she's the only thing that feels, well, still upright. What I do know is that I want to spend time with her, that I panicked when I watched her go over the side of that boat, and the idea of her making eyes at some ... some ... cowboy ..."

"Perhaps she's more your type than you know. I didn't think I was destined for anything but acting, but here I am content as a Mexican *hotelero*. Sometimes happiness is found in unexpected places."

"All right then, let's say that's the case." Mark leaned forward. "What the bloody hell do I do now?"

"I'd say you wait until she returns from her ranch visit and you tell her how you feel. You said you were planning to have her over for dinner. Seems like a perfect opportunity."

"And if she doesn't feel the same? I often get the distinct impression she's just tolerating me."

"That is possible. She's rather down-to-earth and you can be a bit of a toff." Paul smiled. "But, you'll have to take that chance. We all have to learn to face rejection at some point, even the great Mark Jeffery."

Mark watched a middle-aged couple walk by hand-in-hand, the woman leaning into the man's shoulder as she laughed at something he'd said. "I seem to be taking a crash course of late."

"I'd say it's about time you caught up with the rest of us who have been in lifelong programs of study. I must have my PhD in Piss Off by now!"

Mark snorted. "And how do you survive it? I thought I was going to go mad after I got dumped for Janzen ... or turn boozer."

"I'd say you did a bit of both, mate. It's as you said, you survive it. I can't tell you much else."

Mark drank down the last of his beer and clunked the bottle on the table top. "Right then, I'll give it a go. I will drive down there and pay Ms. Lyall a visit."

Paul rolled his eyes and leaned back in his chair. "Oh hell, did you not hear what I said? *Wait until she returns.* You'll just frighten her if you show up there, not to mention set yourself up for complete embarrassment."

"What's that delightful American expression? 'Go big or go home'. I believe it suits the occasion."

"But how you proceed should suit her as well as you."

"I haven't known her long, but I'd say I know this much about Ms. Lyall, that a grand gesture would please her more than you think." Mark placed his hand over the left side of his chest. "There's a woman of passion under that quiet, Canadian exterior."

"Oh please, enough with the drama." Paul stood and pointed a finger at Mark, "If this goes sideways, don't say I didn't warn you."

With few towns or other established areas in the East Cape region, the research had been easy enough. He still wasn't certain he had the right place, since the web site showed a Mexican national as the owner and head trainer, but Alejandro Torres had spent many years in America, only returning to Mexico five years ago. He raised Azteca horses and specialized in a discipline called western dressage at his facility south of La Ribera. Mark was familiar with dressage but not the cowboy version of it. Somehow he'd imagined Sandra doing something more traditional, and less western.

The road was quiet as he rolled through Los Barriles. He'd gotten an early start, unable to return to sleep after waking at six. Sandra had been gone for two days and he was feeling anxious about what he might discover at Rancho Azteca. The horse trainer was about Mark's age, good looking, successful, and quite a catch for someone with an interest in horses. He'd been hoping to find some bandy-legged old cowboy on the website, and a bio for a Mrs. Torres. It wasn't Mark's style, putting himself in awkward situations, but he knew he'd only pace his beach house until Sandra returned and then struggle to find a way to ask her about Alejandro anyway. Better to face it head on and get it over with. He was prepared for possible rejection at the end of this journey.

Two hours and three cups of coffee later, Mark pulled onto

the dirt road indicated by his GPS. The sign at the turn read "Rancho Azteca 3 km". His hands were moist on the steering wheel and he had to take deep breaths to keep his stomach from climbing into his chest. He stopped after two kilometres and stared ahead at the road, the engine purring in the quiet desert. He was tempted to turn around. Why was he putting himself through this? For what? *Go back to your life, Jeffery, and let this woman to her own.* Five minutes went by, then ten, and still he sat and stared at the road, one hand on the wheel, the other on the gear shift. He didn't want to turn back and yet he couldn't drive forward. What if she were on some kind of romantic getaway with this Alejandro? What if he walked into the middle of something desperately uncomfortable? How to extricate himself in that event?

Mark put the car in gear and turned the wheel sharply to the left, the passenger's side tires climbing the sandy berm on the side of the road as he made his u-turn. He stopped the car a few hundred feet back the way he'd come and banged his hand on the steering wheel. "Damn it, Jeffery. Don't be such a bloody coward!" He pulled another u-turn and set off on the final kilometre to Rancho Azteca.

# Twenty-One

The sun had been up for an hour when Sandra led La Tormenta from the paddock. She was a solidly-built grey mare, still dark and dappled at seven years old, and Sandra's favourite mount at the ranch. The past two days had been grounding, helping Sandra reconnect with that inner peace she'd come to value so highly. When she'd called, Alejandro was quick to welcome her to the ranch for a few days, fitting her in between clinics.

Rancho Azteca had two main streams of business, breeding fabulous horses and offering riding and horsemanship clinics. Almost ten years earlier, Sandra had seen Alejandro give a western dressage demonstration at an equine expo, and when she saw his brochure pinned to a board in La Paz she could hardly believe her good fortune. That was during her second visit to Baja and she'd managed to grab the last spot in one of his clinics that year. She'd returned for a week each of the last two years and this year's stay was scheduled for mid-March. Alejandro was a gifted horseman and an even more gifted teacher. His clinics were small, just eight students, each paired with one of his Azteca horses. He would work with each person individually as well as conduct group sessions and, no matter what the level of the student, each one took something away from six days under his guidance.

The year before was the first time Sandra had come to the ranch outside of a scheduled clinic. She'd registered for a February session and, at the end of the six days, Alejandro invited her to return for some one-on-one coaching. It had been a rewarding experience that she'd hoped to repeat and she was feeling fortunate to be sandwiched into his busy winter schedule this year, especially at a time when she needed a place to regroup.

La Tormenta raised her head and nickered and Sandra looked up to see Alejandro walking toward the barn, his white cowboy hat dangling from his hand. He was not a tall man, but he walked with authority, giving the impression of a much larger person. This was one of the keys to communicating successfully with horses, projecting a larger self than your physical size when you needed to. He smiled as he approached, his teeth bright against his brown skin and dark moustache. Sandra had thought him handsome when she first met him and as she got to know the inner workings of the man, he only became more attractive.

"Buenas días, Sandra. You are out earlier even than yesterday." He walked up to La Tormenta and stroked her shoulder. The mare turned her head toward him, curving her elegant neck around her trainer.

Sandra continued grooming the grey horse. "She loves to be brushed so I thought I'd give her a little more spa time before our morning lesson."

"And this in addition to the thorough grooming she will no doubt have after the ride?"

"Of course."

Alejandro chuckled as he continued to caress the mare. "*Suerte chica.* You are a lucky girl, Tormenta. You will gleam like the sun by the time señora leaves us." He turned to Sandra. "She is still for sale you know. And she likes you, which is very important to me."

Sandra continued to brush the mare's legs from her crouched position. "I know she is. I saw her listed on your website. But it's a very long ride home."

Alejandro laughed, a deep sound that seemed to come from

his very core. "Not to worry on that account. I have *muchos amigos* who would be happy to deliver her to Alberta for you. She does not enjoy the heat so she would like it in Canada."

"I'm betting she doesn't like the cold either, at least not the kind of cold we get. Poor girl would be looking south at the first sign of Canadian winter." Sandra rubbed Tormenta's neck as she stood up. "Wouldn't you, beautiful?"

"For the first winter, perhaps, but they are extremely adaptable, our equine friends, and you need a mount of your own. It has been how many years?"

"I put my old gelding down five years ago."

"Then it is time. Think about it. I will give you a very, very good price." Alejandro looked at his watch. "See you in the arena in twenty minutes?"

He placed his hat on his head and disappeared around the side of the barn, a deep nicker greeting him. That would be Caliente no doubt, his Andalusian stallion. They had a relationship like no other man-horse team that Sandra had seen and she loved to watch the two of them work. It was Caliente who had travelled around North America with Alejandro, giving demonstrations in liberty work and western dressage. She hoped she'd have a chance to see him work with the big, black horse while she was here. This afternoon they were planning a beach ride. Maybe Alejandro would ride him then.

She laid the saddle blanket on Tormenta's back, followed by the western saddle. It was so much lighter than the one she had at home. She'd have to ask Alejandro where he got it. At fifteen hands, Tormenta wasn't a tall horse, but it would still be a heave to throw her own thirty-five pounds of leather, fibreglass and silver onto the horse's back. This saddle didn't weigh more than twenty-five.

Bridle adjusted, hands gloved, helmet on head, Sandra led Tormenta from the hitching rail to the outdoor riding ring. Rancho Azteca had a small covered arena for when the weather was hot, but this morning it was pleasant even in the sun. The outdoor arena was edged with a rustic-looking post and rail fence, the desert providing the perfect sandy footing. She checked her cinch one more time before putting her left foot in the brass-clad stirrup and mounting. That first moment of sliding into the saddle, the smoothness of the leather against the back of her jeans, felt like coming home. Sandra settled into the deep seat and picked up her reins, the rawhide and leather poppers hanging down below Tormenta's shoulder. She closed her eyes and let the mingled scents of leather, horse and desert embrace her.

Absorbed in her lesson, Sandra didn't notice the man standing ringside until Alejandro was quiet for an unusual amount of time. He often paused his instruction to give students the opportunity to feel the work they were doing without interruption, but this pause seemed extraordinarily long. She brought Tormenta down to a walk before looking around the arena. He was by the gate at the far end, talking to a man in khakis and a white shirt. The man didn't look like someone here to ride; maybe he was lost. As Sandra rode closer, recognition set in. *No. It can't be. Not here.* Alejandro turned and smiled, waving her over. Yes, it was definitely Mark.

"Sandra, a friend has come in search of you." Alejandro was smiling but confusion showed in his eyes.

"I see that. What a surprise." She looked at Mark, forcing a pleasant expression on her face.

"Good morning. Paul mentioned you were down here doing cowboy dressage, something I'd not heard of, and my curiosity got the better of me," Mark said, his eyes going from Sandra to Alejandro and back again.

Sandra couldn't speak. She didn't know what to say. Why would he do this? Showing up at Mar Azul nearly every day was one thing but following her down here without an invite. What the hell?

"Don't let me interrupt your ride. I won't be a bother," Mark said.

*You have already interrupted and you're absolutely a bother*, Sandra wanted to shout at him.

Alejandro seemed to sense the awkwardness and spoke. "Well, back to work then, Sandra. You have thirty minutes yet to ride."

As she rode away she heard Mark's voice but didn't catch the words. She turned her head to look at him. "Pardon me?"

"I said, lovely horse!"

"Yes, she certainly is." Sandra lay her hand on Tormenta's neck, hoping the smoothness and warmth would settle her jangled nerves.

She'd tried to remain focused on the balance of the lesson but was distracted, and the horse felt it. The latter part of the ride had been a sharp contrast to the first. She removed the halter from Tormenta's head and watched her walk away to join the herd. The mare paused and pawed at the earth but decided against a roll, Sandra's vigorous post-ride grooming enough to remove the need.

Sandra walked toward the barn to put away her gear and as she rounded the corner, there was Mark, leaning against the hitching rail. "Howdy, cowgirl." He gave a slow wave.

"Howdy yourself, city slicker. Nice ranch attire."

Mark looked down at his clothing. "Yes, I can see now that a white shirt was perhaps not the best choice."

"Not to worry. It won't be white for long."

"I did bring a spare of a darker colour."

"So you're planning on staying, then?" Sandra heard the tension in her own voice.

"Well ... I ... no, of course not. But your cowboy friend did invite me to stay for lunch. I hope—"

"Yes, Alejandro is a true gentleman. Excuse me. I need to put my things away." Sandra pulled her saddle from where it rested on the hitching rail and stalked into the barn.

# Twenty-Two

Mark stood alone on the verandah of the ranch house survey-ing the setup of Rancho Azteca. The house was surrounded by horses, the split rail fences dividing the property into paddocks for the various groupings. The group closest to Mark appeared to be youngsters, their skinny necks and gangly legs reminding him of adolescent boys. There were five of them. The black one was determined to get a game going while the other four looked ready for a nap in the sun. He would trot into the group swinging his head in the air and then rear in front of one of the sunbathers. The other horse would flatten his ears, not joining in the game. The little black would then trot away only to return to his friends and nip one of his herd mates on the cheek.

Mark heard the screen door behind him. "He is a trouble-maker my Caballero, always trying to stir things up." It was Alejandro.

"He certainly is. I wish I had his energy. I feel more like the other four, just wanting an afternoon nap."

"Ah, but he has just one year and the zest for life we all do as boys. When he has to work he will appreciate his rest time." Alejandro set down a basket of tortillas and a steaming bowl of some kind of meat. "*Tacos de carne*. I hope you are not a vegetarian."

"No, not at all."

"It is a simple meal but I am on my own here so we will have to manage. Have a seat." Alejandro smiled at Mark, his perfect, white teeth lighting up in his dark face. Mark half expected a star-shaped glint at the corner of his mouth like you see when the cartoon hero smiles. And then there was that Mexican accent—all Ricardo Montalbán. No doubt most of Alejandro's students were women.

"Am I late?" Sandra came around the corner from behind the house.

"Not at all." Alejandro pulled out a chair for her. "Your timing is perfecto. As the Americans say ... dig in." He made a flourish with his hands over the food on the table. "Ay! I am a terrible host. I have brought you nothing to drink. *Para la bebida* there is wine, cerveza, iced tea, and water, of course. Sandra, can I get you something?"

They both requested iced tea and waited in awkward silence until Alejandro returned. When he did, he stood beside the table holding the two tumblers of blue Mexican glass, each with a lemon slice on the rim. His eyes went from Sandra to Mark. "Everything is fine here?"

"Yes, fine," said Sandra. She pulled the napkin from the plate and placed it on her lap.

Okay, so perhaps Paul had been right, showing up here was not a good idea. When lunch was over he'd be on his way and leave Sandra and her cowboy to whatever it was they had going on. He thought back to her lesson and how Alejandro had placed his hand on her knee when he went over to speak to her, his other hand stroking the neck of the horse. It seemed an intimate gesture from where Mark stood.

"So, Señor Jeffery ..." Alejandro started.

"Call me Mark." He spooned the meat mixture into a tortilla, added what looked like a coleslaw from another bowl, and folded it in half.

"Sí ... Mark. How is it you know the lovely Sandra?" Alejandro took a bite of his taco and fixed his gaze on Mark.

"She is staying at Mar Azul, which is owned by a friend of mine."

"Ah, Paul is a friend of yours! I have not had opportunity to meet him but Sandra speaks very well of your friend."

"Yes, he's a good fellow. We've known each other since we were lads."

Sandra was quietly eating her lunch and sipping on her iced tea, her eyes travelling back and forth between the two men as they spoke.

"And what brings you to Rancho Azteca? You wish to ride?" Alejandro asked.

"No, no riding. I came to see how Sandra was getting along." As the words left his mouth, Mark realized that checking up on a woman he hardly knew was not a good reason to show up unannounced. "And I ... needed to ... run an errand ... in Cabo ... and so, here I am." He flashed a look at Sandra and took a large bite of his taco, chewing rapidly. "Mm, very good," he said, mouth full. It was a fair question; just what was he doing here at Rancho Azteca?

"Cabo?" Alejandro laughed. "I am not exactly on the way, unless you were planning to drive that expensive car around the cape, and I would not recommend it. Horse would be a better way to travel that road. Perhaps you would like to join us this afternoon. We are going down to the beach with the horses and it is not so hot today," Alejandro said.

"I'm not much of a rider, at least not without a stunt double." Mark glanced at Sandra to see if he'd made her smile. He hadn't. He cleared his throat and shifted in his seat.

Alejandro squinted at Mark. "A stunt double? I don't understand."

"Mark is an actor, so his riding in movies is no doubt done by someone else, someone who can ride well." She looked at Mark, her eyes hard. "Is that about right?"

"Well, yes, but I do ride ... some."

"Well, join us then." Alejandro was smiling with all those teeth again—*glint*. "It is an easy half hour down to the beach."

"Followed by a gallop on the sand," Sandra cut in.

"*But*—I have a nice older mare who will go at whatever speed you like. Her name is Tranquilo, at least that is what she has been called for many years. She could use the exercise to prepare for her next clinic."

"I don't want to intrude." Mark glanced at Sandra, who gave nothing away with her expression.

Alejandro jumped in. "Not at all. Everyone who comes to Azteca must ride one of my horses. *Es obligatorio*! More tea?"


They rode along the well-worn trail three in a line with Alejandro leading on his striking black stallion. He and the horse were well matched: the shiny black hair, the dark eyes, the male energy that seemed to pour off of them. Mark wondered if Caliente had the same dazzling smile when he opened his big horsey lips.

The trail wound its way through the many cactus, ocotillo and acacia that filled this part of the Baja landscape. Alejandro turned in his saddle and gestured to a large cactus as he rode past it. "Do you know the cardón can grow to seventy feet high and weigh more than twenty-five tons? Its name comes from the Spanish word for thistle. It is said when Hernando Cortes came to establish a settlement in Baja, he named it "Isla de Cardón" for all of the spiky plants and because, at the time, they believed the peninsula was actually an island."

"So these are not saguaro?" Mark called from the back of the line of horses.

"No, although they are close cousins. The saguaro do not grow this far south on the peninsula; believe it or not, there is too much moisture." Alejandro faced forward again.

From his position behind her, Mark watched as Sandra's

shoulders rose and fell, one and then the other, with the movement of Tormenta's walk. Her hair was pulled into a bundle of curls that stuck out from beneath her brown riding helmet and she wore a denim shirt that bunched up at the cantle of the saddle and hung over legs dressed in light blue Wranglers. They'd not spoken since lunch. His uncertainty about her feelings and about her relationship with Alejandro had stopped his words every time he started to explain his presence at Rancho Azteca. And now here he was on a horse. Every wretched period drama he'd been cast in seemed to involve at least one horseback scene, so he had learned to ride out of necessity, but he'd never felt comfortable astride. If all of those swooning, horse-loving females had seen some of the riding scene out-takes they surely would have been far less enamoured with the equestrian prowess of Mr. Rochester. At least he was in a western saddle today so there was something to grab hold of if the need arose.

The trail wound between two hills and then the sea was before them, blue and sparkling in the midday sun. Down one more low hill, across a road, and they were on the beach. *Right, splendid, the gallop part Sandra mentioned.* Western saddle or not, he didn't think he was up for a beach run, or the embarrassment and potential injury that would come if he landed head first in the sand.

Alejandro stopped and turned, waving them over so he could be heard over the sound of the surf. "The waves are quite large today so we will ride higher on the beach, but stay on the hard sand to make it easier for the horses. Tranquilo is getting a little long in the tooth."

"I know the feeling," Mark responded. "She and I are happy to bring up the rear."

Alejandro patted Caliente's shoulder. "And this boy was a bit sore last week so I will also take it easy. You go on ahead Sandra, I will ride back here with Mark. Tormenta is never reluctant to leave her friends for a bit of fun."

They continued to the water's edge and turned left, away from the houses that could be seen in the other direction. The horses expectantly broke into a slow trot, ears forward, energy up. "Take a bit more rein and sit deep in your saddle. She will stay in a nice jog once you get her there," Alejandro said to Mark. As Mark brought the rein toward his abdomen he felt the horse's back rise beneath him, her neck arched, and she slowed into a smooth, easy, two-beat gait.

"*Bueno!*" Alejandro was smiling, matching Mark's speed on his own horse. "Caliente is not quite so keen to go at a slow pace but it is good exercise for him. We all need to learn to keep ourselves in check from time to time."

Tormenta was trotting fast, putting distance between her and her companions. Sandra raised her arm in the air and called, "See you at the end of the beach!" With that she pushed Tormenta up into a canter. She sat easily in the saddle, her body moving with the rhythm of the mare, Tormenta's dark grey mane blowing in the wind. When she was a hundred yards down the beach, Sandra rose from her seat, leaned forward and found another gear. Divets of wet sand flew from the mare's hooves as she galloped away.

Alejandro said something in Spanish that Mark couldn't quite make out.

"Sorry?" Mark asked.

Alejandro turned to him and said in English with more volume, "She is quite a woman."

"Right. Yes. She certainly is." Mark's eyes went back to Sandra. Apparently he wasn't the only one who'd noticed.

Tormenta was drifting right, into the breakers, the water spraying up around her as she continued to gallop. Some of the waves were just foam running up the beach, others a foot or more of water, and the horse's gait became more animated whenever the water went as high as her knees.

"Should she be out in the waves?" Mark asked as they

jogged along.

"Well, as long as they stay that size she is fine. Tormenta has done this many times before. But ... that one," Alejandro pointed out further into the sea, "could be a problem."

Mark followed Alejandro's gaze and saw a large wave, at least a foot taller than the others, rolling toward the beach. When it reached Tormenta, the mare's legs were washed from under her and both horse and rider disappeared into the surf. Alejandro's black stallion responded instantly to his cues and they were galloping away from Mark toward the spot where Sandra had gone down. Tranquilo continued to jog along, not fussed by the urgency of her companion. "Damn it," Mark said to himself as he squeezed the horse's sides to ask her for more speed. "All right girl, help me out here. We can't hang back and let Don Juan do all the rescuing." Tranquilo broke into a rolling canter that Mark found surprisingly easy to sit. No wonder it was required that everyone ride one of Alejandro's horses when they came to the ranch.

Sandra was standing now, holding Tormenta's reins, wiping her face with the other hand. And then Alejandro was there, sliding to a stop and vaulting off his horse. *For Christ's sake, it's like a scene out of a Hollywood romance.* As Mark and Tranquilo cantered toward the others, he could hear Sandra's voice and her laughter. At least she wasn't hurt.

Mark spoke as he rode up. "You do realize that not every activity has to involve a plunge in the sea?"

Sandra smiled at him for the first time since he'd arrived. "Yes, smart-ass, I do."

Both woman and horse were soaked, and he couldn't help but notice how Sandra's clothes clung to her body.

"You didn't happen to bring that spare shirt with you, did you?" Sandra asked.

"No, I'm afraid not, but I'd be happy to give you this one," he said, completely serious.

"I'm kidding. I'm fine. It's the sand more than the wet." She shook one arm and then the other, followed by each leg. "My clothes are filled with it."

They had moved up out of the water and Alejandro was inspecting the mare, running his hands down each of her legs. "She seems fine," he said. "I will take her for a little jog to make sure." Alejandro passed Caliente's reins to Sandra and trotted off down the beach with Tormenta.

"As you see, he's more concerned about the horse than the rider." Sandra chuckled.

"Does that bother you?" Mark asked.

"No, of course not. He can see that I'm fine, and his horses are his most prized possessions; well, unless you count wife and children as possessions."

Mark looked to where Alejandro was trotting with Tormenta. "So, he's married?"

Sandra was still shaking her legs, trying to get the sand to fall out of her jeans. "*Very*. Martina is in Cabo, visiting her sister."

"Why do you say *very?*"

"They're just one of those couples that's more like one person than two. Know what I mean?"

Mark found himself wishing he did.

The return ride was quiet, each rider caught up in his or her own thoughts. Mark brought up the rear again, Tranquilo content to walk more slowly than the others. Every now and then she would break into a jog to bridge the gap. Mark reached forward and ran his hand over the hair on the mare's neck. It was smooth and warm on the surface with the muscles tight underneath, the black mane sliding forward and back on its red-brown backdrop. He'd never ridden a horse just for pleasure; there had always been a purpose, a goal—and horses could be the most difficult creatures when you were working on a schedule.

Sandra and Tormenta were ahead of him on the trail. She was still soaking wet, her bright orange t-shirt showing through the light denim of her outer layer. He couldn't imagine riding a horse in wet, sandy jeans, but she didn't seem to mind, remaining cheerful and amused since her dive into the sea. Finding out that Alejandro was married had given Mark some relief, but he still wasn't sure if Sandra wanted him here. The frostiness that met him when he first arrived seemed to have melted some, but she continued to be distant, like she'd placed some kind of invisible shield between them. It had been that way since they'd met, at least off and on, but now the barrier seemed more intentional.

They reached the dirt road that would take them the final mile to the ranch and Alejandro fell back beside Sandra. "Mark!" he called. "Come and ride with us, amigo." Mark tapped Tranquilo's sides with his heels and she moved up into a jog. He caught up to the others and slipped into the space next to Alejandro.

"You are enjoying my precious girl?" Alejandro asked Mark, looking at the bay mare.

"She's lovely. I was just thinking how I'd never had the pleasure of this kind of ride before. And, truly, if all of my movie horses had been as easy as this one, I wouldn't have needed the stunt doubles so often." He glanced at Sandra. Her lips pressed together with the corners turned up slightly.

"Ah yes, she is a favourite of my more novice students. Often they will request her when they register for a clinic. If only I had half a dozen exactly like her."

"I rode her the first year I came," Sandra said, "and then I met Tormenta." She patted the mare's shoulder.

"Sandra prefers a less predictable ride," Alejandro said.

"Like an unplanned swim, you mean?" Sandra chuckled. "She brought that on herself you know. I didn't ask her to move out into the waves."

"I am certain you didn't. She has a little of the devil in her, from her sire." Alejandro looked to Mark. "My other stallion can be troublesome, always full of mischief. Even at twenty-two he is a handful."

"But incredibly gorgeous," Sandra said.

"Yes, that as well. If only he didn't know it."

"I've known many an actor like that, far too aware of their own good looks to be manageable," Mark said.

"So, Mark, tell me about your work. I am not a watcher of movies or television—there are always too many horses to tend or train—so I apologize if I should have recognized you." Alejandro reined in the dark stallion, trying to stay in step with Tranquilo's steady gait.

"I'm not exactly a household name, at least not in America. I'm more often recognized in Britain."

"For movies or for television?" Alejandro asked.

"Some of both, more movies in recent years."

"Is that why you are in Mexico? Are you making a movie? If you require any horses …" Alejandro offered his blinding smile.

"You would be the first one I'd recommend, but no, I'm here taking some time off. I'll be starting on a new project very soon."

Sandra stopped Tormenta to allow the others to catch up. "So it's done then? You liked the script and it's all settled?"

"Well no, not quite yet, but I'm expecting the script to arrive in the next couple of days. They've been doing some rewrites. It sounds very promising."

"And you will go to England when it is done?" Alejandro asked.

"No, likely Los Angeles, at least to start. I'm not certain where they're planning to do the filming. Somewhere in the mid-west."

"Sounds exciting, but I do not envy a travelling life. I had my share for twenty years and I am happy to stay home now." Alejandro stroked Caliente's neck as his eyes rested on the horizon. "I will not leave."

"Ever?" Sandra asked. "Not even for a vacation?"

"*Vacaciones?* Now what would I possibly want a vacation *from?* All the years I travelled I only desired to be back in Mexico, settled on land of my own. Now here I am, so there is no need to go anywhere else."

"And you have no wish to travel, to see places you haven't been?" Sandra asked.

Alejandro closed his eyes, his body moving with the motion of the horse. "You must only stop concerning yourself with what you are missing elsewhere to appreciate what is here and now." Alejandro opened his eyes and smiled as Rancho Azteca came into view.

# Twenty-Three

The warm water felt luxurious streaming down her face and through her hair, washing away the salt and sand from her unplanned swim. There was sand in every nook and cranny of her body—between her toes, in her ears, under her fingernails, and in places that made her chuckle as she watched the tiny grains swirl around the drain in the red tile floor.

In the end it had been a fun afternoon and, despite her initial resistance, she had enjoyed Mark's company. Why did he have to be so charming at times? It was easier to keep him at arm's length when he was tossing chairs or going on about his celebrity life, so foreign to her own. He'd actually offered her his shirt, and it seemed he meant it. And now Alejandro had invited him for dinner and to stay over—damn his over-developed sense of hospitality! Mark would have been on his merry way this afternoon and Sandra could have continued with her ranch retreat. But, then again, he had been rather dashing astride the big bay mare, wearing that pair of borrowed Wranglers. What was it with movie stars that they could wear clothes so well? She spent hours trying on umpteen styles and sizes of jeans before finding a pair that looked half decent on her 49-year-old butt, and Mark looked like *that* in a random pair of jeans Alejandro had around the place. And, on top of that, he'd sat a horse rather well. She was feeling a bit guilty about her comments at lunch, mocking his riding ability and need for stunt doubles. But, so what, he could wear a pair of jeans and sit a horse, he was still not her type and she was still not interested in getting involved with him. Was that why he was here? The sailing, the art show, Pablo's could all be chocked up to diversions from his troubles but driving down here to seek her out, that seemed something quite different.

"Again, you must excuse my lack of expertise in the kitchen. The barbecue is the only cooking appliance I am well acquainted with and so, tonight, we have steak with grilled vegetables and potatoes. However, to make up for my limited culinary skills, to accompany our meal …" Alejandro pulled a bottle from behind his back and set it on the table with a flourish, "*el vino tinto* from my personal cellar."

Mark picked up the bottle and read the label. "Temecula. I don't know this area."

"It is a small valley southeast of Los Angeles. Many of its wines are only available locally, but I have a good friend there who is a sommelier, and he makes shipping arrangements for what he considers the *best* of Temecula. I am fortunate to have such a friend, and tonight, I share my good fortune." Alejandro gave a slight bow. "And now, how would you like your steaks prepared? It is organic beef from a neighboring ranch. They raise the Corriente cattle."

"And is there a best way to eat this organic Corriente?" Mark asked.

"With a fork and a knife is my preference." Alejandro responded with a straight face.

"Well yes, of course, but what I meant was—"

Alejandro's smile danced in his eyes before lighting up his face. "*Perdón*, amigo, I am only having some entertainment at your expense. In my opinion, it is a shame to cook the Corriente too much and so I prefer it cooked to medium rare, at most. But, if you don't like your meat a little bloody, then I can certainly leave it on the grill longer, and will not be offended. I will simply feel sad for you to miss out on the full experience."

"Medium rare is good for me," Sandra cut in. "Leaning slightly toward the rare."

"Sounds perfect. I'll have the same," Mark said.

"Enjoy some wine while I start the steaks. Perhaps Mark, you can open it? I apologize I did not allow it time to breathe. When Martina is not here to remind me ..." Alejandro shrugged and flashed a smile before turning and heading around the corner of the house.

"Is he always so ... animated?" Mark asked, still looking at the spot where Alejandro had disappeared.

"You know, he isn't, but then this is a role I've not seen him in. Martina and her helper usually deal with the meals and serving. And with the horses, he is much more ..." Sandra searched for the word, "serene, I guess. He has this quietness around the students and horses, but a quietness filled with strength. He's a remarkable person."

"Paul said you were scheduled to come here next month, for a clinic or something."

So he had been asking Paul questions. She'd assumed that's how he'd found her. "Right, I was. I am. I'm coming back in mid-March to take a week-long session."

"I was surprised you didn't stay to attend more of the art show. I saw Pascual yesterday and he was disappointed to hear you'd gone away."

"Yes, well, I felt like doing some riding and Alejandro had this one small window." *And, I was trying to get away from you, as it happens.* "It was good of him to fit me in, especially without Martina here to help. He wasn't anticipating two guests."

"I hadn't intended to stay the night. He seemed genuine with his invitation. Was I wrong to accept?"

"Alejandro is very genuine. If he invited you, he wanted to, and he's accustomed to having guests. I'm just feeling responsible for his extra workload, since I'm guessing you wouldn't be here if I weren't." Sandra meant it more like a question than a statement.

Mark's cheeks flushed with colour. "I suppose I'd best get this wine breathing before our host returns to find it still suffocating in there." He stood and picked up the corkscrew, winding it into the top of the bottle. It was a simple tool, a t-shape with the bottom end a screw and a solid silver bar across it for pulling. With it fully screwed into the cork, Mark grabbed it with his right hand and held the bottle down with his left. His hands were broad, almost working hands, which struck Sandra as odd given his line of work. But then an actor probably had to get his hands dirty from time to time, depending on the role. His shirtsleeves were rolled up and a simple, silver-banded watch was on his left wrist, standing out brightly against tanned skin. He pulled on the corkscrew, the cork not wanting to leave its home, and the muscles in his hand and forearm flexed with the effort.

"You have a better method maybe?" His words came out strained.

Sandra didn't respond, not understanding the question.

"You just looked like you might be sorting out another way of getting the job done."

"Only a different kind of corkscrew, one of the little guys with the pull-down arms." She motioned with her hands. "This type must have been developed for men to show off their strength."

"Well it's not working in my case." Mark adjusted the bottle and pulled on the cork again. He gave one final tug, extracting the cork from its secure position. "Ah! There, you confounded thing!"

Sandra clapped her hands. "Well done, Sir Mark. You have saved the day."

"Wine, m'lady?" Mark extended the bottle toward her glass.

"It will breathe all the better out of this vitreous prison."

He was smiling at her, with his eyes as much as his lips. His hair was lying in curls at his forehead giving him a boyish, vulnerable appearance. She met his gaze and felt pulled into those eyes the camera loved to show in close-up. "Yes ... please."

Despite Alejandro's professed lack of culinary skills, dinner was delicious: steak grilled to perfection, potatoes seasoned in a blend of spices he'd not divulge, and a mix of winter vegetables that tasted fresh from the garden.

"You sell yourself short, Alejandro. Your cooking skills rival your horsemanship," Sandra said before putting the final bite of steak in her mouth.

"Well, thank you." Alejandro gave a gracious nod of his head. "I do my best."

"And the wine ... I don't know what to say about that; simply ... perfect." Sandra picked up her glass.

"Perhaps I will let Martina lead the next clinic and I will prepare the meals."

"I wouldn't go that far." Sandra laughed. "I think Martina is still master of the kitchen."

"You are correct, *but* she is also a very good horsewoman. Many people do not know this because she is chained to the stove when a clinic is running."

Mark was quiet during dinner, but in an easy, pleasant way, seemingly content to savour the food and the surroundings, and listen to Sandra and Alejandro chatter about horses. He smiled and nodded where appropriate, laughed at the right spots, and when he finished his meal ahead of the other two, he sat back in his chair and slowly sipped his wine.

"You are very quiet, amigo," Alejandro said.

"I am made speechless by the meal and the company, not to mention this splendid location. I haven't felt so satisfied in a long while. Thank you for having me." Mark raised his glass in a toast.

"You are quite welcome. I hope you will return one day, perhaps participate in one of our clinics."

"I don't know about that, but you never know. Life is full of surprises." His eyes went to Sandra with a look that sent tingles up the backs of her arms.

"Well ..." Alejandro looked from Mark to Sandra, "I must now get to the less enjoyable portion of the meal." He stood and began picking up dishes from the table. "This is where Martina relies on her help but I have not such good fortune tonight."

Sandra started to rise from her chair. "I can assist. Put me to work."

He motioned for her to sit. "No, no. You sit, enjoy the rest of the wine, and I will rejoin you for tea in a short while. It is a small task to clean up after only three, especially when all of the food was cooked on a grill." Alejandro's smile shone in the fading evening light. He stacked the dishes into the grilling pans and went into the house.

The light was mostly gone from the sky, leaving a faint glow to the west. Caliente grazed in his paddock, a silhouette against the twilight. The screen door creaked open and Alejandro was back, carrying four votives of multi-coloured stained glass. "I almost forgot to give you some light. Soon you will be sitting in darkness." He set the candles on the table and lit them before lighting a lantern that rested on a side table. Warm light filled the space. "*Mucho mejor.* Now you can see who you are talking to."

Sandra felt one of those jittery Mark-Jeffery-fan-club moments coming on. She wished Alejandro would stay, or had taken her up on her offer of assistance with cleanup. But, as he said, cleaning up after a three-person barbecue wouldn't take long. The screen door banged behind him. He'd be back soon enough.

"It's a great spot here. I can see why you come," Mark said.

"I love it. Between here and Mar Azul I feel I've scored the peaceful places jackpot."

"I'm not sure I'd call galloping down a beach and diving into the surf peaceful."

"Now that's true, but it wasn't my typical beach ride. It's usually a much more relaxed experience, cantering along the sand with the waves rolling in *beside* me."

"And yet you seemed to enjoy it, even with the sand down your pants."

"I did. Sometimes it's good to have something shake up your world a bit. Don't you think?" Sandra asked.

"I'd like to say yes, since that would make me seem much more daring, but in truth, I don't deal well with being shaken, as you've witnessed. Boring, really. One of the challenges of being an actor ... measuring up to characters who are unequivocally more exciting or interesting than you are." He took a drink of wine and set the glass back on the table.

"Hm, I'd not thought of that. Admittedly, I'd say I did have some expectation you would be kind of like the characters you've played."

"It's the me you know."

"Or did."

He looked down at his hands resting in his lap and adjusted his watch band lower on the wrist. "So, have you been riding since you were a child? You ride well."

"I've worked hard at it, partly because I took it up as an adult. The first summer I was out west I thought a pack trip in the Rockies seemed like the 'quintessentially western' thing to do. After five days on the back of a horse, despite the inability to walk normally for a week, I was hooked, completely and forever it seems. Once I was working and settled, I got a horse of my own." Sandra swirled the wine in the bottom of her glass, watching its crimson legs linger on the sides before disappearing back into the pool. "He was a special guy. I lost him five years ago and I haven't had the heart to replace him yet." Sandra could feel tears filling her lower lids, threatening to spill down her cheeks.

"So now you only ride in the winter when you come here? That seems a shame."

"Oh, I ride at home too. I have friends with horses and they are quite happy to have me exercise one or two of them. It's not the same as having my own but it's been very good experience after riding one horse for so long. It's less predictable."

"We can grow quite comfortable in our own little world without a wave or two to mix things up." His face darkened. "And sometimes we don't realize just how complacent we've become until the water is over our heads."

*Oh, oh, clouds forming.* "I'm going to take Tormenta a carrot. Would you like to come?"

"In the dark?"

"Oh come on, we'll take the lantern. Mr. Rochester wouldn't have batted an eye!"

"You see, this is exactly what I was speaking of. Some author creates a fantastical hero that I am constantly held up to. And where is he now, Edward Fairfax Rochester? Safely in the pages of Bronte's book, that's where!" He stood and banged one hand on the table top.

"Nice performance. Now, let's go."

Sandra held the lantern ahead of them as they walked, the twilight now faded into night. "There are lights once we get to the barn."

"How very modern. The place only looks like something out of the old west."

"It does, doesn't it? I always feel a bit like I've stepped onto one of John Wayne's movie sets."

Sandra set the lantern on the ground in front of the barn and went in for the lights. "Alejandro would kill me if I took the lantern into his barn." She felt her way to the panel and switched on the overhead lights before heading into the feed room for the carrots.

Mark followed, hands in his pockets, looking around at the various bins and bags of feed. "Quite the equine smorgasbord in here. Do they eat *all* this stuff?" Mark lifted the lid from a plastic bin and stuck his hand into the oats, letting them fall through his fingers.

"Different horses have different dietary needs. Most of this is for the breeding stock and young horses. The average adult horse gets by on hay or grass, although Alejandro gives them extra during the clinics."

She handed Mark a few large carrots from the bunch she carried. "For Tranquilo."

"Ah yes, my trusty steed."

Sandra pulled the switch for the lights as they left the barn and Mark retrieved the lantern from where they'd left it. "Shouldn't there be a fairly full moon tonight?" Mark asked, looking up at the sky.

"I think it's just not up yet. It was late last night, around ten."

Mark held the lantern aloft. "I guess this will have to do then. I hope we don't frighten the poor beasts, lurking about in the dark."

"They're used to it. The students often visit the horses after dark, mostly trying to strike bargains for the next day's riding."

"And how does that work out for them?"

Sandra laughed. "From experience I can say, not very well."

A soft nicker met them as they neared Tormenta's paddock, followed by another and then a third.

"Did we bring enough carrots? Sounds like a mob."

"Tormenta and Tranquilo are both in this area, along with two other mares." Sandra squeezed between the fence rails, straddling a middle rail for a moment before touching ground on the other side.

"I think I'd best go over the top or you might have to pry me out from between those rails." Mark handed the lantern to Sandra before climbing up and vaulting over the top rail, landing squarely on both feet.

"Nicely done, Mr. Rochester." She could see his smile in the lantern light, a little crooked, but somehow perfect.

"I have my moments."

The horses were a few feet away, waiting in the darkness. Tormenta nickered and stepped forward, taking a bite from the carrot Sandra offered. She stroked the mare's neck and kissed her muzzle. "I wonder if I can fit you in my Toyota. What do you think, girl?"

The other three mares were crowded around Mark as he held the lantern high above his head with one hand, the carrots grasped in the other. The mares quickly located the treats and were reaching and grabbing. "All right girls, no pushing now. Be gentle."

Sandra went to his rescue, moving the horses back and taking the lantern. She showed him how to offer the carrots so they could take a bite without sucking the entire thing into their mouths. He talked to the horses, stroking their faces as they chewed while Sandra leaned on the fence and watched. He was good with them.

"Did you have animals when you were growing up?" she asked.

"We had an Alsation when I was a young boy. He was my father's dog from before my parents married. When Sig was gone there were no more pets, my mother saw to that. Although my brother did talk her into a turtle at some point, until she found out about the diseases they can carry. The turtle was banished to a cousin's pond."

"So your mother wasn't an animal person."

"That's an understatement. She was barely a child person. Anything that upset her perfect house and busy calendar were not worth having. They were an unlikely pair, my parents, the nutty professor and the socialite. I was never sure what made it work."

The carrots were gone and one horse and then another wandered off to seek out the last morsels of Alejandro's night feeding. Mark snorted. "Typical women—they take all you've got and then head off in search of something more."

"What? I'd say that's much more typical of men. We women are the hearth keepers."

"So you say."

"I take it that hasn't been your experience?"

"Not exactly, no." He climbed up and over the fence, not risking the vault this time but instead climbing down one rail at a time. He held out his hand and took the lantern from Sandra so she could squeeze back through the rails. They walked along in silence, Sandra waiting for him to continue.

"My ex-wife, Serena, definitely not a hearth keeper, although she wasn't entirely to blame. It's tough to keep a hearth for someone who's never home, if she'd been so inclined. But she wasn't very ... domestic, or maternal."

"So you don't have children?"

"No, she was never interested, too busy with her career, although I hear she's pregnant now. She's back in America, in Montana, married to a screenwriter. It's like she's turned into a different person than the one I knew. I'm not sure which one was real."

"Maybe they both were. Some people bring out qualities in us that others don't."

Mark looked over at her, the lantern lighting his face from below. "Very true."

When they got back to the house there was a new bottle of wine on the table, as well as some chocolate-dipped fruit and a note from Alejandro: *Gone to bed. Enjoy the rest of the evening!*

"To bed? It's barely nine o'clock," Mark said, looking at his watch.

"For all his energy, Alejandro is an early-to-bed kind of guy. But then he's up long before dawn doing chores."

"I guess it's just us then."

"I guess it is." Sandra felt a rush of nerves.

"More wine?"

*That might help.* "I don't ride until ten tomorrow morning so, why not."

"How long are you staying at the ranch?" Mark asked, filling Sandra's glass.

"Until day after tomorrow. There's a group coming in so I need to clear out by Sunday afternoon to give them time to prepare. Martina will be home Sunday morning."

"And you'll do some more riding?"

"Yes, definitely. Two morning lessons and I'm hoping for another canter down the beach— maybe without the swim this time."

"Well here's to enjoyable, and dry, riding." Mark held up his glass and clinked it against Sandra's.

"And you? What's your plan?" Sandra asked.

"I'll head back to San Leandro tomorrow, but I'd like to stay to watch you ride in the morning, if you don't mind."

Sandra hesitated, thinking back to the morning's ride and her hyper awareness of Mark looking on. "No, I don't mind."

"You're sure?"

She wasn't, but if Mark was managing a horse of his own. … "Maybe you'd like to ride with me. Alejandro is a marvelous teacher."

"I'm sure he is, but I think I'll just spectate. I'd like to see more of this 'western dressage'."

"This morning wasn't a very good example. Tormenta and I weren't clicking like we usually do." Sandra examined her wine glass. Tomorrow morning it would be challenging again but she was determined to focus on her riding rather than who was watching and what he might be thinking.

Mark was leaning back in his chair with one foot resting on the other knee, his hands folded around the bowl of his wineglass. He seemed different than the guy who'd sat across from her at breakfast less than two weeks ago. He was more at ease now, more real, far less prickly, and not so furry and rumpled of course. Grey was showing around his temples and peppered through the rest of his dark hair but his face appeared more youthful and less clouded than it had then, like some deep trouble had been erased.

"You seem happier than you were a couple of weeks ago," Sandra said.

His eyes lifted to hers and he nodded slowly. "I suppose I am. And I believe I have you to thank for that."

"Me?"

"Yes, you. You're a good influence, and you seem to have a calming effect on me." He paused. "I see that expression and I know what you're thinking but, knocking over chairs and hitting table tops aside, you do, maybe partially because you poke at exactly the things I need to think about in a less self-pitying way."

"You make me sound like your therapist."

"Well, I suppose you have been, in a sense. But I'm not cured yet so don't think your work is finished. And, I still owe you a dinner."

"Oh, don't worry about that. I wanted to give you the painting."

"I know, and I want to make you dinner." His face became serious and the intensity of his gaze made Sandra look down at the hands in her lap.

Sandra felt her stomach dance at the thought of being alone with Mark in his house. Excitement or fear? She wasn't sure. "All right then, dinner."

"You're home Sunday, so, Monday next?"

"How about Wednesday, or Thursday? I'd like a couple

of days to wash the horses out of my clothes and get back to painting."

"Wednesday it is then. I can't offer quite the surroundings of Alejandro's ranch but— Have you painted here? It seems the ideal spot."

"I've done a few sketches but I left my painting things back at Mar Azul. I like to stay focused on the horses while I'm here. There's so much to learn from Alejandro and he doesn't mind me following him around, picking up everything I can."

They sat in silence for a time, sipping their wine, watching the candles burn down, the flames flickering with each whisper of breeze.

Mark spoke suddenly, like he'd been working the words in his head, "So you've been married?"

Sandra was startled by the question, running back over their conversations for any mention she'd made of Nick. "I was. But how did you know that?"

"You mentioned your in-laws, the sailors."

Her tension faded. "Of course. Yes. I was married."

He waited.

"And it feels like it was someone else's life, a very long time ago. We married right out of high school."

"How romantic." Again he waited for her to go on. It seemed he wanted to hear the whole story.

"I suppose it was at the time. He was my first love, a senior in high school when I was still a junior. Graham Benson. He was athletic and popular and very handsome—blonde hair, blue eyes, broad shoulders—you know the type. I was so flattered when he noticed me and started flirting." Sandra swirled the wine in her glass, memories flooding in. "At first I thought he was interested in my friend Annie, because she was much prettier than me, and then he asked me to the dance. He picked me up in his red Chevy convertible, met my parents, brought a corsage. It was a scene straight out of one of your movies." She tilted her head back and closed her eyes, a picture of Graham appearing on the backs of her lids. "He wore a blue corduroy blazer with patches at the elbows, a white shirt and Levi jeans. And he smelled like Aqua Velva." She took a breath through her nose and opened her eyes to look at Mark. *"There's something about an Aqua Velva Man."* Sandra sang. "Did you have that commercial in England?"

Mark smiled but said nothing.

Sandra continued, "I was so excited walking into the dance hall on Graham's arm. I still couldn't believe he'd asked me. I began to wonder why, if it was maybe some sort of bet with his friends or a trick he was put up to by Ginnie Maxwell. She hated me for some reason, even before Graham chose me over her. But then we danced, song after song, never missing the slow ones, and my disbelief just faded away. The last dance was 'Beth' by Kiss—and at the end he looked down into my eyes and kissed me on the lips. I melted. I was instantly and completely in love."

Mark chuckled. "It does sound like one of my movies."

"We were inseparable through his remaining year of high school and when I was in grade twelve, he would come to the school to take me for lunch every day. He was working by then, for his father's automotive business. We married as soon as I graduated. He worked and I went to university."

"And lived happily ever after?"

"For about a week." She laughed. "But then we started to drift apart. I think he was intimidated by my becoming more educated than he was. He started spending more time with his friends who were still single, staying out later and later on weekends, and then one night he didn't come home at all. He'd slept with Ginnie Maxwell after a party at his friend Frank's. Good old Ginnie. She must have been waiting all those years for her chance."

"Ah, the ever-important villain."

"No, it wasn't her, she was just convenient. I forgave him

but we were never the same after that. Things were better for a while but I felt I couldn't trust him and he wasn't comfortable around me. He needed to be that hero he was in high school but it was gone after graduation. His drinking increased and I stopped caring whether he came home or not. One night I woke up in the wee hours, his side of the bed still empty, and I knew it was time to go. I packed a suitcase and went to my parents. And that, as they say, was the end of that." Sandra took another drink from her glass, realizing she was feeling a bit light-headed. "Sorry, that was a rather long answer to a simple question."

"No, not at all. It's a good night for storytelling and it gives me some insight on what makes Sandra Lyall tick." Mark raised his glass before taking a drink.

"Is that something you've been trying to sort out?" The wine was making her bold.

A corner of Mark's mouth lifted into a lop-sided smile. "I suppose I have."

"Now I'm nervous."

"Oh don't be, I have no devious intentions."

"Well, that's good to know. So just what are your intentions then?" She was surprised by her own question and felt her face warming. She'd always been plagued by lips easily loosened by a bit of alcohol.

Mark seemed even more surprised. "Well ... I ... simply ... was curious about this western dressage Paul said you were doing down here."

"I see. And that's what brought you to Rancho Azteca, curiosity?"

"Partially," Mark paused, "and I wanted to invite you to dinner."

"Of course, dinner."

"And ... I ... enjoy your company. I've been enjoying your company." And then the words came tumbling out like stones down a hill. "I went to see you the morning you went away and

Paul didn't seem to know how long you'd be gone or just where you were and I suddenly felt a little … lost." He reached his hand across the table placing it on hers. "I like you very much, Sandra Lyall, and I want to know you better."

# Twenty-Four

Back in his chinos and white shirt, Mark walked across the yard to the verandah of the main house where Sandra and Alejandro were already seated at the breakfast table. "Good morning," he called as he approached.

"Buenos días. I see you are none the worse for wear despite the extra bottle of wine I left you," said Alejandro.

"Well I don't know about that. I slept rather late." He draped the pair of jeans he was carrying across the back of an empty chair. "Thank you for the loan."

"I was just thinking yesterday how unfair it is that I spend days searching for jeans that fit well and you can throw on a borrowed pair and look like ... well ... like you did." Sandra's cheeks reddened at her own words.

Mark grinned. "Well, thank you."

Alejandro was watching them, his eyes going to one face and then the other. "Sit, sit." Once Mark was seated Alejandro asked, "So, what did my guests get up to in the late hours of last night?" He was leaning forward, eyebrows raised.

"Just enjoying the wine, and the evening. And we took carrots to the girls," Sandra answered quickly.

Mark remembered the warmth of her hand under his and that she hadn't pulled it away as he'd half expected, but allowed it to rest there for a few moments. He was disappointed when she then announced it was time for bed, but she had taken his arm when he offered it on their way back to the bunkhouse.

Alejandro's smile seeped into his features. "I see. It was a lovely evening indeed." He looked directly at Mark, his dark eyes dancing.

"I suppose it was." The words came out stiff.

Alejandro laughed and pulled a cover from the plate in the middle of the table. "A specialty from my days north of the border ... pancakes and sausages, or here in Mexico, *los tortitas y salchichas.*"

Sandra was tightening the cinch on her saddle as Mark walked up. "All set it looks like," he said.

She turned as he approached, her expression a sharp contrast to yesterday's cool reception. "Almost—just need to get my bridle." She patted La Tormenta's neck and went into the barn. He watched her as she walked away, her slim body filling out her bootcut Wranglers. *Well, the jeans were certainly worth the extra shopping time.* She was an attractive woman, he'd noticed before, but this morning she seemed alight, and he wasn't sure if it was coming from her or from him. When he'd first looked out his window this morning he'd seen her on her yoga mat, sitting with legs crossed, eyes closed facing the rising sun. Her hair was pulled back in a ponytail but one strand was free and wisped across the cheek that faced his direction. Her head was tilted back and the corners of her mouth turned up slightly. He wondered what she was thinking, about the source of her smile.

Sandra stepped back into the sunlight from the dark of the barn. "And you? You're ready to travel?"

"Alas, she can't wait to see the back of me." Mark hung his head in mock despair.

"Always performing." Sandra arranged the bridle in her hands.

"I'm hoping Alejandro will invite me to one more meal, after you ride, and before I hit the road."

"Alejandro will keep inviting you until you say no, so unless you'd like to stay another night, and perhaps right through his upcoming clinic, you'll have to stop him." Sandra held the bridle to Tormenta's face and the mare opened her mouth, willingly taking the bit.

"I should get back, although ... I'd like to stay." He waited for Sandra to respond. She continued to focus on the horse and the adjustments to the bridle. "But, there's likely a script waiting for me and an eager agent awaiting my response."

Sandra turned toward him. "Well that's worth heading back for. Isn't it?"

Right here, right now, it didn't seem so. "Yes, of course."


Mark sat on a folding chair next to the arena, a glass of lemonade in his hand. The sun and wind were to his back, keeping his eyes shaded and the dust from drifting into his face. The day was already warm and Tormenta's chest and flanks were growing dark with sweat as she worked. The mare was incredible to watch as Sandra put her through her paces under Alejandro's guidance. One moment she was jogging nearly in place with an elevated stride, and the next extending down the side of the arena, her elegant forelegs stretching out ahead of her as she seemed to float the length of the rail. Sandra seemed in another world, one of horse and him—Alejandro. Yesterday, Mark would have been jealous, but now that he understood their relationship and her admiration of the man, he envied her. It had been a long time since he'd looked up to someone that way.

When he was first on the stage after drama school, he'd worked with an actor then in his fifties, an actor who had spent his career on the London stage. His performances were captivating to the point where Mark was always at risk of losing himself in Robert's work and forgetting his own lines. And Robert had taken him under his wing in those early years, becoming a mentor, coach and dear friend. He wondered if he was still acting, or even alive. Surely he'd have heard if Robert had died. They'd fallen out of touch many years ago. He realized he missed his old friend.

Sandra loped past in front of him, her body rocking with the rhythm of the horse's stride. Her face shone with the slight perspiration of her efforts and, despite the intensity of her expression, a smile played on her lips. Alejandro spoke and Sandra slowed her pace and walked into the centre of the ring to talk with him. He placed one hand on the small of her back and the other on her knee, adjusting the position of each ever so slightly before looking up at her and speaking. She smiled down at him and laughed. Her laugh—it wasn't its physical sound as much as its genuine nature. Alejandro was gesturing and talking animatedly, acting out some movement he was no doubt asking her to perform. She laughed again. He wished he could stir a similar combination of admiration and amusement. So far he'd mostly had to settle for tolerance.

Sandra and Tormenta jogged off and Alejandro remained quiet and still, just watching. She pushed the horse into an easy lope and then loped a tight circle. Alejandro nodded. She continued down the arena, this time taking the horse into such a tight arc that the mare's front legs seemed to be loping a circle around the rears, her rear hooves hopping a tiny pattern in the sand. Sandra let out a whoop when she finished the circle, pushing the horse into a longer stride toward Alejandro who was grinning and clapping. "*Maravilloso!* Very well done!" Alejandro called.

She loped past him, stroking Tormenta's neck and then turned the horse toward Mark. She rode up with an ear-to-ear grin and stopped right in front of him, a cloud of dust rising from under the horse's hooves. "Did you see that?" she asked, breathless.

"I did indeed, and I take it that manoeuvre calls for a certain amount of celebration?"

"Absolutely! I've only been trying to pull it off since I started coming here." She rubbed Tormenta's neck. "She's known how to do it all along, of course."

A streak of dust lay across one cheek where she'd wiped a gloved hand and her freckles were more pronounced with the increased heat of her face. Her hair was mostly tucked underneath her helmet but a few rogue wisps curled in front of her ears. She seemed almost child-like in her moment of accomplishment and Mark found himself wanting to take her in his arms and swing her around, sharing in her joy. Instead, he stood, and reached his hand up toward her. "Well, congratulations then. Even from my perspective as a complete neophyte, it looked impressive."

She shook his hand, grinning all the while. "Thank you." She started to ride away but then turned her head back to him. "Staying for lunch?"


As Mark drove north toward San Leandro, the images of the previous twenty-eight hours replayed in his mind like a movie. Lunch had been a festive affair after Sandra's successful riding lesson, and Alejandro was glowing right along with his jubilant student. It would have been easy to stay on but the invitation hadn't come. Sandra had mentioned a final "quiet" afternoon on the ranch and a chance to spend more time with Tormenta, and Alejandro was also not quick to invite, perhaps beginning to mentally prepare for his wife's return and the group expected in two days. But Mark was happy that Sandra had warmed to him since his arrival yesterday; that in itself had been worth the journey.

The dry landscape rolled by on each side, the hills hiding the Sea of Cortez just a few miles to the east and the Pacific Ocean thirty to the west. He smiled as he recognized a cardón cactus, its multiple pillars extending up from a thick base and flowers beginning to appear on the upper stems. His thoughts returned to the view of Sandra's back, riding ahead of him on her grey mare, her body swaying with Tormenta's long stride. Maybe that was what drew him, how she always seemed to be easily moving forward, not in a hurry but with purpose and grace. His path through life seemed much more irregular, with his speed varying from a standstill to warp and back again. Being with her seemed to moderate the tempo. A month ago he would have thought that boring, but something was shifting.

He spotted riders on the hill, moving a herd of cattle in front of them. The dust rose up around the herd and the cloud blended with smaller dust clouds created by each of the horses. He wondered if they were some of Alejandro's organic Corriente. It had been so easy to stay longer than he'd planned and so difficult to leave, but she would be back tomorrow, and he'd find a reason to drop by Mar Azul. His new script should be arriving and he could pop by to share the good news with Paul … and maybe bump into Sandra and buy her a drink.

The road opened up into a long straight stretch and Mark pressed his foot to the accelerator. The car surged ahead and the wind pulled at his hair, whipping it around his face. The ever-present sun was pleasant this afternoon, its warmth resting like a hat on his head—and then it appeared, on his right, beyond the scraggly desert shrubs, the sparkling pale blue of the sea. He chuckled out loud as he thought of Sandra's plunge into the waves the day before and her jovial response. From what he'd seen, the only thing that seemed to ripple her calm surface was him. What he couldn't quite make out was whether that was a good thing or a bad thing.

# Twenty-Five

Alejandro was working a young horse in the arena as Sandra approached on Tormenta. "I'm going to ride up the hill a short way. I won't go far," she called to him.

He rode over at an easy jog, the buckskin's chest and neck soaked with sweat. "This one has worked hard and would benefit from a little time on the trail. May we join you? There is still enough sun to go to the sea."

Sandra looked to the west, the sun already beginning its descent toward the hills.

"Okay, so perhaps it will be a little dark by the time we return," Alejandro said, "but I know the way very well, even in the dark."

"You're on." She patted Tormenta's neck. "What do you think, girl? Have you got another hour in you?"

"That mare will be going long after you and I have had enough of this day. I should have named her for a soldier instead of a storm."

Alejandro opened the gate from astride, moved his horse through, and then pulled the gate closed behind him. "*Muy buena chica*," he said with enthusiasm to his horse. "You are my best student."

"And who is this one?" Sandra asked. "She's lovely."

"This is a daughter of Caliente and La Belleza. She is just four. La Mantequilla—she was the colour of butter when she was born. She has grown darker since then."

"I love her colour, and that incredible head of hair."

Alejandro caressed the horse's shoulder. "Yes, she has the colour of her dam, her sire's beautiful mane, and the intelligence of both. This one is special." He continued to gaze at the top of the black mane. "Well, shall we see how she likes the big water?"

"She's never been to the beach?"

"Not yet!" Alejandro put Mantequilla into a lope, the mare's stride animated and rolling. Tormenta's ears flashed forward and then back to Sandra, awaiting direction. She didn't have to wait long, as Sandra gave the cue to follow the buckskin along the cactus-lined trail to Cortez.

The air was almost still when they reached the water, just a suggestion of a breeze carrying the scent of seaweed ashore. The waves were smaller than they had been the day prior, and they rolled in rhythmically, their thump and whoosh interspersed with near quiet. They rode at the edge of the surf, Alejandro's mare stepping higher each time the leading edge of the froth threatened to touch her hooves. Tormenta and Sandra jogged next to them on the sea side, the grey mare content to move at a slow pace, the water splashing up from under her feet whenever a wave came far enough up the beach. Sandra couldn't help smiling: the warm air, the smell of the sea, the sun low in the sky, and the power of the animal beneath her. One of life's perfect moments. The kind you want to put in a jar and take home for a cold winter's night. She drew the soft sea air into her nostrils and closed her eyes as Tormenta slowed to a walk.

She could feel Alejandro looking at her before she opened her eyes. She turned her head to see him grinning at her. "Yes?" she asked.

"You are enjoying yourself." He slowed the buckskin to a walk but she began to prance again as soon as a wave rolled under her feet.

"She doesn't like the water on her toes."

"She will get used to it. Remember that she is a creature of the desert. I usually bring them to the beach when they are still beside their dams, but her mother does not like the water and I didn't want that to influence this one."

The water was darkening as the sun fell, creating a dramatic contrast to the colouring sky. Wisps of light cloud lay in bands and the edges were beginning to glow as sunset neared. "I could stay here for my entire Baja visit."

"But surely you would miss Casa del Mar Azul and your friends there."

Sandra pulled her fingers through the smooth, dark hair of Tormenta's mane. "I suppose. It's just so peaceful here. I hate to leave, even for a couple of weeks."

"Then something has changed at Señor Paul's. I recall your tales of how magical a place it is, how very *peaceful*, I believe you said."

"Your memory is too good."

"I remember what is important, what people tell me about themselves. So what has changed—at Mar Azul?"

"It's the same. It's still very good. Paul is wonderful. I enjoy the pace. It's great ... really." Sandra's gaze went to the sea.

"Is it now?" Alejandro's words were tinged with laughter. "And who are you trying to convince of this, me or you?" He sat easily in his saddle as the mare's pace quickened and eased again with each passing wave.

"I don't know what you mean," Sandra said.

"I think you do. You know how I always tell you to listen to the horse, even though she does not speak? It is the same with people and you are saying much more than your words."

Sandra could feel the movement of Tormenta's back underneath her, causing her hips to rise and fall with each step, the simple rhythm soothing.

"Tell me about your friend," Alejandro said.

"My friend?"

"Yes, your friend Mark, who followed you here to Cabo del Este."

"There's not much to tell. He's a friend of Paul's, and we've spent a bit of time together. We went sailing."

"I sense that he is much more, or would like to be."

"That might be true of him, but not of me."

"I disagree with that as well." Alejandro picked up the reins and pushed Mantequilla into a jog. "I think it is time to see what this young girl can do." He flashed his smile at Sandra before turning forward, rising up in his stirrups and galloping off ahead.

She caught up to him at the end of the beach, where the headland rose before them. The young mare was blowing hard through her flaring nostrils, excited by the environment and the run. Alejandro had eased her toward the water as she galloped, and by the end of the beach she was throwing up water with each stride.

"I told you this was a special one." He was beaming.

"You were right about the water. After a few strides it seemed she forgot it was there."

"And, after a few more, she was enjoying it." He leaned to the side and his eyes went to the mare's face. "Weren't you, *mi amor?*"

"So I take it this one is not for sale?"

"*Ay, Dios mío!* Not even to you, amiga." Alejandro looked west. "We had best be making our way home. Let's see how my girl likes the waves now at a walk."

Alejandro rode the mare in and out of the surf as they walked the length of the beach. She reacted only once, jumping sideways when a wave touched her belly. He just chuckled and urged her forward, stroking her neck to reassure her. He slowed the horse and let Sandra come up beside him. "So, you were about to tell me more about your friend Mark, before I so rudely galloped off."

"I don't think I was."

He turned sideways in his saddle to face her. "So there is nothing to tell of the famous and handsome man who followed you here from San Leandro? I see. It is true this happens often, movie stars showing up without announcement. Perhaps it is the lure of the Rancho Azteca." He made a sweeping gesture with his right arm in the direction of the ranch as he faced forward again.

Sandra continued to look at the beach between Tormenta's ears, saying nothing.

"You do not have to talk to me about him. I am only a curious old romantic," Alejandro said, "and I recognize *la chispa* when I see it."

"La chispa?"

"The spark, the energy, the life that is between two people who share a connection. It is not so different from the energy between horse and human, and what I use to pair my students with their mounts. It does not come from attraction on the side of one or the other, only when it is mutual. Just because I think this mare is the most beautiful horse I have raised does not mean she will work with me. But, this time I am fortunate." His hand trailed along the crest of Mantequilla's neck, his fingers lifting the mane from its resting place like a curtain being drawn aside.

"And you sense this energy, between Mark and me?"

His gaze fixed on her and he was no longer smiling. "From the moment he arrived; even though I also sensed your anger with him." His smile returned. "I have not seen you so chilly toward anyone before. I knew he must be special. It is why I invited him to stay."

"So that's what gave me away was it, my giving him the cold shoulder?"

"Ah, so you admit it then!"

"No, I don't. I admit I feel some attraction to him, but he frustrates me, scares me actually. I often feel very uncomfortable around him."

Alejandro laughed. "It sounds like love, then."

"Love? What kind of love makes you want to run away from someone. He's the reason I came here in the first place."

"I assumed so."

"You did? When I came?"

"Sí. I did not know what you were running from, but I knew there was something. And when I saw his car roll into the yard …"

Sandra let out a long sigh and looked to the sea, even darker now against the pink sky. "I didn't know what to do. I felt like he wouldn't let me be and I couldn't seem to say no."

"Or did not want to?"

"No, I did want to … I think I wanted to."

"Ah, and there is the question. Were you running from Mark or from something else, perhaps?"

"But there was nothing else, just Mar Azul, my painting, my friends there …"

"And yourself?"

Was that it? Was she running from her own feelings? She hadn't felt inclined to run since her first unplanned visit here to Baja four years ago. She thought she'd put that behind her.

"Do you *always* feel uncomfortable in his presence? Because, now and then, I saw a light from you that I have not seen before. A little flash."

"Sometimes I enjoy being with him. He makes me laugh. He can be quite kind. And last night after dinner he seemed more down-to-earth than he has before, warmer somehow, and deeper."

"He is a troubled man, that I sense, but never would I think him shallow, and certainly not cold."

"So you think he's a good person?"

Alejandro cocked his head, a serious expression on his face. "I would never want to influence anyone's decision in matters of the heart for they are such personal affairs; but, yes, I think your

Mark is one of the special ones." He glanced down at Mantequilla and then back to Sandra. "Of course, I am just an old horseman. What do I know of love?"

Sandra traced the cactus pattern with her thumb, the mug warm in her hands. She could hear the horses moving about in the darkness, scouring the earth for the final remnants of the night feeding. It felt good to sit in the quiet, alone. She drank in the scents of Azteca—the horses, the desert and the sea drifting in from Cortez. Tomorrow she'd be back at Mar Azul, her Baja home, and, although she was happy to return to her painting and the beach, she felt some anxiety, about Mark of course. She thought back to the night before, when she sat in this same chair, but with a glass of wine in her hand and Mark sitting across from her. He'd looked so inviting in the lamplight, his tanned face and neck dark above his white shirt, his eyes like pools of ink. She wondered if he was at Pablo's tonight. She could picture him sitting at the bar, laughing with Paul, talking with Arturo. Now why was she thinking of him when she finally had some time to herself?

"You look very deep in your thoughts," Alejandro said from behind the screen door.

Sandra could barely make out his shape in the low light. He pushed open the door and came to stand next to the table. "You are still out here," he said.

"Just finishing my tea, enjoying the evening. I thought you'd gone to bed."

"I am missing my Martina tonight so I am too restless for sleep just yet. May I interrupt your enjoyment of the evening?" Alejandro asked, nodding toward the closest chair.

"Of course, join me. I believe this is your deck."

Alejandro pulled out the chair and sat down. He sighed as he leaned back. "So, where were your thoughts taking you this night? Any place an old romantic might find interesting?"

Sandra lifted her eyes from her mug and furrowed her brow. "So now you can read minds?"

"I have always been good at reading the minds of horses so I thought I might try humans. They are such interesting creatures; much more complicated and less predictable than horses."

"I know. I think I prefer horses."

Alejandro laughed, a rumble that rolled up from his abdomen like distant thunder. "Ah, but you cannot share a wonderful meal, or a fine glass of wine with your horse ..." his voice became playful, "or your bed."

"Alejandro!"

"What? You are too pure for such things, amiga?"

"No, it's just not something I want to discuss with *you*."

He laughed again. "I am only trying to lighten what seems to be a burdensome subject for you." He pushed his chair onto its back legs and placed his hands behind his head.

His eyes continued to meet hers, not challenging, not questioning, only waiting. The sound of a horse blowing through its nostrils echoed in the darkness behind her. "What did you mean at the beach, when you said that Mark was one of the special ones? How do you mean, special?"

Alejandro sat quietly for a time before speaking. "When I first met Caliente, he had been labelled a dangerous animal. He had changed hands many times, for he was incredibly striking, and each new owner was going to make him into a magnificent horse for the show ring and then the breeding pen. By the time I first saw him he was eight, and offered to me for one of my expo demonstrations. It is possible the person who offered him was trying to set me up for failure, but it didn't matter, when I looked into his eyes I saw the years of confusion and pain deep within them. The others had seen his handsome exterior. I saw what was inside, even buried as it was beneath so much hurt. I knew in an instant that he had what I would call that *special* something. Perhaps it is a gift, perhaps a willingness to look, but I see it in people also, even when it tries to hide itself. I see it in you, which is why I invited you to come and spend some time with me last year, and why you're here now."

"And you see this in Mark?"

"Sí. It is perhaps what has made him successful as an actor, that quality within that people are drawn to without knowing what it is. He is handsome, yes, but if you look beyond that, there is more, much more I think."

"So how did you fix Caliente?"

Alejandro snorted. "By not fixing him at all. I simply gave attention to all that was good and ignored all that was bad. Very soon, only the good remained."

"It's hard to imagine him being dangerous."

"That is because he was never dangerous, only afraid."

"Is that what you think about Mark, that he's afraid?"

"Terrified."

"But of what? What does someone like him have to be afraid of?"

"And what did big, powerful Caliente have to be afraid of? Everything that threatened him, or seemed to threaten him, even me at first."

Sandra traced the ceramic cactus again, exploring its engraved lines. She looked up at Alejandro and tried to smile. "So what do I do now?"

"It is simple, and yet so very difficult. You ignore what is in here." He tapped his head. "And listen to what is here," he said, placing his hand across the left side of his chest. "Your heart will not lead you wrong." He reached across the table and laid his hand on her wrist. "I see the hurt deep in your eyes also. It has eased since you first came to Azteca, but still it is there. Do not let it determine your path in this life."

# Twenty-Six

Mark took the steps down to the beach level and followed the lighted path to Pablo's entrance. Its warm light poured out onto the sand and the sounds of music and conversation blended with the ever-present rumble of the sea. He smoothed the front of his shirt and pulled one hand through his hair before entering. The place was full, mostly with couples seated at tables of two, the flickering candle flames lighting their faces. He looked to the bar and there she was, sitting sideways on a stool, her back to him, her fair hair loose and covering her neck with waves and ringlets. She was talking to Arturo and he was laughing as he mixed a trio of drinks.

Mark had expected to find her here the previous night following her return from the ranch, so he'd arrived early and stayed until almost closing. Just before he left, Paul finally saw fit to announce that, by the way, Sandra had ordered room service around seven o'clock, in case he was interested. Bastard. He'd thought about knocking on her door, inviting her down for a drink, but didn't want to risk another icy reception. She did like her privacy and he felt he was making some progress, even though he hadn't completely divulged his reasons for following her to Alejandro's. He'd never been very good at expressing himself, unless the lines were printed on the page in front of him. When they had to come from his own head and heart they just weren't there, and borrowing from one of his movies would be far too tacky. That, and the risk that she'd seen the film and would recognize the dialogue.

As Mark moved toward the bar, he considered how best to greet her. Had he not recently become acquainted with the wretchedness of rejection, he might walk right up, wrap his arms around her from behind and plant a kiss on the tanned shoulder left exposed by her pale green dress.

"Señor Mark!" Arturo had spotted him. Sandra turned on her stool and smiled as he approached.

He leaned in and kissed her cheek. Not quite as demonstrative as his first idea but it would do. "I thought I might find you here," he said.

"The bar right below my hotel room is a pretty safe bet."

"True. So much for being the next Sherlock Holmes." He took the stool beside her. "May I join you?"

"It seems you already have."

He smiled at her without saying any more.

"A drink?" Arturo was still standing opposite them.

"Yes, please. I will have a beer—whatever is coldest." He continued to look at Sandra.

"But, they are all cold …"

Mark looked to Arturo. "Of course they are. Bring me a Sol, please." Maybe the beer would help settle his nerves. "So, you have come back to us. How was your final day with Alejandro and his fine horses?"

"It was perfect, once my stalker cleared out." Her expression was serious.

Mark felt his face flush.

"I'm teasing." Sandra leaned toward him and placed a hand on his thigh, immediately pulling it back and reddening a little. "And did you get your new script?"

"No, not yet. Wednesday, I'm told. I'll read you an excerpt over dinner."

"A sneak preview. I feel special."

"So you're still coming to dinner then?"

"I am, and looking forward to it." Her eyes reflected the tiny lights strung behind the bar.

He felt his face flush again. "Well, good then. So am I." He took another drink. *Really Jeffery, try not to sound like a nervous school boy.*

Paul came through the swinging door from the kitchen, wiping his hands on the apron tied around his waist. "Ah, my two favourite customers!"

"I've heard you say that to every table in this room," Sandra said.

"Perhaps yes, but not with such feeling as I did just now." He put his hand to the left side of his chest and bowed.

"Oh please, Hutchings." Mark snorted. "I feel as though I'm back in drama school."

"Still in a fine mood, are we?" Paul leaned to Sandra as if in confidence. "You should have seen him last night, in here watching the door like a dog waiting for his master to come home, getting more and more bearish as the hours went by." He flashed a smile at Mark.

"Mark, a bear? I can't imagine. He seems quite pleasant this evening," Sandra said.

"Ah, then perhaps what he was waiting on has finally arrived?" He raised his eyebrows.

"Don't you have work to do?" Mark asked. "The place does look rather busy tonight. I'm sure some of these other guests might enjoy a visit from their wonderfully entertaining host."

"I'll get to them. For the moment I think there's more fun to be had here." His eyes were bright as he leaned on the bar, settling in. "So, Sandra, I hear you had uninvited company while you were away on your little ranch sojourn? Did he manage to embarrass himself from the back of a horse? He is so very good at it." Paul grinned at Mark.

"It was actually me who fell off my horse," Sandra responded. "Mark rode quite well, even without his stunt double."

Mark gave a nod of his head. "Why thank you, my lady."

"I'm just thinking back to when he was working on *Jane Eyre* and the stories he told about having to work with the *monstrous* black horse that frightened the daylights out of him." Paul was snickering.

"Mesrour," Sandra said.

"Excuse me?" Paul asked.

"Mesrour, the name of Rochester's horse in *Jane Eyre*. It was a fabulous animal they used in the series, but I can see how he might have been intimidating. They needed one with some size and fire to portray the horse according to Bronte's description."

There she was, going to his defense again. He wanted to kiss her. He watched her as she spoke, describing the horse during Rochester's opening scene where it rears and he falls off. She was quite lovely. He couldn't imagine how he'd ever thought her average-looking. Her smile put creases at the corners of her mouth and her eyes that somehow made her whole face lift and brighten. The creases were a mark of age but on her they only seemed echoes of the many smiles that had come before this one.

"Isn't that true, Jeffery?" Paul was speaking to him.

"Sorry. What?"

"That you turned down a part because it required a lot of … equestrian activity."

Mark was tiring of Paul's efforts to embarrass him. "That is true, but I also turned it down because you were trying for the same part and I felt my declining would be best for our friendship."

Paul's smile faded.

"Is that true? You did that?" Sandra asked.

Mark continued to look at his friend. "I did, fool that I was in those days." His bottle of Sol landed on the bar with a clunk, its fizzy contents climbing up the neck.

A minute of silence felt stretched into five. "Well … I'm

going to take a walk on the beach. Goodnight, gentlemen." Sandra lifted her glass toward them and swallowed the last of her margarita. She slid off her stool and left the restaurant.

"Nicely done, old *friend.*" Mark said as he watched Sandra disappear into the night outside Pablo's. "What the hell was that about?"

"Nothing. Just making conversation. Helping her get to know you."

"By embarrassing me?"

"If need be," Paul said.

"And what is it you think I'm up to with this woman?"

"I don't think you're *up to* anything, only that you're good at hurting people, especially women, whether you intend to or not."

"So that's what you think of me, that I'm some insensitive lout who goes around stepping on the hearts of others."

"Yes, but not because you are ill-intentioned—you're just used to getting everything you want. I'm not sure you can appreciate something, or someone, of genuine value anymore."

"Well, I know I've certainly come to appreciate the value of Sandra. I confess, I didn't at first, she was simply a nice diversion, but that's changed." He looked down the neck of his beer bottle and sighed.

When he looked up, Paul was examining his face. "You mean that, don't you?"

"I do indeed." Mark nodded slowly. "I'm afraid I'm coming to understand all too well some of the characters I've played, the ones all muddled up over someone who seems less than interested."

"Well, I'm enjoying this even more then. Mark Jeffery, arse over tip. How delightful." Paul was grinning.

"You are a cruel man for one's best friend, you do know that." He pushed his empty bottle toward Paul. "I might as well have another beer."

"Might I suggest a walk instead?"

"A walk?"

"Yes," Paul inclined his head toward the entrance, "a walk. For such a worldly individual, you really are quite thick when it comes to matters of the heart. She's probably not far off at this hour of the evening."

"Right, good thought." Mark stood. "Depending on how this goes, I may be back for that second beer very soon. I forgive you for being such a bastard."

Paul laughed. "Go!"


The moon was three-quarters full and well above the horizon as Mark left Pablo's behind him. As his eyes adjusted to the diminished light, he made out the shape of someone walking at the edge of the waves. As he got closer he could see she was holding her calf-length dress up above her knees, kicking the water out ahead of her as she walked. The splashes lit up like diamonds in the moonlight. She stopped walking and stood still as a wave rolled up her legs, climbing to just below the fabric of her dress. She'd seen him and started to move in his direction. When she reached dry sand she let her skirt fall back around her legs and waved.

As they approached one another, again he had that urge to take her in his arms.

"Hi," she said when they were ten feet apart.

He stopped. "Hello." It was like he had a scene from one of his romance movies playing over and over in his head, but the actors refused to follow the script.

"It's tough to tell in this light but no bruises? No black eye? I thought your little chat with Paul might come to blows the way it was going."

He snorted. "No, we got it sorted. We always do."

"It seemed he was on a mission of mockery."

"Good way to put it."

"I hope it wasn't on my account."

"Well, it was." He met her eyes, not sure how much to reveal. "But not to worry, we've come to an understanding."

She waited but he didn't know what else to say. What was he going to tell her, that he'd compared her to vanilla ice cream but changed his mind, or that Paul thought him destined to break her heart? There didn't seem much he could share that wouldn't extinguish the tiny flame he was doing his best to shelter.

"Care to join me for a walk in the waves?" she asked.

Mark looked down at his socks and shoes.

"Oh, don't let those stop you. My shoes are back at the first palapa."

"All right." He bent down and pulled off his shoes and then his socks, stuffing the socks inside the empty loafers and rolling his pant legs up to just below the knees. "Shall we be off then?" He held his shoes in one hand and offered the other to Sandra.

She hesitated a moment but then accepted it. Her hand felt small and warm in his as they walked the edge of the waves without talking. There seemed so much to say and yet nothing that was ready to leave his lips. He turned his head to observe her walking alongside him, the moonlight casting a shadow over her down-turned face. Her full skirt had become a snug mini the way she had it pulled up around her thighs away from the rising and falling water. She looked up just then, directly at him, her expression difficult to read. He felt her hand loosen its grip for a moment before it tightened again.

He had to say something. "That's a lovely dress you're wearing." Not exactly profound or heartfelt but it would do.

Sandra ruffled the fabric of her bunched skirt forward and back. "Thank you. It's nicer when it's not balled up in my fist."

"Oh, I don't know. It certainly shows off your legs like that."

She smiled and he was relieved. Good. She didn't think he'd jumped from schoolboy to letch. He couldn't remember the last time he was so careful of every word he uttered.

"Just don't go tumbling off into the waves on me, as I know you're inclined to do," he said.

"True. Ian and Tormenta can both vouch for that."

"Ian?"

"Oh, I surprised him with a dip in the ocean when we were out walking one night. I think he was worried I'd drown myself in my rather margarita'd state."

"Ah, I see. And he rescued you, no doubt?" Mark felt the muscles tighten around his jaw.

"He came out after me, but I wasn't in need of rescuing. He was quite upset with me, actually."

Mark had forgotten about Ian. Here he'd run off to Rancho Azteca worrying about the Mexican cowboy when there was someone right here in San Leandro that posed more of a threat. Alejandro was married, Ian wasn't.

"So. Ian. You've known him long?"

"Since my first trip to Baja. We've been keeping in touch ever since, and of course I see him here in the winter. He's a good friend."

"Seems to me he behaves like more than a friend." *For God's sake, Jeffery, try to maintain some dignity.* He'd never been the jealous sort and had no idea why it was happening to him now. What was it about this woman that brought out these ridiculous adolescent tendencies?

Sandra didn't seem to notice. "Ian? No, he's just a flirt. I'm far too blonde and Canadian for his tastes. He usually has a Mexican girlfriend, but not this year, for some reason."

"Perhaps his interests have gone elsewhere."

Sandra missed his meaning. "Possibly. He does seem to be focused on his songwriting at the moment. There's a Canadian country singer who's planning to record one of his songs. Did he tell you that?"

"No, but we're not exactly mates."

"Anyway, it could mean big things for his career. He seems to be more and more inclined to be at home these days so a steady stream of royalties would be a big help."

"Is he planning to return to Canada?" Mark could hear the tightness in his own voice.

"I doubt it. He's far too happy down here. And that, I completely understand. He was talking to me about buying property."

"With him?"

Sandra stopped and looked at him. "No, of course not with me. I told you—he and I are just good friends."

"So you keep saying." He wasn't caring anymore if she heard jealousy in his words.

She squeezed his hand and continued walking. "But I'm not interested in buying property in Mexico. I love my home and have no plans to move to Baja. Besides, how could I come here and not stay at Mar Azul?"

They continued on in silence until they were in front of the hotel. "Well, I have a painting to get to in the morning so I think I'm going to call it a night. Thank you for the walk." She let go of his hand as they moved up the beach, smoothing the fabric of her dress down over her legs. When they reached the palapa, he sat down to brush the sand from his feet before putting on his socks and shoes. He stood and offered his arm and she put her hand through the triangle it made at his side, dangling her sandals from her free hand. They walked up the stairs past Pablo`s and stopped outside the entrance to the guest area.

Again, the movie played in his head, this time the goodnight kiss scene. Sandra pulled her arm from his and stepped toward the door. "So, good night then. I guess I'll see you Wednesday for dinner."

He wanted to move toward her but his feet refused to move; once again, the screenplay falling apart. "Yes, Wednesday." *At least there's that*, he thought, as she turned and disappeared into Mar Azul.

# Twenty-Seven

Even though it was feeling very much like a first date, something she'd been avoiding for years, Sandra was looking forward to dinner at Mark's. Officially, it was payment of a debt, but she knew there was more to it than that, on both sides. She felt she'd crossed some sort of threshold when he'd offered his hand on the beach and she'd accepted. A man offering his arm seemed like chivalry, a hand felt intimate. And it had been nice, even romantic, walking hand-in-hand with him through the waves in the moonlight. She couldn't deny it anymore; she was drawn to him and it wasn't just a movie star crush. In fact, the more she got to know him, the more he became Mark the man instead of Mark Jeffery the actor. She was still feeling nervous about the evening, but mostly due to the date factor, not because of who or what he was in life.

Sandra enjoyed the walk to San Leandro, so Mark had offered to drive her home at the end of the night. It was a good area, quite safe, but a lone woman on a beach at night was still vulnerable. The beach was quiet now in the late afternoon; vacationers were settling in for dinner or cocktails. There were a number of homes along the stretch between Mar Azul and San Leandro, all fairly small and in keeping with an environment that felt more remote than touristy. Sandra spotted a man and woman seated at a table in front of an orange stuccoed house. There was a white tablecloth and what looked like fine dinnerware and a bouquet of red roses. It appeared they were celebrating something—maybe an anniversary? It had been a long time since she'd had anything to celebrate with a man, unless you counted her brother's fiftieth birthday.

At the top of the headland Sandra sat down on the bench. To her right stretched the mile of beach past the vacation homes and Mar Azul, to her left the bay of San Leandro, and straight ahead the Gulf of California. Mainland Mexico rested somewhere beyond the horizon, the curve of the earth hiding it from view. Looking at the ocean from a high vantage point always reminded Sandra of the earth's vastness and, despite the feeling it brought of being a small part of a very large system, it gave her a sense of her own power. Powerful, that was a good way to head into the evening.

She pulled Paul's hand-drawn map from her shoulder bag. It showed the trail as it went over the headland and down into San Leandro Bay. Amusing, since she'd walked the trail to the village many times and certainly didn't need a map to find her way there. Paul was so meticulous. It looked as though Mark's place was a short distance from the main beach area, the house right on the water, third place down from where the main street of the village dead-ended at the sea, and golden yellow. It would be hard to miss. She tucked the map into her bag and set off down the trail.


Third house—golden yellow—must be the place. There was a staircase off the beach leading to a wide deck but she wasn't sure if the French doors would take her to a main entrance or a bedroom. Showing up in his bedroom might be awkward; better to go around the back and find the door off the street. A narrow stone pathway took her up past the house, flowering shrubs crowding in on both sides. The scent of the generous pink blossoms reminded her of a perfume her aunt used to wear too much of. The smell was quite pleasing when it wasn't wrapping itself around her in a bear hug. A tile staircase climbed to the second level and the wrought iron railing was hung with ceramic pots, each an explosion of red, purple and yellow flowers. She climbed the stairs and knocked on the heavy wood door. No answer. She looked around for a doorbell but, seeing none, she knocked again, more firmly this time.

"Yes, yes, I said come in," she heard Mark call from inside the house.

Surprised by his tone, Sandra hesitated. Maybe he was just in the middle of some difficult task in the kitchen. She squared her shoulders and turned the doorknob.

When she stepped inside, the smell of something burnt met her nostrils and the air was thick with smoke. *Ah, that may explain the tone.* The kitchen was to her left, in the back corner of the house, and the main living area was open to it across a counter. French doors led from there onto the high deck she'd seen from the beach. The house, while not large, was appealing, with its wooden open-beam ceiling and red tiled floors. The walls were a sunshine yellow, less gold than the exterior of the house, and the kitchen cupboards a sky blue.

Mark had his back to her, focusing on something on the stove. He didn't turn around when she came in. She stopped half way between the entrance and the kitchen. "Hello."

He still didn't turn around. "Blast!" He picked up whatever was burning on the stove top and threw it into the sink, pan and all.

"Not going well?" Sandra tried to keep her voice cheerful.

"Is it that bloody obvious?" Whatever he'd put in the sink was steaming and spitting and when he turned on the tap it got worse.

She was trying not to laugh. "Can I help?"

"You can help by not standing there gawking at this cock-up that was supposed to be our dinner!" He went back to the stove and was stirring something in a large saucepan.

Still amused, she said, "We could always go over to the hotel for something. Maybe clean this up later?"

He whirled around. "So that's your solution, is it? Just walk away and do something different?" It was then Sandra heard the slur in his speech, the sound of a voice steeped in alcohol.

"I'm sorry. Have I missed something? Are we still talking about dinner?"

He stared at her, a tomato sauce covered spoon in his raised hand. The sauce ran down the handle of the spoon onto his wrist. "Bugger and blast!" He threw the spoon into the sink with the still steaming pan and wiped his hands on a towel that lay bunched up on the counter. Beside the towel was an empty wine bottle and a half full glass of red wine. It seemed he'd gotten a head start.

"Are you okay?" she asked.

"Do I seem *okay*? Is this what *okay* looks like where you come from?" He held his hands out wide to give her a good view.

"I'd have to say, definitely no."

He turned to look back at the water-filled pan, blackened chunks of something unrecognizable floating in it.

"It's just dinner, Mark. We'll find something to eat."

"It's not the blasted meal, for Christ's sake!" He continued to stare into the sink.

She waited, watching him, wanting to offer some kind of comfort but, at the same time, afraid to move or speak. "So, what is it then? What's happened?"

He spun and pointed to a manuscript lying on the floor; it was open and standing like a pup tent next to the dining room table. "You see that?"

She nodded.

"*That* is the script I've been waiting for. Do you remember? The masterpiece that was going to lift my career from the gutter and launch me to Oscar stardom? The one my feckless agent assured me was the perfect part for me?"

"I take it it's not what you were expecting." Sandra walked over and picked up the script. The cover read One More Chance. *There's a bit of irony.*

"What I was expecting? No, I'd have to say I wasn't expecting that piece of absolute rubbish, a dreadful waste of the paper it's printed on. They should have saved a tree and not bothered!" He turned back to the stove for a moment and then whirled around again. "And to top it off, the role they assured me was equal to the one I had ripped out from under me?—supporting flunky to a couple of near-teenagers. They want me to play the loser father, a character who is so far-fetched and annoying the audience will undoubtedly fast-forward through every one of his scenes if they're fortunate enough to be watching at home!"

"So, can't you just say no?"

Mark picked up his wineglass and took a large swallow. "Oh, of course, so simple. I did! I called him immediately and do you know what he said to me? He told me I might not be offered anything better and the clock is ticking. The clock is ticking! So, basically, he's saying I'm second rate and my career is over."

"I don't think he was calling you second rate, maybe just trying to protect your career. That is his job isn't it?" She tried to sound as conciliatory as possible.

"Oh, and precisely when did you become an expert on the movie industry and what the job of my agent might be?" He set down his glass and placed his hands on the counter top.

*Okay, wrong approach.* She attempted to recover. "All right, I know nothing about your business. All I'm saying is that he might just be trying to do his job—"

"He's trying to cover his own ass is what he's doing. If I don't work he doesn't get paid! And that, that ..." Mark pointed at the script in Sandra's hands, "insult, happens to pay very well.

Why anyone would put money up for this crap baffles the hell out of me."

His intensity seemed to ease a bit on the last statement; she forged ahead. "So, tell him no, again," she placed the script on the table, "and wait for something that suits you."

"Well isn't that great counsel coming from the artist who has no ambition or desire to do anything more than sit on a beach and paint pretty pictures—for herself! She's giving me advice on something she knows bugger all about, advice that, followed, could very well end my career. What the hell do you know of my life?"

Sandra felt the heat rush to her face. She placed a hand on the table to steady herself. So, this is what he thinks of her. She wasn't sure whether she should stay and argue or run for the door. The door was more appealing, but then she remembered Trisha's words from their call this morning: "Don't let him frighten you." This probably wasn't what she had in mind when she'd said it but the advice seemed to fit the situation. "I don't see how attacking me is going to help you. I—"

"Attacking you? So now this has become about you, has it? My wretched life is in shreds and you want me to be *polite*. Is that how you deal with things in Canada? Everyone is polite and all the problems magically disappear?" He waved his hands in the air above his head, the volume of his voice building. "Or is that just how it works in your own little sheltered world of ordinary?"

Sandra stood and stared at him. She felt her chest tightening and the tears welling up. No, she would not cry and let him see that he'd hurt her. "Well, excuse me Mr. Rich and Famous. I can't imagine why I thought you would take my comments as those of a friend, rather than some *ordinary* drone trying to tell you what to do with your illustrious career. I'll leave you to your self-pity and go back to my sheltered world where people are fucking polite!"

She turned and strode toward the French doors that were open to the deck. She stopped in the open doorway and glared back at him. "Oh, and maybe open another bottle of wine. The first one seems to have done wonders for your perspective."

"So that's the solution, is it? Run away? Just like you're telling me to do? At least I have a career and take my work seriously. You, who dabbles about with your interests, unwilling to let …"

His voice faded as she plunged down the stairs. By the time her feet touched sand he was on the deck, continuing to shout at her retreating back. She couldn't get out of range of his voice quickly enough. She wiped the tears from her eyes as she jogged toward the headland.

By the time Sandra reached Mar Azul she was feeling less shaky but still in shock. She'd seen Mark's temper before but never directed at her like it was tonight. She'd been right from the beginning, stay away, the man was nothing but hurt waiting for a place to happen, and she'd stepped right into it. *Stupid, stupid girl, Sandra.* She was tempted to go straight into Pablo's but decided to freshen up in her room first. She'd been crying on the walk back and her mascara probably had her looking like a raccoon by now. She rounded the corner to the stairs leading to the main level and nearly ran straight into Paul.

"Hey! What are you doing back so early?" he asked cheerily. His tone changed when he saw her face. "Oh no, what happened?"

"I'm okay, really. I'll be down for dinner in a minute, just need to freshen up."

"No, no. You need to tell me what he's done." He looked past her toward San Leandro. "Damn him!"

Sandra touched Paul's arm. "Paul, I'm okay. He's having a bad day I think. I'll be fine as soon as I have some dinner and one of Arturo's gigantic margs."

Paul searched her face. "I'm sorry. I told him ..."

"It's got nothing to do with you. If I walked into something I shouldn't have, it's my own doing. See you downstairs in a few minutes?"

Paul stepped aside to let her pass. "Okay, but over dinner you have to tell me what's happened."

"Deal," Sandra said as she took to the stairs.

When she got to her room she threw her bag on the desk and flopped face down on the bed. The smell of the clean pillowcase was soothing and the comforter felt soft underneath her body. If not for her growling stomach she'd be content to lie here until at least the morning. She could always order room service; but no, she'd promised Paul. What was she going to tell him? *Your friend is an arrogant, thoughtless ass?* She didn't want to cause a rift between them, although it was possible that was already done. Besides, it wasn't her job to protect Mark Jeffery from the consequences of his behaviour. Mark Jeffery ... as soon as she'd known who he was she'd wanted to run away, and the first time he'd shown his temper she'd wanted to run faster. Why had she not listened to her own good instincts? But, no real damage done, it wasn't like she'd fallen in love with the guy. She rolled over on her back and stared up at the ceiling, blue starfish swimming across it. Had she? The tears started then, running down her cheeks and into her ears. The tightness moved from her stomach to her chest to her throat, its grip making it difficult to breathe. She released a loud sob, then another, and rolled over pressing her face into the pillow.

Face washed and make-up reapplied, Sandra went downstairs an hour later. Her eyes were a bit puffy and red but she hoped no one would notice in the low light of Pablo's. She stopped near the bottom of the stairs. *Oh God, what if he's here?* She couldn't face him right now and didn't want to hear some smarmy, drunken apology. She edged over to the wall and peeked around the corner of the entrance, scanning the people inside. No Mark. Good, perhaps he'd passed out. If there was justice in this world he'd have a mother of a hangover tomorrow.

Sandra squared her shoulders, put a smile on her face and walked straight up to the seashell bar. Arturo was taking a drink order and glanced at her, smiling, as she climbed onto a stool. No Paul either; so far, a perfect evening. Then she felt warm hands on her shoulders and her heart thudded in her chest.

"Good evening, mademoiselle. I haven't seen you for ages," said a familiar voice in her ear.

She spun her stool to face him and gave Ian a firm hug.

"Well, I guess you missed me too?" He chuckled.

"It's just good to see you; a sight for sore eyes." *Literally*.

"May I join you? Or, should we get a table? I'm here for dinner."

They took a small table at the front of the restaurant, only a wooden railing separating them from the beach. "Where on earth have you been?" asked Ian as he settled into the cane-backed chair.

"I decided to go to the ranch for a few days of riding with Alejandro. It was fabulous. You really should come down there sometime. Even if you don't ride, it's such a fantastic place, and you'd love Alejandro and Martina."

"And, you never know, you might even get me on a horse."

"Now *that* I'd like to see. Have you ever ridden a horse?"

"Once. No, twice, at my great uncle's farm near Quebec City. Dolly was a work horse, but she didn't mind packing a few kids around. I was the oldest of the cousins so I rode in front and did the steering. So you see, I'm an experienced horseman."

Sandra laughed. "Well, you're all set then." She was feeling better already. Ian was smiling at her from across the table, filling the hole Mark had torn in her earlier.

She saw Paul coming toward their table. She prayed he

wouldn't say anything about her early return to Mar Azul.

"I see you've found a dinner companion," he said, looking at Sandra. "Good." His eyes searched her face.

"Yes, and a welcome one." She glanced at Ian.

Paul took their order and started to leave but then turned back and spoke directly to Sandra. "So ... you're good here then?"

"Yes Paul, I'm good here. Thank you."

Paul moved on to the next table and began reciting the special to the couple seated there. "What was that about?" Ian asked. "Are you good here. Why wouldn't you be?"

"Oh, he and I were talking earlier and I was feeling like staying in my room. I think he's just making sure I'm okay. You know how he is."

Ian's eyes went to Paul who was writing down the couple's order and nodding. "So, you weren't feeling well?"

"No, not really, but I just needed a short rest. I'm fine; and even better now that you're here." She glanced around at the tables neighbouring theirs. "There are always so many couples in this place. It's nice to have someone to share a table with."

"Where's your friendly neighborhood celebrity? I thought he might be skulking around. He was in here all Sunday night from the time I arrived for setup until closing."

"I'm not sure where he is tonight."

"Oh, I somehow thought you two might be—"

"No, we're not. We spent some time together, but that's all. I think he found me a bit too ordinary for his tastes."

"What did I say? Arrogant prig! Ordinary? What, because you don't make the pages of the tabloids?"

"I shouldn't have said that; please forget I did. Let's leave it at I'm not planning on spending any more time with him. Okay?"

"Okay, but I'm here to listen if you need to talk about it."

"Thank you, but tonight, I'd rather talk about anything else.

I don't want to waste the best table in the place." She swept her hand in the direction of the sea.

"Done. The best table and the most beautiful woman; how lucky am I?"

Ian was perfect salve for all that was hurting. She could tell he wanted to know more, and he could probably see she'd been crying at this close range, but for now she simply wanted to enjoy the evening and forget Mark had ever walked into her world.

Paul arrived with their drinks, a margarita for Sandra and a beer for Ian. "I had Arturo throw an extra splash of tequila in there ... in case it was needed." He looked at Sandra. "Oh, and I'll bring your dinner, but don't forget our deal."

"I won't. Later."

Paul moved on to another table.

"Deal?" Ian asked.

"Nothing, just a little joke between us."

"I see." Ian didn't sound convinced. "You two have something going on?"

"No, of course not." She was hoping Paul would go back to the kitchen and let Elena serve their table. "We started a discussion earlier that he wants to finish. Nothing important. So, what's been happening with you?"


The restaurant was emptying as it neared eleven o'clock but Sandra felt reluctant to leave the comfort of the beachside table for two. "I think I'm going to have some tea. Can you stay?" she asked Ian.

"After a lifetime of playing gigs my clock is permanently set on late to bed and late to rise. So tea, sure. Does he have Red Rose?"

"Sorry, only in Canada."

"Pity." They both laughed. "You know, that reminds me of

an idea I had." Ian said. "What do you think about an All-Canada party, here in Baja?"

"As long as you're not planning to bring in snow."

"No, I think I'll leave the weather where it is, but have everything else Canadian—food, drink, music …"

"Beavers and maple leaves?"

"Them too."

"Sounds like fun. We could have it right here at this table, or maybe one of the tables for four," Sandra said.

"Oh no, we are far from alone. Do you know how many Canadians are around San Leandro either as permanent residents or snowbirds? A pile."

"I didn't know that. I've met a few here at Mar Azul but they're usually only staying for a week or two. Do you think you'll remember what we eat and drink in Canada?"

"Well, super-Canuck, I guess I'll get you to help me out there, since you think me so un-Canadian."

"Would we hold it here at Mar Azul?" Sandra asked.

"We could, but it might be better suited to a house party. My place is pretty small but there's a couple who winter in one of the beach houses between here and the village, Doug and Jeremy. Maybe you've met them? They come in here quite often."

"Mid-forties, one blonde, one greying brown, fit looking?"

"That sounds like them. Good guys, Canadian enough to meet your standards," he smirked, "and the house is great."

"So, when?"

"I've got a gig in La Paz mid next week, so how about Friday, the thirteenth."

"The thirteenth …" Sandra looked out toward the water.

"You're not superstitious are you?"

She turned back to Ian and attempted a smile. "No, it's fine. The thirteenth is a perfect day for a party."

# Twenty-Eight

Mark's head was pounding as he climbed into the driver's seat of the convertible. He'd been trying to get in the habit of walking to Mar Azul, but it wasn't even a consideration this morning. He took a swallow of coffee from his travel mug and slid it into the holder beside the console. A bouquet of flowers rested on the seat beside him, picked from the small flower garden the landlord kept behind his house. Mark didn't spend much time back there anyway. Might as well put the flowers to good use.

He'd followed Sandra's advice and opened another bottle of wine after she'd left, but it had done nothing to erase the words he'd spoken to her, they were all too clear; "sheltered world of ordinary". *Where in hell had that come from?* Sandra was far from ordinary, and far from deserving the things he'd said to her last night.

The road was quiet, as it often was in the morning; only one vehicle passed him as he drove the short distance to the hotel. He pulled into the parking area and took another drink from his coffee, hoping to pull some strength from the bitter brew. He picked up the flowers and got out of the car, standing for a moment and listening to the sound of the waves hitting the beach. Last night could have ended so differently.

The lobby was empty when he walked in so he stuck his head out onto the breakfast patio. Three tables of diners, none of them Sandra, and Arturo serving. Arturo walked over to

Mark when he'd finished taking the customers' orders. "Buenos días. You are here for breakfast?"

"No, not very hungry this morning. Have you seen Sandra Lyall around?"

"Not since an hour ago when she ordered breakfast. Would you like I should call her room?"

"No, no, that's all right. Is Paul here?"

"Sí. He is in the kitchen. I'm going there now if you'd like to come."

Paul was at the grill when they entered the kitchen. He looked up from his work. "I need to talk to you." He pointed a metal flipper at Mark. "Arturo, can you handle things here or should I call Carmelita to help?"

"Got it covered, boss." Arturo gave Paul a salute. He was very capable, and pleased anytime he had the opportunity to prove himself to his employer.

"You're a star, amigo." Paul walked past Mark and motioned for him to follow. "Come with me."

"I feel I'm being summoned to the principal's office," Mark said as he followed Paul up the stairs to his suite. He still clutched the bouquet of flowers in his hand.

Paul's suite was on the same level as the guest rooms but at the back of the hotel overlooking the parking area and the hills. It was a small, one-bedroom unit with a refrigerator, sink and microwave serving as the kitchen. He'd never had need of anything more with the full commercial version just down the stairs. A cushioned blue and white sofa and a large-screen television filled one side of the living area with a desk and chair opposite.

"Sit. Let me put those in some water before they're even more pathetic looking." Paul took the flowers from Mark, pulled a large coffee mug from the cupboard, and filled it with water. "Sit," he said, without turning from his task.

Mark took a seat on the sofa, knowing what it was about but not knowing where it was going. He almost wished Paul would just hit him and get it over with. It might make them both feel better.

Paul turned and leaned against the short counter, placing his hands behind him at its edge. "So, what the hell did you do?"

"What did she tell you?"

"She told me absolutely nothing, that's the problem. But she didn't need to. The look on her face when she came back to the hotel said it all. So, again, what the hell did you do?" Paul's face was reddening.

Mark sat forward and rested his elbows on his thighs. He looked down at his hands. "I was pissed off at Nate, I had too much to drink, and I took it out on her." He paused, waiting for Paul's reaction. "I can tell you're not surprised."

"Should I be? You know, somewhere in there you're a good guy—I wouldn't still be here if you weren't— but Christ, you can be one self-centered, inconsiderate son-of-a-bitch. What did you say to her?"

"I'm surprised you didn't get that from her."

"I was going to, in the bar last night, but she was sitting with Ian LeRoy and I couldn't very well bring him into it."

Mark dropped his face into his hands. "Well isn't that great. Mr. LeRoy there to pick up the pieces. I imagine she's filled him in on the whole unfortunate incident. "

"So why don't you fill me in?"

Mark hadn't cried since he was a boy but he was feeling very close to it now. He told Paul the whole story: the script, the conversation with Nate, the too much wine, and the details of his argument with Sandra. Paul stood, expressionless, shaking his head from time to time. When Mark finished, he leaned back into the couch, letting his head drop back and his eyes close.

Paul started to clap. "Bravo Jeffery; stellar performance. So, what are you going to do for an encore?"

"I'd like to start by talking to her, apologizing of course." He pointed to the mug of flowers. "Give her those."

"And you think that will do it?"

"No, I don't, but it's all I've got for the moment. It's a place to start."

"Okay, I'll tell you what, even though I'd rather just punch that screen idol mug of yours, I will take her the flowers and tell her you're here and would like to speak with her."

Mark jumped up from the couch and went to Paul, grabbing his right hand and shaking it between his two. "You're a good mate, Hutchings. I owe you one."

"One? Are you kidding me? I'll add it to your forty-year tab." He picked up the cup with the flowers. "This was the best you could come up with, huh?" He shook his head and left the suite.

Mark stood in the middle of the living area, hands jammed in his pockets, watching the door. The minutes crawled by into what felt like an hour. He started to pace. On his sixth or seventh pass, the door opened, but it was Paul, alone, and he was still carrying the flowers, an orange lily drooping over the side of the mug. "Sorry old friend, she doesn't want to talk to you," he set the flowers on the counter, "and she doesn't want these."

Mark dropped back onto the couch with an audible out breath. "What did she say?"

"Well, she was very polite." Mark flinched at the word polite. "She said she doesn't feel you have anything to say that she wants to hear. She'd basically like you to leave her alone."

"You were gone for at least ten minutes. She must have said more than that."

"It was less than three, and she didn't say much else. Sorry ..."

"But?

"But what did you expect? Sandra Lyall is an independent woman who knows what she wants—and what she doesn't. And I'd say, what she definitely doesn't want is to be mistreated by you, or any other wanker who thinks she's not good enough for him. You blew it. Admit it. Move on."

"Just like that?"

"Just like that. Come on Jeffery, it's not like your heart is broken. I'll admit you nearly had me convinced you had real feelings when you set off for the horse ranch," Paul shrugged his shoulders, "but it's only ego, and it will heal the next time a woman throws herself at you or your agent calls with an appealing offer. Let this fish go. Let her enjoy the rest of her holiday. Find yourself some other form of entertainment."

"Is that what you think?" Mark stood up. "That Sandra was some kind of meaningless form of amusement for me?"

"What else?"

Mark took two long strides to put himself right in front of Paul. He glared at him, fists clenched at his sides. "That's just the thing. I don't bloody well know, and it seems now I never will!" He slammed the door behind him as he made for the stairs.

When Mark returned home, the house seemed emptier than usual, even though he was accustomed to being there alone. He surveyed the mess from the night before: the empty wine bottles, the red stained glass, the pan of burnt offerings still in the sink. He just didn't have the energy for cleaning. The script lay on the table where Sandra had left it, the worthless instigator of the entire train wreck. Mark picked it up and flipped through the pages without seeing them. He stood for a moment and again came the burning sensation in his eyes. He stalked across the kitchen to the rubbish bin and hurled the bundle of pages through its spinning lid.

After two days of mostly sleeping and reading, Mark's hangover of alcohol and emotion was gone and he was feeling more himself. It was time to clean the kitchen and get this thing sorted with Sandra. Sure, she'd said she didn't want to talk to him, but that was the morning after, when the wound was fresh. He thought he knew her well enough to believe that she'd be more open to forgiving him by now. He'd go to Pablo's tonight. Ian LeRoy would be playing, so no fear of the Frenchman keeping him from talking to her. He pulled the crusted, blackened pan from the sink, floating bits of congealed fat on the dark water. "Blimey," he said out loud. "This would have been easier a few days ago, Jeffery." But there was no gain in regretting the making of a mess, only a time to start cleaning it up.

He waited until after eight o'clock to go to Pablo's, when he knew Ian would be on stage. He heard the music as he descended the stairs. When he stepped inside, his eyes went to the bar, counting on Sandra to be occupying one of the stools. A young couple sat at one end sipping at two straws from the same over-sized margarita glass, an older woman with short spiky hair was two spots down from them, and a Mexican gentleman had the end stool. *Damn.* He took a quick look around the room but saw no tables of one, only twos, threes and fours. Well, maybe she was coming down later. He'd wait.

Mark took the stool halfway between the spiky-haired woman and the solo gent, leaning forward and resting his forearms on the bar. Arturo came from the kitchen and gave him a broad smile. Well, at least someone was happy to see him. "Señor, good evening. What can I get for you?"

"Hello Arturo. I'll have a Corona—no, wait, just bring me a coffee, please."

"Coffee?"

"Yes, coffee." He wanted to keep his thoughts clear. "Have you seen Ms. Lyall tonight?"

"Sí, she is over there." Arturo pointed his chin toward a table behind Mark and opposite the stage. Sandra was seated with two other women, both in their forties or fifties, dressed in the tropical tourist uniform of loose cotton shirts and capri pants. Sandra was talking, her hands moving along with her lips, her companions nodding and laughing. He wondered what story she was telling them and if it was one he'd heard, or maybe even one he'd been part of. Just then she glanced toward the bar and spotted him. Her hands stopped moving for an instant. He smiled at her but there was no acknowledgment of his presence, only an averting of her eyes and a return to the conversation.

*So, now what?* He was certain she'd seen him but her response was far less than encouraging. Should he go over and ask to talk to her? Maybe he'd wait awhile to see if her friends would leave.

During the break, Ian joined the table of three women. Behind him, Mark could hear Ian speaking French in a dramatic fashion, the laughter of the women, the conversation lively and cheerful. He continued to face forward, nursing a second cup of coffee. Sandra's companions weren't going anywhere now that they'd met the performer; that much he knew. He'd just have to go over and say hello. The thought made his throat constrict and caused his stomach to churn. What was it Paul had said when he was bound for the horse ranch, you'll survive it? And he would, even if she spat in his face, he'd survive it. What he wouldn't survive were the feelings of guilt and regret.

Ian was playing again, a tune that had the table of three women clapping along and completely focused on the music. It seemed as good a time as any. He slid off the stool and made his way across the restaurant, coming around to Sandra's side. He touched her shoulder and her head turned toward him and up. The smile fell from her face and she stopped clapping. One of her friends turned briefly to Mark but then refocused on the stage. *Not a Jane Eyre fan apparently—lucky break.*

Mark leaned toward Sandra's ear. "Can we talk?"

She said nothing, just shaking her head and looking back to Ian.

"Please? A few minutes, that's all I ask."

She looked at him then and he saw the pools forming in her green eyes. "I can't. Please go." She turned away.

There was no anger in her expression or words, something worse, something he didn't know how to respond to. He straightened and stood looking at the top of her head for a moment. So that was that.

# Twenty-Nine

The sky wasn't looking right and she couldn't sort out why. Sandra dabbed more cerulean on parts of the canvas. *No, that's not it.* She stepped back from the painting, looking from it to the horizon and again to the canvas. The late afternoon sky was streaked with trailing clouds, giving it a striped appearance. A sailboat was heeled over and beating upwind on Sandra's canvas where none existed on the sea in front of her. She'd set up at the palapa farthest from the hotel, hoping to be left alone. It had been a few days since she'd seen Mark, but she'd been keeping to herself and spending less time in Pablo's so she wasn't sure if he'd been around or not. Out of the corner of her eye she spotted a man leaving the hotel and heading in her direction. Her breath shortened and she felt her chest go tight, but he had far too little hair to be Mark. It was Paul. She waved the hand that held her paint brush.

"Ah, the artist at work on another masterpiece?" Paul asked when he was close enough to be heard over the surf.

"I don't know about that, but another painting. I'm having some difficulty getting the sky right."

Paul came around beside her to view the canvas. "Not enough white," he said, matter-of-factly.

Sandra continued to look at the painting, her eyes travelling from it back to the clouds. "You know, I think you're right." She turned to Paul. "How did you figure that out so quickly?"

"Fresh eyes maybe, and I've seen a lot of your work. I'm

always amazed with how you use white to bring out the colours. It's what I love about your latest painting of Mar Azul. I've been chastised many times for leaving the hotel white and not making it more colourful and 'Mexican looking', but I've always loved it just the way it is." His eyes went to the whitewashed hotel with its blue accents. "And in your painting, it's white, but it reflects the colours that surround it—the sky, the water, the sand—" he swept his arm in an arc over his head, "and the colours leap off the canvas like they're alive. It's phenomenal, which is why I now own it, of course."

"I'm so glad you like it. I was tempted to keep it for myself but I'm happy to have it hanging here. And I don't believe I ever thanked you for buying it, so thank you. You helped make my first show a sell-out success."

Paul gave a nod of his head. "But I didn't come down here to talk to you about your painting. Do you have a moment?"

"Of course." Sandra put her brush in water and placed the cover on her stay-wet palette.

Paul pulled the two canvas chairs around to the far side of the palapa and they sat sideways across the outstretched lounging sections. "Is there a problem?" Sandra asked.

"There is, but it's not your problem, so I completely understand if you don't want to involve yourself." His eyes dropped to his feet in the sand. "It's Mark. I had written this whole thing off as rather typical moody movie star behaviour, but I'm worried about him."

Sandra looked out to the waves rolling onto the shore, squinting at the sun reflecting on the water. *What on earth am I supposed to learn from all of this? It better be good.*

He continued. "I know. I have no business asking, and I'm not suggesting you involve yourself in a relationship with him, more the opposite in truth, but I'm hoping you'll talk to him. This whole business with his agent and with you is messing him up in a way I've not seen before, and if he had a chance to

unburden himself, apologize, it might help him move forward."
Paul's eyes searched Sandra's face.

"Has he been here? Did he ask to see me again? I thought
I was clear."

"No, he hasn't been back, other than to drop off the balance
of a case of wine. He's never been much of a drinker until this
past month, you know. I'm hoping he's figured out it's not the
solution he's looking for."

"Well, that's something," Sandra said. "But I don't see how I
can help. In fact, I seem to be good at setting him off."

"And it may not seem like it, but that's a *good* thing. Mark
has so rarely been challenged; it's been a pretty easy ride until
recently. And he's reacted rather predictably like a spoiled child,
which is why I haven't been inclined toward sympathy until I
saw him this morning." Paul's voice caught and he paused. "I
dropped by on my way to pick up fish down at the docks. He's
looking and sounding ... broken. I don't know what else to call
it. He'd hardly meet my eye, just kept looking at his iPad, scrolling through page after page of tabloids. I couldn't draw him
out, couldn't even make him angry, and I've always been good at
that." The corner of his mouth turned up a little. "So, will you
talk to him? He didn't ask. I don't think he will again. And I'm
betting you won't see him before you leave if you don't want to."

Despite her anger, the thought of a beaten Mark immediately brought a tightness to Sandra's throat. Damn it! How could
she feel sorry for this guy after the things he'd said, after he'd
used her the way he had. She'd started to feel that he liked her
for who she was, not simply as filler for some void in his life,
but a bottle of wine makes a good polygraph. She felt the tears
coming and looked away toward the water again. "I really don't
know that I can help."

"I don't either, but I have a sense that you can."

She continued to watch the waves rolling and cresting as
they ascended the beach. Such a simple, reliable rhythm they

made. Simple rhythms, that was how she'd rebuilt her life these past four years, a life that remained fragile and needed protecting. "I'm sorry, Paul, I just don't think it's a good idea. I don't think I can."

"You're braver than you believe, stronger than you seem, and smarter than you think. The wise words of A.A. Milne, via Christopher Robin. I don't like to push, really I don't, but give him ten minutes, leave at the first angry word, that's all I ask."

Paul and his hotel had been the light at the end of a long tunnel and he had never asked anything of her. Maybe she could do it for him. Maybe she was stronger than she seemed. "All right, I'll go, because you've asked, but I can't promise it won't make the situation worse."

Paul reached out and took Sandra's hands between his. "Thank you. You're a good person, and a much better friend than he deserves."

Sandra chose mid-morning as timing for a visit to Mark. Paul offered to let him know she was coming but she felt it better to show up unannounced. If she was going to be of any help she needed to see him real, not with time to put on his actor face. As she walked along the beach toward San Leandro, vacationers were out making the most of their time away from winter— walking, swimming, or just lying in the Mexican sun. She noted the house that Ian had described as belonging to the two Canadians hosting the Canada party. It was one story of pale orange stucco with a wide front of windows and a covered deck facing the beach. The deck area alone was large enough to accommodate the number of people expected at the gathering and its low height would make it easy for the party to spill onto the sand if needed. It was perfect—as Ian said it would be—and Doug and Jeremy, excited about the idea, were happy to play hosts. The party was tomorrow. She'd have to stop in San Leandro after her visit with Mark to pick up the ingredients for her food contribution.

Sandra stopped on top of the headland and took a seat on the bench. It had been just over a week since she had last sat here. The view out to sea was almost identical but how different her view of her relationship with Mark was today. Both times she felt hopeful, both times anxious, but today there was no sense of a future with him beyond the next hour or so. She wondered if a future that included a man was in the cards for her at all. Despite the hurt it caused, Mark's absence the past week had certainly brought simplicity and clarity back to her life. Trisha claimed both were synonyms for boredom, and instructed Sandra to not let one bad dating experience send her scuttling back into her shell, or something to that effect. Sandra smiled and shook her head as she remembered the conversation with Trisha two days ago. At least she finally agreed, reluctantly, that Mark Jeffery was maybe not a good bet, at least not for Sandra. But, now that the dating ice was broken, Trisha was likely lining up prospects for when Sandra returned home. Oh joy.

*Well, best get this over with.* She stood and took one last look at the blue waters of Cortez, feeling a bit like Daniel entering the lion's den.

# Thirty

As Sandra approached the house she debated on whether to go around back or climb the stairs to the deck. *Might as well try coming at it from a different angle.* The French doors were closed this morning and the blinds across the front of the house completely drawn. *Is he even here anymore?* You didn't see blinds closed to the beach in Baja. Sandra was inclined to cover windows only when absolutely necessary, especially here by the sea. She remembered years ago her grandmother joking about the lack of blinds on her bedroom window at the lake house, *"If someone in a boat wants to see an old lady undress, they can be my guest".* She was a wise woman.

Sandra reached the top of the stairs and knocked, tentatively at first, then hard enough to rattle the panes of glass in the door. There was no point in tip-toeing around. She heard a sound from inside and then a hand pulled the slats of the blind down at eye level. The hand let go and the blinds returned to their orderly state. The door opened and there was Mark, looking well on his way to how he'd appeared when she first met him: rumpled and bearded.

"Hi," Sandra said. "I was in the neighbourhood …" She didn't know what else to say.

He stood looking stunned for a moment and then stepped aside to let her in. "Come in. Please. Sorry, I'm just surprised to see you."

"I maybe should have called first but I needed to come to

the village this morning and—"

"And Paul asked you to look in on me."

She tried to respond with words but then just shrugged.

"I thought so," he said. "But no worries, I'm glad you're here, no matter how it came to be. I've been wanting to talk to you." Sandra saw his face tighten and he turned away, taking steps toward the kitchen. "I was making some tea. Would you like a cup?"

"I'd love some tea."

Sandra wandered the living area of the house as Mark boiled water and heated cups. Her painting hung on the wall behind a sofa, a reminder of how all this had begun. The two people in the painting were still walking along the beach toward one another, still a mystery. Mark's iPad sat on a small table next to a wingback chair that would normally give a beautiful view of Cortez, but not with the blinds shut tight.

"Can I ask why you have the blinds closed on such a beautiful day?"

"Precisely."

"Precisely what?"

"Precisely because it's such a beautiful day. Don't you ever get tired of it, the weather here?"

"Never, and you're the first person I've heard complain about it being too nice."

Mark brought a tray from the kitchen and set it on a large square ottoman. "It's just so interminably pleasant—drives me mad." He gestured to a double-wide leather and brocade chair. None of the furniture in the living room matched and yet it all came together in a harmonious way. "Sit. Please. That over-stuffed thing there is quite comfortable." He poured two cups of tea, offering cream and sugar from a matching bowl and pitcher.

Sandra picked up her cup, blew on the surface of the tea and took a sip. "I've not seen you drink tea before. I wouldn't have pegged you a tea drinker."

"Oh, I'm true to my heritage that way, a proud supporter of the British tea culture. I don't remember ever *not* drinking it. Well, except when I stupidly decided to try substituting with wine. A rather dull-witted idea as it turned out." He attempted a smile but it couldn't break through the darkness clouding his features.

"Paul told me you made a donation to the cellar at Mar Azul."

Mark nodded and took a drink from his steaming cup. "So, exactly what did my old friend Paul put you up to?"

"He asked me to come and see you, hear you out. He thought it might help."

"You know I didn't ask him to do that."

"I do. And I know you tried to speak with me before. I'm sorry I wasn't able—"

"*Please* don't apologize to me for anything. I feel dreadful enough." He set his cup down and took a long, slow breath before lifting his eyes to Sandra's. "My behaviour the last time you were here was unforgivable and boorish and I am terribly, terribly sorry. Whenever I think about the unkind words that came out of my stupid, arrogant mouth, I ... you, of all people, didn`t deserve a bit of it." His head dropped forward into hands propped in prayer position, his index fingers pressing into the space between his eyebrows. "I was angry with Nate, with myself, and I directed it at you." He lifted his head and his eyes met hers again. "Please, forgive me."

Sandra had always considered herself an understanding person, but could she forgive him his words? "Of course," she said.

"Thank you. I don't believe those things I said. Please know that I don't. I can't imagine where they came from. As you know, my life has been in a bit of a state lately but it's no excuse. I have nowhere to lay blame but here." He patted his chest with his hand.

"I believe you. Thank you," she said.

Their two chairs were angled toward each other and to the shuttered view of the sea, close enough their hands could touch if they both reached out. They sat in silence, each sipping their tea, Sandra glancing at Mark every so often. He held his cup in both hands, his eyes fixed on it, his gaze drifting to the tea service whenever he lifted the cup to his lips.

Sandra spoke first. "You know, to paraphrase Jane Eyre, from this distance you're looking rather alarming, Mr. Jeffery."

He snorted, nearly spitting tea. "I'm quite certain I am." He set his cup down and ran both hands through his tangled curls. "Any better?"

"Not really. Sorry. Did you lose your razor again?"

He rubbed a hand over the growth on his face. "I can go shave if it would make you more comfortable." He sounded serious.

"No, of course not."

He looked around the room and then back at Sandra. "I'm leaving in a few days. I've accepted my fate and taken the part. I'm off to London to finalize things and then to America to begin filming."

"I see. And you're happy with that decision?"

"Happy? Good God no, but what choice do I have?"

Sandra was afraid to say what seemed so obvious to her but had launched him into a fury only a week ago.

"I can tell you have something to say. Out with it. Go ahead. I promise to remain civil," Mark said.

"Only what I've said before. Don't do something that goes against your better judgement and instincts."

"And throw away a thirty-year career? Because that's basic-ally what it comes down to, tossing success out the window."

"Is what you have right here, right now, success? An agent who doesn't know who you are or what you want and is trying to get you to do something to pad his own bank account? If you're right, and he believes you're second rate, then get rid of him. If you don't believe in your own worth, no one else will, and people like Nate will only drag you down. There is more to you than what he sees."

"And what more is that then? The bit that's around my mid-section, this extra chin I've been developing, or maybe the crow's feet next to my eyes." He pointed a finger at the side of his face. "I'm sure he can see them just as well as everyone else can … including all the wonderful friends I have, who seem to have forgotten I'm alive and don't give a fig that my life is crashing down around my ears. In fact, it's more like they're afraid they'll get some on them if they get too close."

He'd leaned forward and his voice was getting louder but Sandra remained in her chair, holding his gaze. "I give a fig," she said quietly.

"And look how I treated you." Mark's head dropped forward and he ran his hands through his hair again, pulling at it. "The thing is, I don't want this part." His eyes met hers, their darkness filled with pain. "The frightening thing is, I'm not sure I want any part."

"So what is it that you do want?"

"And that is exactly the bloody question I've been wrestling with and still don't know the answer to. I've thought about doing something completely different, although I don't know what that would be. Problem is, when you've got people following your every move, it's difficult to walk away from your work." Mark leaned toward her, resting his elbows on his knees. "Tell me, when you left your job as a curator you set out to do something entirely different, reinvent yourself. Is that about right?"

"Yes."

"And how many magazines and newspapers printed the story of your departure? How many people speculated unkindly about where you'd gone and why? How many headlines reported your has-been status? How many reporters called your friends and family to dig out your hard luck story so they could splash it all over the tabloids?"

Sandra nodded, considering his words.

"Because that's what happens to a celebrity. When we disappear, even intentionally, we must have done it because we've crashed and burned and, even if we didn't, they'll report it that way. Why? Because they like to see us fail. It sells magazines." He leaned back with a thump that moved the chair backward an inch.

"I can see how that would happen. But you know, I would have done it anyway. I felt trapped in my job. I'd never chosen it and, once my father was gone, I had no reason to continue; not that he was a good reason to do it in the first place."

"So even if you knew your life would be portrayed as a complete fall-out, you'd have walked away."

"I would have. As for the tabloids, I've only experienced them as a reader, but people forget very quickly. And, those who are true fans, like my friend Trisha or Pascual's wife, will still sit and watch *Jane Eyre*, fall in love with your Mr. Rochester and cry their eyes out, just like they did the first time—or second, or third. That's the beauty of what you've done for the last thirty years, no matter where you go, or what you do next, the best of that work will live on."

Mark was silent for a moment. She could almost hear the thoughts turning like rusty cogs and wheels. "Thank you for that." His voice wavered on the last word. "I've been having this recurring dream, about a dog, an Alsation of all things."

"Didn't you tell me you had a German Shepherd when you were a child?"

He nodded slowly as he explored the back of his left hand with the fingers of his right. "Sig."

"And do you think it's Sig in the dream?"

"I'm not sure. Probably. In the dream, the dog needs saving and I seem to be his last chance."

"Dogs can mean all kinds of things in dreams, according to the experts," Sandra said. "What does Sig represent to you?"

"I don't know … childhood maybe, strength, unconditional love. He was my father's dog, but in truth he was mine." Mark was smiling slightly, still examining his hands. "I used to imagine we were a search and rescue team on missions of great importance. I recall we once rescued Queen Elizabeth." He chuckled but then his face fell. "But he got old and died before I was ten."

"And what happened to the dream of being a search and rescue guy?"

"Nothing. It was just a boyish game."

"Are you sure? Didn't you tell me you wanted to be a doctor? Kind of similar, don't you think? Both involve saving lives."

Mark nodded without looking up.

"So what happens to the dog, in your dream?" Sandra asked.

"I don't know. He's right there, so close I feel his breath on my face. I think he's dying but I'm not sure how or why and I don't know how to help him."

"I think it's kind of obvious, and quite ironic that your dog's name was Sig, Sigmund Freud being the father of dream interpretation."

Mark looked up finally. "Well tell me then, student of Sigmund, what do you see?"

"Well, to be honest I have no idea what Freud would have said about your dream, but I think the dog represents the dreams you had as a boy, the dreams you left behind when you went to acting school instead of medical school. I think Sig is trying to tell you that it's time to do something or it will be too late to save it, the dream."

"So I'm supposed to get a German Shepherd and join a search and rescue team?" Mark raised his eyebrows.

"Possibly." Sandra shrugged her shoulders. "Although I'm sure there are opportunities better-suited to someone of your circumstances."

"Ah, you mean my age," he put his hands on his stomach, "and my physique."

"So sensitive. No, I didn't mean that. Well, maybe your age a wee bit." She smiled at him. "But I was thinking more about your position in life, your influence."

"I'm afraid I don't feel very influential at the moment. Other than a model for how not to live your life ... or treat your friends."

"Well, as a starting place, tell me what you liked about acting, when you first started."

"I certainly liked the attention."

"I'm sure you did, but what else?"

He thought for a moment, looking up at the ceiling. "I liked having an impact on people and the way they think. It's why I wanted to do films with substance, not a never-ending stream of romcoms and period flicks." He poured more tea for himself and offered some to Sandra. She shook her head.

"So, since there are a lot of things you could do that have the potential to impact or change people—art, writing, teaching, counselling, charitable work, health care, I could go on and on— why acting?"

"I was good at it I guess, and the money was extraordinary as time went on."

"Well, I was a very good curator; I have a memory for historical details that suited the job incredibly well. At the time I left I'd been offered a position with the National Gallery in Ottawa, about as high up as I could go in my career and for a significant salary increase. That was what sent me west. I knew it wasn't what I wanted and that if I took it I'd be selling out."

"So that's what you think I'm doing, selling out?" He asked the question calmly, without anger in his voice.

"No, I only know it's what I would have been doing, continuing down a course I'd set myself on because I kept being rewarded along the way. Somehow the National Gallery felt like the point of no return, when it should have felt like reaching some kind of pinnacle. I knew I had to leave."

"And you've never regretted it?"

"Not for an instant."

"Then you're a braver soul than I'll ever be," Mark said.

"Oh, I don't know about that. You're older now than I was then, and I think that makes it harder. We're more courageous when we're young. We don't feel quite so mortal."

"Ah yes, mortality. The growing awareness of the mark we leave on the world, or don't."

"No pun intended?"

He smiled for the first time since she'd arrived. It seemed her work here was done. "Well, I should get going." Sandra rose from the armchair. "I have to come up with the ingredients for poutine."

"Poutine? Isn't that chips smothered in cheese and gravy?" Mark stood and followed her the few steps to the French doors.

"You know it."

"And why are you making poutine? Wouldn't it be simpler to eat at Pablo's? If you're homesick I'm sure Paul would even make it for you," Mark said.

"There's an all-Canada party tomorrow night, and foolish me offered to make poutine. It was the most uniquely Canadian dish I could think of, but not the easiest to make from a hotel room. Fortunately, Paul has offered me the use of his kitchen for some of the prep work." Sandra opened the door and stepped out into the sun. She pulled the sunglasses from the top of her head and placed them on the bridge of her nose. "My, it's bright out here," she said with a smirk.

"Now you see why I keep the blinds closed." Mark held his hand to his forehead, shading his eyes.

"Be careful not to turn into a troll. They like dark places too, you know." She began descending the stairs.

"Sandra."

She stopped and turned.

"Thank you for coming. You didn't have to and I know you didn't want to." He took a step toward her.

"I'm glad I came. Really." She took three more steps before pausing and turning around again. She said the words before she allowed her mind to question her spontaneity. "Would you like to come tomorrow night, to the party?"

"But I'm not Canadian."

"No, but you know what poutine is, and we were part of your empire."

"Ah, so the lone Brit at a Canadian party. I'll likely be strung up as a display of your independence!"

"Why do you think I'm inviting you?" She lifted the sunglasses from her nose and winked.

He chuckled. "I'll think about it."

"Well, great. If you decide to come, it's the fourth house beyond the headland going toward Mar Azul, a pale orange place with a big deck out front. You'll see the red and white flag stuck in the sand. Eight o'clock." Sandra continued down the stairs to the beach. She glanced back before rounding the corner of the house and waved. Mark lifted his hand from the railing in response.

# Thirty-One

The sun had been down more than an hour and all remnants of its light were gone from the sky. Mark sat on his verandah, sipping a cup of tea and looking out at the dark water. He could just make out the white froth on the cresting waves illuminated by shore lights. It had rained in the morning but turned into a hot, sunny afternoon and a warm evening. He looked at his watch. Ten to eight. Sandra and Ian would be getting ready for the arrival of their guests; he envisioned them preparing plates piled high with chips and cheese curd.

His thoughts returned again to Sandra's invitation the day before. Was she just being polite or did she genuinely want him to go? He wondered if it was a good idea, whether he was game for an evening of Ian LeRoy. Ian was probably a good chap—Sandra liked him—but something about the guy grated on Mark, and now there was the added discomfort of whatever Ian might know of last week's cock-up. Mark took another swallow of tea and closed his eyes. He listened to the rumble of the surf and felt its fine mist on his face. There was so much more he'd wanted to talk about yesterday, beyond the dismal state of his career. It bothered him that she had gone away thinking all of his gloom was a result of Nate and the movie nonsense. Well, there'd be time to talk later. No harm in taking it slow and careful. He would be better off to stay home tonight and arrange to see her another time, without the distractions of Ian and a room full of Sandra's fellow Canadians.

But, then again, it was a nice evening for a walk. He looked at his watch—eight o'clock on the nose. He thought of Sandra and how she'd looked when they walked on the beach that night, the moon on her face and her skirt hiked up around her thighs. He remembered the warmth of her hand when he held it and how his stomach danced when he thought about kissing her goodnight. Maybe he'd wander down the beach and see if he felt like going in when he arrived at the house Sandra had described. He ran his hand over the whiskers on his face and realized he'd need to clean up if he was going to a party.

As Mark drew closer he could hear the music and voices fading in and out with the ebb and flow of the surf. A large Canadian flag was stuck in the sand in front of a pale orange house, and the long, covered verandah was strung with tiny red and white lights. He stopped and stood for a moment outside the circle of light extending from the house and squinted at the twenty or so people mingling on the verandah. There was a blonde woman, but her hair hung long and straight, and another who was about the right shape and size, but with darker hair than Sandra's. He also didn't see Ian LeRoy, which meant they were both inside, together, as he so often found them.

On his way over it occurred to him that Ian and Sandra may have become more than just friends in the past week and the last thing he wanted was to walk in on them draped around one another. He moved a bit closer, just inside the reach of light. No one seemed to notice him. From this closer vantage point, he could see the kitchen was on the right side of the house and a window spilled light out onto the adjacent palms. *Maybe I'll go and have a quick peek before announcing myself.*

Mark crept around to the side of the house, staying beyond the lighted area of sand, and looked in through the kitchen window. There were four people inside: three men, one of them Ian, and Sandra. All seemed to be busy with various tasks—one at the sink, another at the stove, a third operating the blender. Sandra was cutting something, her back to the window. She was wearing a red dress that hung to about mid-thigh in a loose skirt, the fabric climbing a third of the way up her back to two spaghetti straps that crossed and disappeared around her neck. On her feet, the sandals he'd convinced her to buy. She turned just then and he stepped back into the safety of darkness. Being caught peeping through the kitchen window wouldn't make for a very charismatic entrance.

He retraced his steps back to the place on the beach that made a natural entry point and walked toward the stairs leading onto the verandah. He marvelled at a string of patio lanterns in the shape of maple leaves hung across the entrance. *Did Canadians travel with such things?* He smiled and nodded at those congregated outside, not recognizing any of the faces. He was hoping to find Paul here but he was quite likely busy at the restaurant. It seemed Mark would be on his own tonight, taking a flyer, and hoping not to crash and burn. He stopped outside the open door to the house, took a deep breath and rubbed his hands on the back of his trousers before entering. Sandra was rinsing off a cutting board at the centre island and was the first to see him. "You made it! Welcome to little Canada ... or," she glanced at Ian, "*petit* Canada." She grabbed a towel and came toward him, drying her hands.

He froze in place, not knowing how to greet her. What was appropriate for two friends who'd moved toward dating, had a falling out and now seemed to be friends again? What did etiquette demand? Fortunately, his body had more sense than his head in the moment and when her arms encircled him in a hug, he hugged her back and brushed a kiss across her cheek. She smelled like lavender with a hint of strawberries. She took him by the arm toward the gentlemen in the kitchen.

"This is Mark Jeffery, the British sacrifice—," she made like she was placing a noose over his neck, "or I mean friend—I told you I'd invited."

Mark stepped forward and shook hands with Doug and then Jeremy, the owners of the house, and then Ian. "Mr. LeRoy, nice to see you again." It wasn't, but it seemed the polite thing to say.

Ian greeted him with forced pleasantness, no doubt for Sandra's benefit. "And you also, Mr. Jeffery. Sandra wasn't sure you'd come."

*And you were probably hoping I wouldn't,* he wanted to say. But instead said, "Wouldn't have missed it. So many friendly people in one place, *and* poutine. How could I say no?"

"Indeed, how could you?" Ian said, his smile vanishing and his words tinged with sarcasm.

Sandra was back at the kitchen counter. "I'm drinking strawberry margaritas. Would you like one? Or, there's also Labatt's Blue—a Canadian beer that Ian found down in Cabo—and Corona, since it's in almost every bar cooler in Canada. And there's wine, from California, which is on the way to Canada." She held a bottle of red wine off to her side, Vanna White style.

"Well, that's quite a selection. But tell me, what part of a margarita is Canadian?"

"Ah, fair question. It's a strawberry margarita, so, the red part and, of course, the ice."

"I'll have one of those then, easy on the tequila please."

Sandra filled a shot glass from a bottle of gold-coloured tequila and poured it into a cocktail glass, topping it up with a frothy red mixture from a pitcher and a split strawberry placed over the lip.

The three men continued to finish up the food preparations and Mark stepped closer to the counter to have a look. Ian was pouring light brown gravy onto two large piles of chips and cheese curd, Jeremy pulled the lid from a baking pan that was filled with what appeared to be small cabbage rolls, and Doug was slicing up a ham and pineapple pizza. In the centre of it all, a cloth-lined basket filled with tiny doughnuts.

Sandra handed Mark his drink. "Well, what do you think of the buffet?"

"Rather fascinating. If I'm not mistaken, the only truly Canadian dish of the lot is the poutine. The others are, let's see—Ukrainian, Italian, and American I believe," he said, pointing to each one.

"True, multi-cultural like those of us who live there, but all distinctly Canadian."

"I'm surprised there's nothing you've borrowed from the British."

"We would have, if you had better food." She lifted her eyebrows at him before she turned toward the door to the verandah. "Come on, I'll introduce you to some of my countrymen and women."

Mark thought he could feel Ian's eyes on his back as he followed her outside.

There were more people on the verandah than when he'd arrived, guests arriving via the beach from San Leandro. The crowd was like a jumbled Canadian flag, everyone dressed in red and white. Mark hadn't thought to ask about dress code and was wearing khaki trousers and a blue and white flowered shirt. He felt a bit like a lone goose in a flock of flamingos.

Sandra introduced him around to everyone she knew, most of whom she'd met in the first hour of the party. Warren and Terri farmed in Saskatchewan and left their grown children in charge of things while they spent the winter in Baja. Barbara and Jennifer, the two women Sandra had been sitting with in Pablo's the week before, were vacationers from Winnipeg, staying at Mar Azul and scheduled to leave in two days. Mark wasn't clear whether they were single friends travelling together or a couple. They didn't give off that couple vibe somehow. Carrie, Mike and their son Leo were enjoying their first winter in Mexico, now that

Leo was finished high school and not yet committed to the next phase of his education. They were from somewhere in British Columbia that Mark hadn't heard of, which could have been almost anywhere since Vancouver was the one city he knew in the province. He'd stupidly asked whether their town was close to Vancouver and Mike had chuckled and replied, "Quite close, yes, just *one* day's drive."

Mark had been to Canada twice, the first time as a young boy and only to Ontario when his father was attending a conference in Toronto. They'd taken a side trip to Ottawa the final two days because Dad felt it important to visit the capital of any country you visited. Mark remembered being surprised that the capital city wasn't Toronto, since it was the largest and most known in the country. It seemed only logical to him, with London the capital of England and Paris the capital of France. But something about Canada had captured his imagination back then, so in his thirties, when one of his ex-wife's films was being shown at the Toronto International Film Festival, he'd jumped at the opportunity to return. Before the trip he did his homework on Canada, learning more of its history and political make-up. More than anything, he hated coming off as some narrow-minded git who knew nothing outside his own borders. He hoped the long-ago education wouldn't fail him tonight. Perhaps he should have done a bit of brush-up.

It was hard to believe Sandra had known these people just an hour, since she remembered their names, where they were from, and usually a little something else. When he had her alone for a moment he asked, "So how do you accomplish that, remembering so much about people you just met?"

"Practice, and a bit of trickery."

"Trickery? A nice girl like you? What sort of—"

"Sandra, you have to introduce us!" A tall bleached blonde was dragging a reluctant-looking gentleman toward them. Apparently Mark had been recognized.

"Lorna, this is Mark Jeffery. Mark, Lorna and her husband Kevin," Sandra said quickly as Lorna pushed past her to shake Mark's hand.

"I love your movies. I didn't realize you were Canadian. You have such an excellent British accent," Lorna gushed.

"Well, you see, I'm actually not—"

Lorna squealed. "Don't you agree, Kevin? Doesn't he sound British?" She was still holding Mark's hand. "You were absolutely fabulous in *Missy's Fortune*, and of course *Jane Eyre* from years ago. What are you doing in Baja? Are you on vacation or do you live here now? I can imagine it's a relief to get away from all the hubbub of Hollywood, fans bothering you everywhere you go. Do you find that? Do you find it quieter here in Mexico or are you here working?" She opened her mouth in a gasp. "You are, aren't you? You're here making a movie. Kevin, isn't that exciting?"

Sandra was standing off to Mark's side barely maintaining her serious expression as he started to open his mouth in answer to Lorna's questions but never managed to get a word out before she was on to the next one. Poor Kevin hung behind her, smiling and nodding where it seemed appropriate.

"So where is your movie set? Surely not right here in quiet little San Leandro?" She turned to Kevin, her eyes wide. "Maybe we can go to the set, honey. Wouldn't that be exciting?" She turned back to Mark. "Do you think that could be arranged? Could we visit the set? I just love movies and to watch you work would be *such* an amazing experience. I guarantee you we'd be no trouble. You wouldn't even know we were—"

"I'll see what I can arrange. It was lovely to meet you. Shall we get another drink, Sandra?" Mark offered his arm to Sandra and turned for the open door to the house. He could hear Lorna still chattering brightly. "Isn't his accent remarkable. You'd never guess he wasn't British."

Sandra burst out laughing as soon as they were in the kitchen and out of earshot. "I can't believe you didn't tell her."

"And spoil her fun, and apparently yours?"

Sandra lowered her eyebrows at him. "Well, aren't you the mischievous one. Now, can I get you a refill?"

She filled their glasses and they returned to the party, heading for the opposite end of the verandah from where Lorna was no doubt spreading the word about the movie being made in San Leandro by the famous Canadian actor, Mark Jeffery.

Before they were drawn into another conversation, Mark said, "I have news. Can we go down to the beach a moment?"

Her eyes met his and he saw the question there. "Sure." She pulled off her heeled sandals and left them sitting on the bottom stair before taking Mark's arm and stepping into the sand.

They walked to the edge of the light, just beyond the flag that was waving gently in the evening breeze. She let go of his arm and turned to him. "Well, enough suspense, out with your news."

She seemed a different Sandra tonight, bolder, more accessible somehow, and she looked dazzling in her red dress that rippled around her legs in concert with the flag behind her. She'd done something new with her hair; it fell in waves around her face and touched the tops of her bare shoulders. He realized he was staring.

"I called Nate yesterday after you left. I told him I wouldn't take the part and ... I fired him."

Sandra's eyes widened. "You did? That's huge. I'm ... well, I'm surprised."

"But not pleased?"

"It's not for me to be pleased."

"Well, I'm relieved, and I haven't had such a good night's sleep in a long while."

"Well then, I am pleased, for you." Sandra extended her glass toward Mark. "I'm sure that wasn't an easy decision to make."

Mark held up a hand. "There's more."

"Okay." Sandra lowered her glass.

"I've agreed to narrate my friend's documentary."

"On Mali. The child mortality film," Sandra said.

Mark raised his eyebrows. "Yes. Precisely. You remember."

"I do. I looked it up. It's a huge issue."

"It is. Norman was thrilled to have me on board. He thinks it will help him get financial support for the project."

"I'm sure it will. Quite a coup for a small organization. And, all of this makes you happy?"

"Terrified, but yes, also happy."

"Well, most definitely congratulations are in order then. To your future; may it shine like the Baja stars." She touched her glass to his and turned her face to the sky.

His eyes rested on her upturned face before following her gaze to the glittering canopy overhead.


Ian was standing at the top of the verandah stairs watching them as they walked back toward the house. "Sandra," he called, "we need your assistance." He signalled her to follow him.

She stopped on the stairs and put on her shoes before turning to Mark, still standing in the sand. "Well, again, I'm happy for you." She took the two remaining steps.

"Thank you," Mark said to her back.

She turned. "You don't have to thank me for being happy for you."

"I'm not. I'm thanking you for being a good friend to an arrogant old sod and guiding him through the forest of his declining career."

"Well that sounds a lot more dramatic than it was."

"Perhaps, but—"

"Sandra." Ian had stepped out onto the verandah again. "We need you."

"Gotta go, duty calls." She shrugged her shoulders before spinning and walking through the open door. She left him with an image of swirling red fabric and flawless legs.

# Thirty-Two

He'd had glimpses of Sandra for the past hour but not an opportunity to talk to her again. Now that Ian had her in his clutches he wasn't letting go. "Just a friend" indeed. It was obvious his intentions went beyond friendship. Why else would he steer her away from Mark at every opportunity? Unless, of course, he thought he was protecting her from the ogre who invited her to dinner and then attacked her. That was a distinct possibility.

The initial call to the kitchen was to prepare the second round of food for the guests who'd arrived late. Then it was drinks, and now it seemed to be some kind of music selection. Sandra and Ian were going around to each of the guests, taking requests for favourite Canadian songs.

Doug and Jeremy brought out more strings of lights and hung them from the verandah to the palapa out on the beach, over to a pole they'd placed in the sand and back to the other corner of the house. It appeared the party space was expanding. Because of the music requests and the speakers propped on the stairs, he assumed the new area was for dancing. Perhaps it was time to leave. Being the single guy in a party filled with couples was plain uncomfortable, and he didn't want to drink as much as it would take to make it easier.

Mark wandered out toward the water, leaving the voices to fade into the sound of the crashing waves. He thought again of the night he and Sandra walked on the beach at Mar Azul, the moonlight shining all around them. He'd felt their relationship turn a corner that night, or thought he had. But maybe all of his hope had been misguided and she was just being kind. It wouldn't be out of character.

He turned to look back at the house as the music grew louder. People were spilling down the steps onto the beach and dancing as soon as their feet touched the sand. He could see Sandra's red dress in the crowd, jumping and twisting to the fast tempo. It was difficult to tell who she was dancing with but he thought he saw Ian's reddish-blonde head of hair in her vicinity. He was a good-looking guy, seemed the intelligent sort, and was, admittedly, talented. Mark could see how a woman would be attracted to him. He was also about Sandra's age and from the same country. She loved music and he seemed to appreciate art. Mark wondered if it would be the most generous thing to take his leave and let Ian make his best move.

He looked down the beach in the direction of San Leandro and his empty house. He groaned as he took a few steps toward home but then stopped and looked up at the points of light twinkling at him from the darkness overhead. Go big or go home; wasn't that what he'd said when he struck off for Rancho Azteca? "Right then. So sorry Mr. LeRoy, but I'm not going to give up that easily," Mark said aloud to himself as he turned back toward the music and the party.

Walking past the throng of dancers, he felt a woman's hands on his arm. He turned with a smile and was disappointed to find a grinning Lorna attached to him, pulling him into the bouncing mob. Oh well, it beat sitting solo on the sidelines, and he could keep a closer eye on Sandra and Ian. He spotted them over Lorna's shoulder, dancing in a foursome with their co-hosts, all singing along with the well-known lyrics, something about the summer of '69. Ian and Jeremy were playing air guitars while their companions bobbed their heads back and forth to the beat. Just then he was grabbed again and pulled in a circle by his partner, his back now to Sandra and her friends.

"I'm onto you, you know," Lorna shouted over the music.

"Are you now?" Mark couldn't help smiling.

"You *are* British!" Lorna threw her arm in his direction and pressed her finger into his chest.

He shrugged his shoulders and lifted his hands from his sides. "You caught me."

"So why are you here?"

"In Baja or at the party?"

Lorna thought for a moment. "Both."

"I'm in Baja on holiday and a Canadian friend invited me to the party."

Lorna danced in closer and leaned toward him. "Don't tell anyone, but I'm not Canadian either."

Mark mocked surprise. "You're not?"

She grinned and leaned in again, her head bouncing close to his swaying shoulder, her hair swinging into his face. "I'm actually American, but I've lived in Canada since I married Kevin. So, you see, we're both strangers in a strange land here tonight." She winked at him.

Being in any kind of alliance with Lorna made Mark uncomfortable. When the song ended he thanked her and went off in search of the loo.

The music had gone up and down in tempo, from folk to rock to country. Some of the songs and artists Mark recognized, others not at all. He'd been back on the dance floor only once since he'd danced with Lorna, when she'd again dragged him into the fray to partner with her new friend Melissa from Nova Scotia. Melissa was also apparently a big fan, but thankfully a much less effusive one. She and her husband were in Baja on holiday, just up from Cabo for a few days, and had met Lorna in the village. Melissa said nothing to him beyond hello when they first met and then continued to smile at him and turn a little pink every time he looked at her. They danced two songs before her husband came to collect her, shaking Mark's hand and then putting his arm around his wife and pulling her close to his side. Mark backed away from them wondering if he was viewed as some kind of playboy home wrecker here on his own.

He sat down on the steps and watched the moving red and white mass of bodies. Dancing was such an odd thing. Take a room full of sane, even conservative adults, put on a rock and roll tune with a good beat, add a few margaritas, and watch the inhibitions fall way. There were at least forty people in the sandy square of dance floor now. He couldn't believe they were all Canadian. How could a country with such a small population have so many people in one place at one time? If it was like this in San Leandro, he could only imagine the numbers in Cabo and the rest of Mexico. Who was minding the store?

As he sat musing about the percentage of the Canadian population present on fifty square metres of Baja beach, he saw Sandra emerge from the crowd at the end of a song and come toward him. She smiled as she walked the few steps from the group of dancers to where he sat. "You're not dancing." She sat down beside him on the step. He could feel the warmth emanating from her.

"No, I was concerned I'd have some Canadian lumberjack clobber me for dancing with his wife."

Sandra laughed. "I don't think there are any lumberjacks here."

"Perhaps not, but the guy who collected his wife after the last dance was big enough to be one, and he *was* wearing plaid."

"That seems like an excuse. What's the real reason you're not dancing?" She tilted her head to the side and gave him a questioning look. "Don't like our Canadian tunes? Can't dance without your stunt double? Maybe had your heart broken by a Russian ballerina?"

She was even more radiant when she was teasing. A song

started with a bouncing piano sound. "I love this one!" Sandra jumped to her feet and started moving backwards into the group of dancers, beckoning him forward with her hands.

Mark followed her onto the dance floor. The other two times he'd been on the square of beach he'd felt inclined to keep his distance, but not so now. It was time to pull out some of the dance moves he'd picked up in his years of playing leading men. He moved in close and placed his right hand in the small of Sandra's back, taking her hand in his left. After only two beats, he pushed her into a three hundred and sixty degree spin before pulling her closer when she faced him again. He could feel the heat between them as they swayed to the song's rhythm.

He spun her a second time, her hair lifting from her shoulders and her eyes closing as she turned. They were open again when she came back to face him, locking onto his with an intensity that nearly made him falter. He took her by both hands and spun her halfway around so that her back was against his chest and his arms around her. The sweet strawberry smell was still there but something else blended with it now, something musky and much sexier than strawberry. Their bodies separated, connected only by their hands and Mark felt the absence of her warmth and an immediate longing for its return. Just as he was about to spin Sandra along his arm and into him again, the song was over, and she pulled away, smiling and clapping.

And then Ian was there, taking her hand and pulling her to the other side of the dance floor, leaving Mark standing alone.

He returned to his perch on the steps but had barely settled when Sandra was back. "I'm sorry about that. I assumed there was urgent party business the way Ian dragged me away but, not so much." She shrugged her shoulders.

"Can I ask what it *was* about?"

She looked at him a moment before taking a seat next to

him. "Only if you promise not to be angry."

"Angry? Me?" He made an "x" across the left side of his chest with his index finger. "I promise."

"Okay." She paused. "He thinks he needs to protect me from you. He's trying to be a good friend."

Mark's eyes went to the crowd and picked Ian out, standing off to the side of the dance floor; he was speaking with a couple that Mark recalled meeting earlier. "I see. So he knows about my unconscionable behaviour last week."

She shook her head. "No, not from me he doesn't. It didn't seem any of his concern."

"In that case, I'm not convinced he's trying to protect you. I'd be more inclined to think he's trying to win you."

"Win me? You make me sound like some kind of carnival prize up for grabs. Step right up, knock over the bowling pins and win yourself a little lady in a red dress."

Mark chuckled. "All right then, woo you or, since you're fond of period drama, court you."

"Oh please. Ian?" She glanced across to where Ian was still standing and he met her gaze and waved.

"You see?"

"What, because he waved?"

"No, because he was instantly aware that you were looking at him."

Sandra didn't wave back. "I've told you before that Ian and I are just friends. He's a flirt, that's all."

"And why is that, why the *just* friends?"

"Are you trying to set me up or something?" Sandra leaned away from him, eyebrows lifted into perfect arches above her eyes.

"Most certainly not. I'm simply curious."

"Okay then." She glanced over at Ian and then back to Mark. "I don't know really. Why does one person inspire feelings of camaraderie and another feelings of passion? One of the great mysteries of human relationships."

At the word passion, Mark felt the hair stand up on the backs of his arms. He was afraid to ask the next question but needed to, and knew it was the right moment. He cleared his throat. "And which do I inspire?"

Sandra eyes darted away then, down to her bare feet on the step. When she turned back to him, her cheeks were flushed and her eyes shone. "You, Mr. Jeffery, have inspired a multitude of feelings in the short time I've known you." A slow, jazzy tune began to play. Sandra stood up and held her hands out to him. "Dance?"

A "multitude of feelings" left a lot to interpretation, but he felt he had his answer in her expression and body language. He took her hands and rose to his feet, following her to the dance floor. The song was an old '50s classic, You Don't Know Me, and he pulled her close, his hand at her back and her palm resting against his. "Isn't this one an *American* classic?" he asked.

She looked up at him as they danced. "I believe you're right, but by one of my favourite Canadian singers, Michael Bublé. Do you know him?"

"As a matter of fact I think I inherited one of his CDs from my ex-wife."

"Part of the divorce settlement?"

"Yes, she got the vacation home in the south of France and I the Michael Bublé CD." He spun them in a slow circle.

"Sounds like you got the best of the deal then."

"If I'd still owned that villa when I needed time away I would have gone there instead of here, so at this moment I would say," he pulled her closer, "yes indeed." He looked down into her eyes, the patio lanterns ringing the sandy dance floor reflecting in them like colourful stars. He searched her upturned face for an invitation to kiss her but she lowered her chin and rested her head on his shoulder. He could feel her forehead against his neck, her hair brushing his ear. They danced that way, saying nothing, for the rest of that song and the next.

Mark tried to remember the last time he'd felt so content to be with another person. He couldn't. Relationships had been calculated and secondary for so long, he'd forgotten the pleasure of being with someone who made you feel complete, made you feel like the moment was enough.

The second waltz ended and Mark dropped Sandra into a low dip, his hand holding her firmly just below her shoulder blades. Her eyes widened and she let out a sharp "Oh!" as her hair touched the sand. When he pulled her upright again, she was laughing and she stepped back from him, still holding his hand. "That was fun. Thank you for not dropping me on my head."

"Entirely my pleasure." He gave a slight bow.

Ian came from behind Sandra and said something in her ear that Mark couldn't hear over the music. She let go of Mark's hand and he thought he was losing her again, but instead she turned and put her hand on Ian's shoulder, leaning in to speak to him. Ian nodded as he listened. When she was finished he offered Mark a half smile before giving Sandra a light kiss on the cheek and turning back into the dancing crowd. He was immediately pulled into a group of three women dancing together.

Sandra turned back to Mark and before he could ask her what had transpired between them she said, "Well? Up for a few more tunes ... or are you getting tired?"

"Tired? Are you joking? Do you know how many hours of dancing might be involved in filming one short dance scene?"

"I do not."

"Well, quite a few, particularly when you're slow to learn the steps." He took her hand, lifting it up and over her head, sending her into a spin.

They danced together the rest of the night and Mark did his best to remember the various steps he'd learned over the years. It had been a long time since he'd used them outside a movie set and here he didn't have the benefit of a choreographer. Sandra was tireless and seemed content to have him as her steady partner, breaking periodically for a song that just didn't seem danceable or when the need for a drink or snack arose. They'd been pulled into more than one group dance during numbers that everyone seemed to know the words to, everyone but the token Brit of course. Even Lorna seemed familiar with the lyrics. But no one questioned his presence at the party and he never felt out of place or unwelcome. He'd always heard that Canada was a friendly place to visit and it seemed they carried their sense of hospitality with them when they travelled.

By one o'clock, the party was winding down and those remaining were lounging around the outdoor fire pit, swapping stories about their shared homeland. Jeremy told a story about a herd of beavers causing a road block that had the rest of the group laughing and glancing Mark's way. He assumed they were wondering if he was buying it, but he'd seen *Men with Brooms*. Nice try. Around two, the last of the guests made their way down the beach toward San Leandro, leaving five around the fire: Jeremy, Doug, Sandra, Ian and Mark. Sandra sat in a low canvas chair, her bare legs stretched out toward the fire and a light shawl wrapped around her shoulders. Ian had kept his distance since the conversation on the dance floor and now sat on the opposite side of the fire. Mark couldn't help but wonder what she'd said to him.

Sandra stretched her arms over her head and then lifted herself from the chair. "Well, it's getting late. I think I'll get started on the clean-up and then head on home."

Jeremy spoke immediately. "Absolutely not! Doug and I are reserving that privilege for tomorrow morning, complete with Mimosas and Michael … Bublé that is." He nudged his partner. "Aren't we, babe?"

Doug nodded in response, never a man of many words.

"You're sure?" Ian asked.

"Absolutely. It's all part of the fun of hosting, but only when it's the next morning. Cleaning up on the night of would be like changing the bed right after great sex. I can't imagine!" Jeremy threw his hands in the air.

"Well then," Sandra continued, "I guess it's home then. Thank you, all of you," her eyes travelled around the circle and rested on each of them, "for a very enjoyable evening."

Sandra headed for the verandah to collect her shoes and Mark wrestled with what to do next. Did she have arrangements with Ian for a ride home? Had she walked? He realized Ian was staring at him, with an expression that said, *Well?* Mark stood and met Sandra outside the circle of the fire as she returned from the house. "Can I walk you home?"

"Thanks, but it's not far, and it's the wrong direction for you. If you recall, you came from thataway." She pointed toward San Leandro.

"I'm quite aware of that but, as you say, it's not far and, after all that cheese curd and gravy, I'm sure I can use the exercise." He patted his belly. "Besides, I don't think you should be walking alone at this hour." *Or, worse yet, with Mr. LeRoy.*

"And what about you, walking alone at this hour?"

Was she concerned or trying to say no? "I'll be fine. I've trained in martial arts you know." He held up his hands karate style.

"For a movie, I'm guessing." She raised one eyebrow. "All right then, I'll take you up on your offer, but I expect to be defended if the need arises."

"On my honour," he said, offering his arm.

They walked over to the three men still sitting at the fire. "Mark's going to walk me home, so I guess it's goodnight, gentlemen."

Doug and Jeremy rose from their chairs and said goodnight to the pair with hugs and waited for Ian to do the same.

Instead, he stayed in his chair, lifted his hand from where it rested on the arm in a low wave and said without emotion, "Happy trails."

Sandra seemed unsure how to respond so Mark offered his arm and led her away from the group, walking toward Mar Azul. After a few minutes of silence he said, "Your friend Ian didn't look very happy."

"He'll be fine. I'm not sure when he became so interested in my affairs. We've always had such an easy friendship."

Her attention through the evening had made him bolder. "It might have happened about the time he noticed what an exceptional woman you are."

"You think?" Sandra laughed. "And just when did *you* notice?"

"Oh, I knew it from the first." Okay, a white lie.

Her grip tightened on his arm and she leaned into him as they walked.

"Thank you for inviting me tonight. I had fun," Mark said.

"I'm glad you came. And they made you an honorary Canadian for your Pierre Trudeau impression! I'm not sure our American guest knew who you were but we Canadians were all very impressed."

He smiled. "There's nothing quite like a live audience."

His comment led to a conversation about his experience of the theatre and the move toward film. How he'd initially found work in film so unrewarding compared to the stage, and the storytelling so disjointed. "By the time it's ready for the screen it's seamless, but not so during filming."

"I can see how that would feel very odd. It would be like painting in many pieces and having someone else put them together for me. I can't imagine how that would be satisfying."

"So what is it you find satisfying about painting, since I know it's not the selling or exhibiting."

"I guess it feels like an expression of myself, like what's in my soul coming out onto the canvas through my brush. Does that make sense?"

"It does. Acting felt like that in the beginning, on the stage, but not for a very long time now."

"Which is precisely why I don't want to sell or exhibit my work. I don't want it to become something I have to do or am expected to do. It's wonderful when people enjoy my paintings, but I don't want to feel their expectations when I paint. I want to create with complete freedom. I'm not sure I could keep that if I were successful in the traditional sense."

"And what if you had someone in your life who encouraged your work? Would that create the same kind of interfering expectations?"

Sandra didn't answer right away, but then spoke with a softness nearly drowned by the sound of the sea. "I did. And no, it didn't."

They walked in silence for a time, Mark mulling over her brief and somewhat confusing answer. She'd pulled away from him a little, her arm no longer linked through his, just her hand resting on the crease of his elbow, and then Mark saw the lights of Mar Azul ahead. He'd managed to extend the evening this far but at some point they needed to say goodnight. He felt the tightness in his throat that came each time they parted, the feeling that had him questioning everything he thought he knew about himself in relationships. They reached the walkway leading into Pablo's, now closed for the night, and Sandra pulled away from him and took a step toward the hotel. She turned to him. "Well, it was a lovely evening. Thank you for the dances and for walking me back," she said.

Mark stepped closer, encircling her wrists with his hands and drawing her toward him. As he bent his head to kiss her, she looked up into his eyes and he saw fear flash across them. She pulled back then and stumbled, dropping her shoes in the sand. She scooped them up and was on her way to the stairs in one swift move. He wanted to follow her but was rooted to the spot, not sure how to proceed. In his movies the leading man would run after her, take her in his arms, kiss her passionately, but this was real life and she was sending a clear message. What was it he'd done now? He waited for her to turn but she disappeared inside Mar Azul without a backward glance.

# Thirty-Three

"And then?" Trisha was leaning in to the camera on her computer, her face large on Sandra's screen.

"Stop doing that! It reminds me of a horror film."

"Horror film? Thanks, friend. Must remember to check my make-up before I head for the gallery. But never mind about that. What happened after he walked you home?"

"I said goodnight and came up to my room," Sandra said.

"That's it? After all the cozy dancing to Michael Bublé and a walk arm-in-arm on the beach, no kiss? What is he, gay?"

"No, he's not gay, and I think he was planning on kissing me goodnight, but I just … couldn't."

"Yes, I've often had that same problem with very handsome men that I've completely fallen for—oh no, don't kiss me, keep your distance." Trisha was pressing her hands toward the screen.

"I couldn't because of Nick. You know that."

"I don't know that, and if I had a way of contacting Nick, I'm sure he'd say the same thing."

"And how can you be so sure?"

"Because he loved you more than anything, and the last thing he would have wanted is for you to be unhappy or lonely or holding back from something because of him."

"But it was the anniversary."

"Yes? And? Is March thirteenth never to be lived or enjoyed again in this lifetime?"

"No, of course not, and I think I proved that by agreeing

to last night for the party. It was all feeling fine until the end."

"So now what are you going to do, now that you've pushed Mr. Gorgeous away, *again*. Sooner or later he's going to take you seriously, you know."

"I know. I just need a day or two to collect myself."

"Really girl, you must be the most collected person I know. I can't see how one or two more days will make a difference. It's time to move on Sandi. High time."

Sandra walked down to the beach after dinner. She'd been half-expecting Mark to appear all day—during her yoga session, at breakfast, on the beach while she was painting, at dinner—and although she felt his absence, she was glad he'd stayed away. Whatever Trisha said, she did need some time to collect herself. She sat down in the sand and dug her toes in, the beach still warm from a day under the sun. She opened her hand, and stared at the two rings that lay on her palm. The tears came without warning, rolling down her cheeks and dropping into the sand between her knees. She knew Trisha was right; Nick would never want her to live without something that made her happy, certainly not on account of him.

She closed her palm around the rings again, feeling the coolness of the metal, the edges digging into her hand ever so slightly. What would he say about all of this? The first time she'd come to Baja it was like his voice was constantly in her head, commenting on the things she saw, keeping her company while she walked on the beach, critiquing her paintings, but four years later she was finding it hard to remember what his voice sounded like. She could describe it to someone—its low, gravelly texture—but she could no longer hear it.

She looked up at the stars, the tears running down her neck and under the front of her collar. *Are you still out there somewhere?* Sandra wasn't sure what she believed about life after death, but she knew that whatever connection Nick had to this life and to her was fading like an old photograph. In some ways it made day-to-day life easier, less painful, but there was a new sense of loss with his growing absence from her thoughts and feelings.

She felt Mark behind her before she heard him. "Paul said I might find you down here. Mind if I pull up some sand?"

Sandra wiped at her face with the back of her hand. "I'm probably not the best company just now."

He stepped up beside her and crouched down, his elbows resting on his knees. "Are you all right? Please tell me I didn't do something that's hurt you."

She turned to him, her face still wet. "No, not at all. I just need some time …"

"To?"

"I'm not sure. To think, maybe."

"Can I sit, while you think?" He was still crouched next to her. "I'd rather not leave you alone on the beach if you're upset."

He really could be thoughtful. Pushy too, but this felt like genuine concern more than trying to get his way. She nodded toward the sand beside her, attempting a smile.

He sat down next to her and they faced the incoming waves in silence for a few minutes. "What have you got there?" He pointed to Sandra's clenched hand.

She examined the ball her fist made, and then opened it to reveal the two silver rings, lying one on the other, one large, one smaller. The tears came again despite her attempts to stop them.

"Can I see?" He held out his hand.

Sandra looked at him then for the first time, his eyes reflecting a depth of caring she'd not seen there before. She turned her hand over and dropped the rings into his outstretched palm.

"They're lovely. Wedding bands, I gather?"

She nodded.

"Yours?"

She nodded again.

"And …?

"Nick's." His name came out strangled.

"The ex-husband you told me about."

Sandra thought for a moment, going back over their conversations. She didn't recall speaking of Nick and certainly wouldn't have referred to him as her ex-husband. "No, I've not talked of him to anyone here in Baja. It seemed to make it easier."

"But the high school sweetheart, the—wait, his name was Graham."

"My first husband. Nick was my second."

Mark's eyes went to the rings resting in his hand. "And Nick …"

"Nick is dead. He died four years ago." The tears started to roll again. She couldn't seem to stop them tonight.

"I'm sorry. I had no idea."

"Of course you didn't." And then came the pain that stabbed at her chest and throat like a dagger. "He died of Lou Gehrig's, ALS."

"Oh dear. I'm sorry. Such a merciless disease." Mark looked out to sea and was silent for a time. "What was he like, your Nick?"

Sandra closed her eyes and breathed deeply. "He was funny. He truly missed his calling as a stand-up comedian. He claimed I was the only one who laughed at his jokes and that was why he married me." She opened her eyes and lifted them skyward. There was no moon and the stars shimmered against the deep black of their canvas. She recognized the three bright points of Orion's belt. "Of course that wasn't true, he made everyone laugh, except his mother. Nick claimed she was born without a sense of humour." Sandra smiled as she thought of Barbara's blank expression whenever Nick was making fun. "I never met his father but Nick must have inherited the funny bone from him."

She looked back to the cresting waves. "He was a good and kind person, always giving a hand to someone, always fair. He gave me a job when I first moved out west, as much because he sensed I needed it as because he thought I was qualified. That's how we met." She glanced over at Mark and thought she saw tears gathering. Her focus returned to the surf. "Nick moved through life so smoothly, like butta', I used to joke. It was like everything made sense to him, everything had a purpose and a reason for being, a reason for happening. I tried to remember that after he died. In the end his free spirit became a prisoner of his body. But even that he managed to reconcile, not at first, but over time." She wiped at her eyes.

"And how long did he live, after he was diagnosed?"

"Almost six years. At first he went on with life as if nothing was happening, like he could will it away if he believed hard enough. If anyone could have done it, it was Nick. But when the symptoms started to increase, after about a year, he fell into as close a thing to depression as was possible for him and, when he came out of that a few months later, he decided we should go travelling and bought an RV." She recalled the day he drove up in front of the house with the thirty foot motorhome and honked the horn until she appeared on the front step. "We drove all over the continent for nearly three years, until he was too sick for us to manage on our own, and on the road. It was time to go home. He seemed to fade more quickly once we were home again, like the adventure of the road had helped to keep the disease at bay." She paused, the words catching in her throat. "During the final year and a half I watched him leave me, watched him fight, watched him lose. It was the most difficult thing I've ever done."

"And that's what brought you here."

She nodded, her body rocking forward and back, comforting her. "Yes … well, not entirely. I could have holed up in my house with my dog and my paints, going for food when the fridge was empty, maybe visiting my friends' ranch to ride a horse now and then. I think I could have healed that way." She picked up a handful of sand and watched it run through her fingers. "This is going to sound terribly ungrateful, but what I couldn't deal with was one more phone call, one more card, one more sympathetic pat on the shoulder, one more well-meaning friend unable to carry on a normal conversation. I needed to grieve in my own way and people seemed determined to help me do it. So, I ran away, drove south in a snow storm, without a destination, my little dog in the passenger seat wondering if I'd lost my mind. We ended up here at Mar Azul."

Mark nodded, like a missing piece had fallen into place. "And so it's a time of remembering."

"It is, but not in the way you'd think. When I came here the first time I was running away from the loss, from the grief, from the community where everyone knew what had happened and approached me with that 'I'm so sorry' look I couldn't stand anymore. I watched my mother fall apart when my father was killed, and I thought a sudden accident must be the worst way to lose someone; never having a chance to say goodbye. But to watch someone you love suffer and fade for years is incredibly painful. When you think you can't take anymore, it keeps coming, day after day after day. You grieve for years before they die and then start all over again when they're gone.

When I came to Baja I felt like I rediscovered myself; remembered the me before the identity of caregiver or grieving widow, the me without Nick. It's why this place is so special." She turned her head to look at Mar Azul. "It feels like it has magic in it."

There was silence then, a long pause. Mark sighed and shook his head slowly, looking down at the sand. "I am such a selfish git. I've been unloading my poor washed-up actor woes on you since the day we met and didn't make the effort to find out what might be troubling you, even though I sensed something now and then."

"I've known Paul and Ian from the first year I came here and, although they might suspect, they don't know about Nick. I didn't want anyone here to know. I wanted to just be Sandra, not Sandra the grieving widow who everyone tiptoes around and is kind to because isn't it so sad what happened to her husband. If you'd have asked, I wouldn't have told you."

"So why are you telling me now?"

Their eyes met and she held his gaze. "I don't know. I guess I feel I owe you an explanation."

"You don't owe me anything. And you've already given me plenty."

And then she knew, realized it in that moment. She didn't feel in debt to him. She wanted him to know who she was, where she'd come from, everything. Despite who he was, despite their differences, she wanted this man to know her. She trusted him, surprising as that seemed. "Okay then, because I wanted you to know."

His face softened, little creases appearing at the corners of his eyes. He looked down at his hand and opened it, revealing the two rings. "Then there's something else I'd like to know. What was your plan for these?"

She grabbed for the rings and he closed his hand around them. "Not so fast. First you have to tell me what you're going to do with them."

"Taking hostages, are we?"

"No, just protecting them from any ill-intent."

"Well, if you must know, I decided it was time to let them go."

"And you were going to toss them into the Sea of Cortez." She nodded.

"Since it sounds to me like your husband and marriage were precious to you, why would you throw away the symbols of that relationship?" Mark inspected the rings, the matching pattern of brush strokes etched into each one, the tiny sapphire in the smaller ring.

She felt the tears coming again and turned back to the water. "I hoped it might release me somehow."

"I'm no expert on these things, far from it, but the way I see it, each person we meet weaves themselves into the fabric of our lives. You can throw the rings in the sea, but it won't change your history, or your heart. You carry it all with you, into the rest of your life, into your next relationship. I know I would never ask you to forget your husband or dispose of things that were meaningful between you. I mean ... if I were in your life ... if you were open to having someone in your life ... again, at some point."

Sandra suppressed a smile. "That's deep stuff Mr. Jeffery, for a selfish git. And, by the way, I'm not sure I like you speaking of a friend of mine in such an unkind way."

He smiled. "So do you promise not to throw them into the sea and instead put them in a safe and special place?"

"All right. I give you my word." She held out her hand.

"You didn't cross your heart or spit."

She gave him a stern look but he continued to hold the rings in his clenched hand.

"Fine then." Sandra crossed her heart with her right hand and turned her head to spit in the sand.

Mark was grinning as he pressed the rings into her outstretched palm, pausing as his fingertips brushed her skin. A tingle ran up the back of her arm at his touch. She placed the rings in the pocket of her shirt and buttoned it closed. "Will that do for now?"

"Right next to your crossed heart—seems appropriate."

They both turned to face the water and sat without speaking, listening to the waves. Sandra could feel him next to her, like his heat was able to radiate through the space between them and warm the left side of her body.

Mark broke the long silence. "You've been a good friend to a ranting, thoughtless wank who has seen nothing but his own troubles. I feel like I can breathe again, thanks to you."

"Now what did I tell you about speaking of my friend like

that? I happen to know he has a good heart; he just needs to listen to it more often. He's helped me too you know, more than he realizes, more than I realized until last night." She turned her face to him then, knowing the tracks of tears were still visible on her cheeks.

"About last night, there is one thing I'm wondering about," said Mark.

She waited.

"All evening it felt like, well, it felt like we were—but then when we said goodnight—I was going to kiss you and—you ran from me."

"I did, but not from you really, more from what I was feeling, from a sudden rush of guilt, kissing another man, or wanting to, on the anniversary of Nick's death. It just felt wrong."

"Ah, it was the anniversary. If I'd known ... I'm sorry."

She searched for the words, wondering how much to say, how much to risk. "Last night was such fun—dancing, laughing, singing. I had the best time, truly." She looked away from the intensity of his expression. "I was feeling like our friendship was, maybe, moving in a new direction, and I couldn't take that step on the anniversary of Nick's death. This day has loomed so large every year for the past four and I realized at the end of the night that I needed to honour it. I'm sorry if I was abrupt or if you felt rejected."

"Not at all, you had every right to act as you did. I would never have—if I had known your history and the significance of the day."

"I didn't see it coming myself until I felt I'd stepped into my own trap."

"And when I asked about your painting, having someone in your life who encouraged you—"

"Nick was there, just like that."

"I wondered about your answer but I couldn't bring myself to ask," Mark said. Again there was only the sound of the surf for a time. "But you wanted to."

She immediately knew what he meant and felt the corners of her mouth lifting; she continued to face the sea. "I did."

"So now ... with the anniversary behind you ... would I send you running for the hotel if I tried to kiss you again?"

Sandra could feel his eyes on her and she turned to meet them. "It's hard to say for sure, but I'm feeling fairly rooted to this bit of beach."

He reached out and touched her face, letting the backs of his fingers slide gently down her cheek, his warmth removing the last of the dampness from her skin. His hand made its way from her cheek to the base of her neck just under her ear and he pulled her toward him as he leaned in. This time there was no fear, no need to run, and no guilt, only the feel of his lips against hers, their softness, their heat. He kissed her gently and then pulled away a little, his eyes asking the question.

"I'm still here," she whispered, as she placed her hand on his shoulder and drew him back to her.


The breeze lifted the hair from her shoulders and pushed it gently across her face. She tucked the stray strands beneath her wide brimmed hat and looked out at the sea. The sun was a hand width above the horizon now, lighting the tops of the waves with golden glitter that disappeared as the water reached the shore. She'd been walking for almost an hour, thinking over the events of the night before. She blushed as she thought of Mark and how they'd sat in the sand kissing and talking and holding each other for the better part of the evening. There had been moments of discomfort, moments of guilt, but they were fleeting, and she'd been determined to banish all such feelings to some faraway place.

A wave rolled over her feet on its way up the beach, the cool water caressing her skin. The tide was coming in. She'd left her paints and her yoga mat in her room this morning, needing some time to herself without the distraction of an activity, and she'd managed to slip away from Mar Azul without anyone spotting her.

What was she going to tell Paul ... or Trisha? After all of her high and mighty "he's so not my type" talk, how would she explain what they'd become? And just what was that anyway? Did this mean they were a couple? Were they dating? Was she his girlfriend? Couple sounded too ... official, dating too formal, and girlfriend/boyfriend too juvenile. They were friends, that was certain, and the thought of it made her chuckle. She was friends, close friends, with Mark Jeffery. At what point would that not sound just a little strange? Probably much sooner than she was dating, or otherwise romantically involved with, Mark Jeffery. That one would take awhile, if it was true. Was it true, or was it some kind of holiday fling for her and pleasant distraction for him? No. She didn't believe that anymore, not after everything that had happened and all that was said. He was no Nick, that was true, and not "her type" in many ways, but she'd come to care for him more and more deeply as she got to know what was under the surface, the real Mark, the person that Alejandro saw. She loved him. She'd been falling in love all along but hadn't seen it, or had chosen not to.

A warm rush of wind met her face and lifted the hat from her head. She jumped up and caught it in mid-air, laughing at her quick reflexes. "Gotcha!" That was when she saw him, walking toward her on the beach. He was too far away to see clearly but she knew him right away, his untucked shirt rippling around him in the breeze, his dark curls dancing. It was Mark Jeffery, the very famous, very handsome British actor, Mark Jeffery. And he was a guy, just a guy, her guy, as it turned out. Sandra smiled and walked just a little faster.

# About the Author

Teresa van Bryce lives on twenty acres of prairie near Calgary, Alberta with her husband, two dogs, three horses, and three cats. She has been published in a number of equine magazines and is a member of the Women's Fiction Writers Association. *House of the Blue Sea* is her first novel.

Visit her website at www.teresavanbryce.com.